WAKE THE HOLLOW

WAKE

THE

HOLLOW

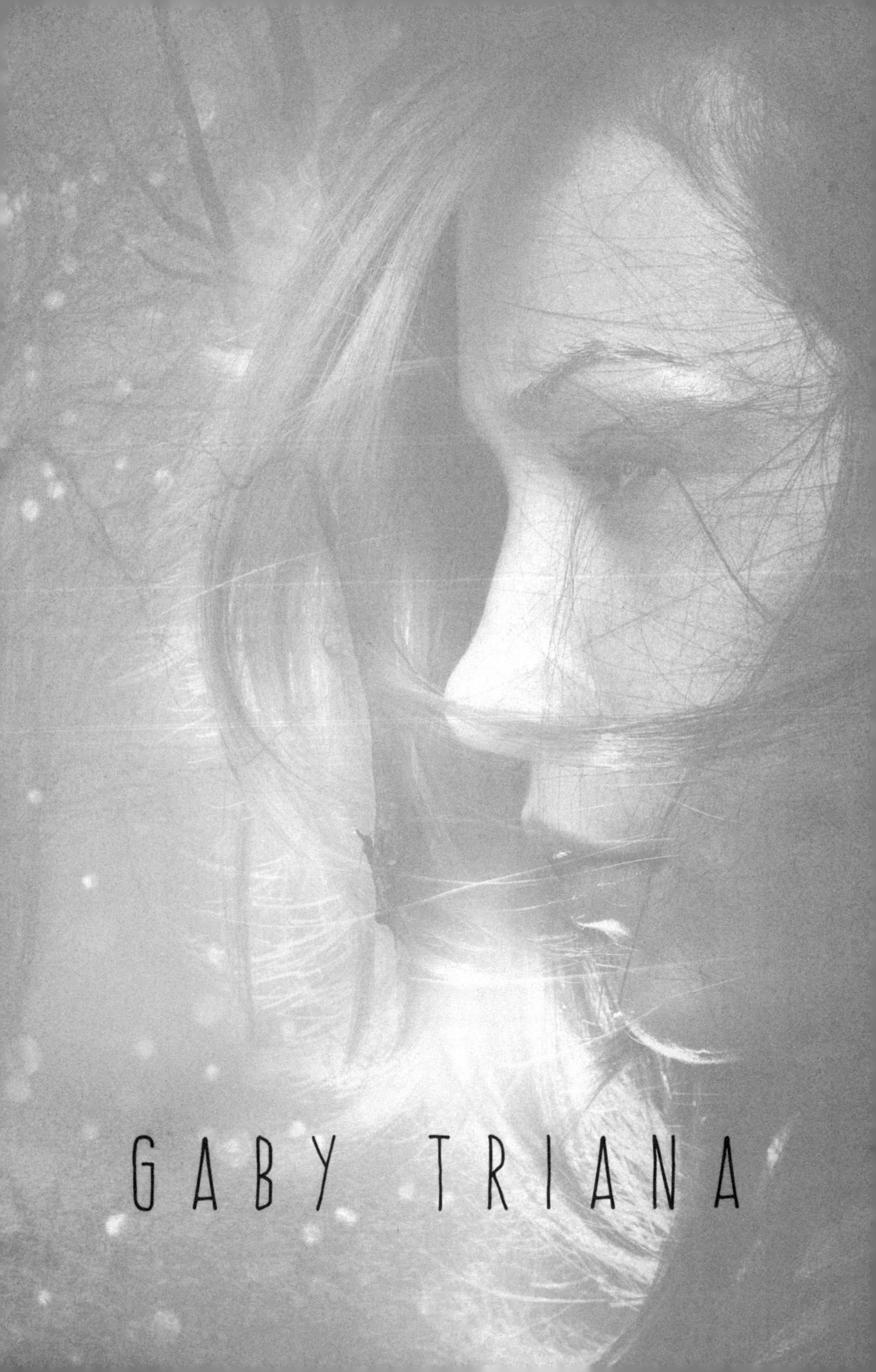
GABY TRIANA

Entangled Publishing, LLC
2614 South Timberline Road
Suite 109
Fort Collins, CO 80525

Entangled Teen is an imprint of Entangled Publishing, LLC.

Visit our website at www.entangledpublishing.com.

Edited by Stacy Abrams and Lydia Sharp
Cover design by Louisa Maggio
Interior design by Toni Kerr

ISBN 9781633753518
Ebook ISBN 9781633753525

Manufactured in the United States of America

First Edition August 2016

10 9 8 7 6 5 4 3 2 1

For my loving mother who traveled with me to Sleepy Hollow and everywhere else I have journeyed in this life.

Lela, please come home.
It's urgent.

CHAPTER ONE

*"A drowsy, dreamy influence seems to hang over the land,
and to pervade the very atmosphere…"*
—*Washington Irving, "The Legend of Sleepy Hollow"*

Follow me, please. The woman's smoky silhouette hovers over me again.

Leave me alone. I cover my eyes, though I can still see her swirling shape through my fingers.

She floats closer, wringing her misty hands. *You mustn't ignore me, Micaela. You must come with me.*

Stop, I won't go with you! I hate that I can never see her face clearly. Why won't she leave me alone? *Wake up!*

A long screech rips me from the hazy dream. My eyes fly open, and my hands grip the first thing ahead of me for balance. Seats. Plastic. Brakes hiss to a stop. A drunk old man asleep in a window seat opposite mine stirs. Where am I? The Metro-North train…that's right. We've pulled into Tarrytown station. 11:28 p.m. I almost slept through my stop.

Hurrying, I stand to gather my bags, try to shake off

the haunting image of the faceless woman. But her voice rings through my brain fog one last time…*need to face the inevitable…*

She got that right.

As difficult as this is for me, I have to do it. For my mom. And my sanity.

The train doors slide open, and I stumble through them onto the platform. The sweet smell of the river mingled with cold, fresh air hits me. I'm transported six years back, waiting for my southbound train to the city, for my plane out of this forsaken place to go live with Dad in Miami. *Don't think about it,* I remind myself. *Just do what you came to do, then get back home.*

The valley hasn't changed much. The station is still the same old cabin from when I was twelve. Boxy, old houses still sit across the street, and behind me, power lines still ruin the view of the Hudson's palisades.

Lumbering into the station with all my stuff, I see the building is empty except for a woman using the ticket machine, in a hurry so she won't miss the train. Her little girl has a teddy bear in the crook of one arm and a jacket in the other, all while trying to play a video game on her handheld. "Let's go, baby." The mother tugs her child by the elbow clutching the teddy bear. The bear drops to the ground without the girl noticing, and the two move on.

I reach down to grab it, my bags slipping off my shoulders and hitting the ground. "Ma'am." I run over and hand the mother the little girl's bear.

"Oh, thank you so much! She would've freaked." The mom smiles at me.

The little girl takes her bear, gives me a shy glance with big brown eyes, and together, they hurry across the platform, jumping onto the train just in time.

The doors slide closed. The train slips into the night. She almost left her bear.

The very memory I told myself to avoid at all costs comes barreling in—my last day here six years ago. The station's honey wood paneling, the lines on my mother's face, how she looked so worn. She'd held a tissue to her stiff lips.

Then the worst part—I'd pushed Sofia, the doll she'd made me when I was little, into her hands. "Take care of her for me," I'd said, though I knew she wouldn't. Just like she hadn't taken care of me.

Her gaze had gripped me, hazel eyes welling up, burning through pain. "Selfish, like your father," she'd said. "Go. You two deserve each other." Then she'd turned and left.

I remember standing there shaking, not knowing what to do, what to think, whether I was making a mistake by leaving. But I needed to go. I needed a parent. Sorrow crushing me, I stepped onto the train, and when I reached my father's arms three thousand miles later, I cried for days.

Yet, despite it all, I'm here. Because she asked me to come. Because I want to make things right with her.

Because I need closure before I can move on with my life.

I wipe my eyes with my sleeve and head outside to find Abraham Derant, my best friend from Sleepy Hollow Past. He'll probably be the only person happy to see me back. We reconnected online recently, where I had the chance to browse through his selfies and discover that everyone now calls him "Bram," which makes me laugh, because he always hated his name. But it suits him, too. He's changed a lot since we were twelve—now he's big and brawny and athletic—a fact that knots my stomach. I can't start anything romantic with him, though. One, he'll always be just *Abraham*—the boy who grew up with me at Sunnyside, the historic home in town where both our moms worked. He did always try too hard, joke too much...plus he didn't bathe every day. So, yeah.

And two, I won't be staying long anyway.

Get in, get out, go home.

All around me, trees rustle in the feisty October breeze. I close my eyes and take in the sounds, breathing deeply. When I reopen them, I spot headlights coming down the hill, then a car turns out of my view and heads into the adjacent parking lot. Nerves flutter in my stomach. In a minute, Abraham—*Bram*—will be live in front of me again after all these years.

Around the corner of the station, a car door slams shut, and heavy boots step onto the wooden walkway leading to the building. I get my friendliest smile ready. "Hey, you."

The sound stops. No one appears. But I heard someone. I know I did. "Hello?"

With my bags, I trudge to the other side of the station where the parking lot is. There's an old blue Eclipse, ticking as its engine cools off in the chilly night, but no Bram. Maybe I should've asked what car he'd be driving. I call him, but it goes straight to voicemail—*Greetings, I'm being held captive by an army of Amazons. Don't try to find me. Beep...*

"Hey. I'm at the station. Call me." I hang up, about to text him, when another text comes in from Nina, my dad's assistant, telling me the townhouse key won't be available until tomorrow, so I should check into a Days Inn instead.

"Ugh." *Hell no.* I'll ask Bram if I can stay with him

before I stay in some cheap motel by myself.

I'm a few letters into my reply when I hear it—"Lela." A whisper.

Nobody calls me that anymore. Only Mami—my mom. Sometimes Bram did, a long time ago. To everyone else, I've always been Micaela or Mica. The chill in the air deepens. I pocket my phone and hug my bags tightly to fight off the cold. Suddenly, I hear something even weirder than the whisper—the clop of a horse's hoof.

But why would... I smirk. Sleepy Hollow, boots, horseman. Okay, I get it.

"Cut it out, I know it's you," I tell the emptiness. It's a small town. In small towns, people make up their own entertainment. And Bram Derant has always been king of entertainment around here. "Where are you?"

I head to the shadowy recesses behind the station, bracing for his surprise attack, but I don't see him. Then, in on the breeze comes mumbling near my ear. I can't understand what it's saying. I swallow softly. The voices are back, torturing me again. Jesus, I've been here less than five minutes, and already, this town is haunting me.

"Bram?" I call out, even though I know it wasn't him.

Nothing. Just wind, crickets, and tinkling chimes from somewhere nearby.

"Fine, I'm leaving, then." I spin and hurry across the road toward Route 9. I still know my way around and will walk to Bram's apartment if I have to, I don't care. I *think* I hear soft footsteps behind me, but when I glance over my shoulder at the army of shadows I'm leaving behind, there's no one.

Faster up the hill, away from the riverbank, I walk in the middle of the street. Visibility is higher here, away from stalkers in bushes and other hiding places. Wow. I'm really thinking like the city girl I've become. No one ever gets attacked in Sleepy Hollow in real life.

The smell of lavender, my mother's favorite, fills my senses. I stop in my tracks. *Mami?* My ears strain to hear. On the street, a crumpled gum wrapper rocks in the wind. Moths dance beneath the dim street lamp, and assorted pumpkins sit on front porches like families gathered in the dark, telling ghost stories.

"Come out already!" I cry aloud.

In the distance, a dog howls a sad reply.

Then, from a side street, a low voice emerges. "Micaela Burgos, as bossy as ever."

Even in the dark, I make out his wide smile, as mischievous as the day he sat in the corner of Ms. Sanstet's Pre-K class for putting sand in my shoes. His hair has darkened since I last saw him, short on the sides, long on top. "God, you scared me." My hand presses against my chest. Because he startled me, or because I'm seeing him again after six years? Not sure.

"Sorry. But finally, you're here!" He pumps his fist in the air and emerges from the shadows into the cone of light cast from a nearby lamppost. I'm hit with the full picture I can't quite get from his pics online. Wearing jeans and a black sweater, keys in hand, Bram makes his way down the street. He's super gorgeous with wide shoulders, over six feet tall, and *sigh*, this will be tough.

"Thank you, thank you. My flight got in late, then I had to wait to take the next train, and…"

His dark brown eyes soak me in underneath heavy brows. He shakes his head.

"What? Why are you looking at me like that?" I ask.

"Nothing, you just…" He blinks a few times. That rascal smile.

I cock my head. "I just what?"

"You don't look twelve anymore." He laughs, letting out a low whistle. "Holy shit, Mica. You are one *fine* woman."

I grin in spite of myself. Apparently, someone learned to flirt while I was away. "Uh, thanks."

"You're so welcome. And what's this?" He gestures to my clothes and purse. His eyes land on the tag hanging from it. "MK? Code for Micaela?"

"Wow, really?" I shake my head. "Michael Kors?"

"Forgive me, Miss Burgos. I keep forgetting you're a *Miami* girl now." He glances down at his clothes. "And me in my Gap jeans and ten-dollar sweater."

"Stop, you look fine." Way more than fine. Hot. Pick-me-up-and-carry-me-straight-into-hell hot. But no. God, no. I can't tell him that. I shouldn't even *think* that. He's good ol' Abraham from back in the day, nothing more, nothing less. "You look...uh...great!" I say instead. "Just like your thousands of selfies."

"Oh? I post too many, do I?" He clucks his tongue and makes silly duck lips. "As if you don't post pics every day from your gleaming white mansion."

Is that all I'm going to be while I'm here? The holes-in-her-Payless-shoes-turned-rich-girl? "Not a mansion. Just a house."

"It's nicer than where I live." He raises an eyebrow, the funny-faced kid I remember poking through.

Ugh, I should've left the bag at home. Then again, it feels strangely satisfying being able to show that we've come such a long way. "Anyway..." I try not to feel his resentful jab. "Come help me with these bags already."

His eyes chastise me.

"Please?"

"Hmm, I was waiting for the magic word." Bram grabs my bags out of my tired hands, but instead of carrying them off to his car, he places them at his feet. Suddenly, his arms are enveloping me, my cheek against his broad chest. Bone-crushing, heartbeat-skipping, a nice...really nice hug. And hey, how about that? He bathes now.

God, he smells good. Like the woods by my old house after an autumn storm.

Still, it takes me a moment to melt into him. I've pushed this corner of the world out of my mind for so long, tried forgetting the pain, that I almost can't give in. But some things are worth remembering. I allow my arms to wrap around him and lean into his solid body.

"There you go," he whispers. *Do not cry*, I tell myself. *Do not.* "Sorry, Mica."

"No, don't. I don't want to talk about it."

"Okay." His clean scent is laced with underlying familiarity. Another memory—us at Kingsland Point Park, by the lighthouse, the day I left. He'd told me he loved me, a pretty bold move for a twelve-year-old. It shocked me at the time. I'd pushed him away gently, not ready to feel that way, but now...

I pull back, reeling, pressing my sleeve against my eyes. "Were you the one sneaking around back there, scaring the crap out of me?"

"Me? I sneak not." He lifts my bags again and hoists them onto his new muscle-man shoulders.

"Over there?" I point toward the station. "You weren't going, *Lellaaaa*?"

"Nope, I just got here. They close the pickup/drop-off area after eleven, so I parked over there." He points down a street. "Voices still torturing you, Mica?"

He always loved teasing me about my peculiar

"talent." I guess he still doesn't believe I can hear them, whoever they belong to. "You're in a blue Eclipse?"

"Black Accord. Mom's old car. Everything okay?"

Black Accord? But then...who was walking around? I could've sworn... I rub my eyes and suck in a deep breath. After the sleepless nights I've had over the last month, it's not hard to believe I might've imagined it all. "Fine. I'm just exhausted. Hey, is it okay if I stay with you tonight? Change of plans. My townhouse key isn't ready for pickup."

"Of course, Princess, you know you can. You'll get to see our amazing palace. Let's get thee off to bed! Your chariot awaits." He struts off toward his car.

Princess. I say nothing about his new nickname for me, but he knows he's hit a nerve.

He cocks an eyebrow back at me. "It was just a joke, Mica. I know you can take the girl out of Sleepy Hollow but not Sleepy Hollow out of the girl. Face it. This town is, and always will be, your home." He pops the trunk and tosses my heavy bags inside like they're filled with nothing but feathers. Then he rounds the car to open the passenger door for me. Before I have the chance to sit down, he kisses my cheek. "So welcome home."

I give him a half smile then stare out at the quiet, sleeping town. *Home.* I don't have the heart to tell him I stopped thinking of this place as home a long time ago. But if anyone can make me think of Sleepy Hollow that way again, it'd be Bram.

Especially now that Mami is dead.

CHAPTER TWO

"If ever I should…steal from the world and its distractions, and dream quietly away the remnant of a troubled life, I know of none more promising than this little valley."

The ceiling in Bram and Jonathan's bedroom features a yellow, cracked water stain, and the industrial carpet throughout the one-bedroom apartment smells like pot. The window is slightly open to let in fresh air, but instead, all I get are the resounding refrains of a couple arguing a few windows away. Jonathan, who had the good sense to move to a friend's house when Bram texted him that I was coming, keeps his half of the room looking like a war zone. Bram never told me what he and his parents fought over to make him move in with Jonathan, but it had to be pretty bad for him to live in this dump.

The yelling couple reaches a new crescendo. There's no way I can sleep.

When I called Bram last month to tell him I was coming back to the Hollow for what could be a week, a month, or more, I threw him for a loop. "Why?" he kept wanting to know, which did nothing for my confidence. I think he was still hurt that I'd turned him down when we were kids and was hoping he wouldn't have to see "the face of rejection" again.

But the more we messaged and exchanged pics, the more comfortable he seemed to be with the idea. "So you finally missed us country bumpkins, huh?" he said one time.

Not really. Him, maybe. And my mom, of course, but that's it.

I'm only here to do good by my mother. I need to understand what happened to her, why she sent me that final note, why she didn't join Dad and me in Miami, why she let other things take precedence over her family. And maybe guilt, too, brought me back. I felt, and still feel, terrible for having left her alone. I can't even tell her anymore. Too late for "I'm sorry."

Since her death six weeks ago, I've tortured myself a million times with the question—why did I leave? And so far, this is all I've come up with:

Her research. Tons of it. Late into the night. Also, I needed a mother. Instead, I lived with an obsessed historian. Finally, everyone hated us. Hated my dad for hitting it big in the South American market and getting the hell out of Sleepy Hollow. They hated my mom for her crazy conspiracy claims, weird handmade dolls, you name it. And they hated me, because...well, hate by association. After Dad left, she asked which parent I wanted to live with. My father—responsible, dependable, financially stable—won, hands down.

My decision didn't mean I didn't love her. She was my *mom*, for Christ's sake. I thought about her, dreamed about her, even drew charcoal pictures of her until I was fourteen. I waited, thinking she'd eventually move down whenever she was done being selfish. Instead, she only called on birthdays and Christmases for a couple of years, then never again. And even then, I *still* loved her.

Then, six weeks ago, her note arrived. In the darkness of Bram's smelly room, I pluck the note from my bag, unfold it, and stare at Mami's shaky handwriting:

Lela, please come home.

It's urgent.

In keeping with the strange abilities that have plagued me since I was little—sensing things before they happen and hearing voices—I knew how the note would read even before I opened it. I was thrilled that she wrote to me, so I started making travel plans without my dad knowing, since he was in Bogotá on business anyway. But then, three days after the note arrived, Nina gave me the news. "I'm so sorry, Mica," she said, handing me her phone with about as much sincerity as her glitter nails, "but your mom's dead."

At that moment, I thought my chest would implode. I thought splinters from my ribs would puncture my lungs, and my breath would escape through fissures in my broken heart. I couldn't breathe. Mami—gone.

On the phone, the officer's formal tone cemented it. "At two thirty p.m. on August twenty-ninth, your mother's neighbor, Mrs. Betty Anne Haworth, noticed your mom's cat begging for food. She knocked on her door. She found her collapsed in the tub, Miss Burgos. I'm terribly sorry for your loss."

And so, my mother's lifeless body remained at the Westchester County morgue for seven days. The big September storm prevented us from flying in, so nobody came to claim her. After that, my father had to fly to Colombia again, said he was waiting for some money he needed before we could travel to New York. Eventually, Dad told me it was over—they cremated her.

I never got to say good-bye.

Staring at the note, I wonder—did Mami know something bad was going to happen to her? The way I know when the phone will ring? If she did, why would she contact *me* when I was too far away to help? Why not Betty Anne? Why snail-mail the note to Emily's house when she'd never even met my best friend before?

I face my restless body to the wall and glance at my phone: 4:37 a.m. I never imagined I'd be sleeping here tonight, but Bram insisted on taking the couch so I could get the "good bed." I don't have the heart to tell him it's not that comfortable, but it does smell like him, which is nice in a weird way. Still, it feels strange sleeping here when my old house is only ten minutes away.

Blunt trauma to the head, the officer's voice echoes in my mind. *She slipped in the bath tub, miss. An accident.* What had it felt like in those last moments before she died?

"I'm sorry I took so long to get here, Mami," I whisper in the dark, wiping away hot tears. I fling the note back into my bag and let go of a big, deep breath. If I think about it too much, it'll consume me.

In and out through the nose. Quiet your mind, like Emily always says during yoga. Still, my disjointed thoughts pester me. Eventually, they blend into something continuous. It's not until the gray, early morning shadows begin melting into streaks of amber, when the image of my mother's ashes floating in the cold wind leaves me, do I finally fall asleep.

...

The woman glides into my dreams—a human in smoke form. She wears dark petticoats and an old-fashioned hairstyle, like buns on the sides of her head. In her arms is a small, soft bundle. No face to speak of again, just a swirling mask of fog, sobs echoing from a distant place.

He's leaving me.

Who? Your husband? I ask her.

She doesn't answer. On a table beside her, a stack of papers lifts into the air and flies about on its own, as if a window has just suddenly opened, letting in a swirling rogue gust of wind. The woman rises from her chair, bundle in arms, and flies high above a busy, foggy cityscape into the countryside, beckoning me to follow.

This is the part that always scares me more than anything. Where does she want to lead me? What if it's the so-called "light"? *Please stop!* I feel the apparition's force pulling me. *I can't go with you!*

Sleep paralysis sets in. I wish my eyes would pry open, wish my legs would budge. I want to scream in my sleep, outside my sleep, anything…but I can't move. *Let me go!*

After more tugs, my real-life body rips forward, catapulting me into the middle of the bedroom. I stumble into the bathroom, covering my eyes, afraid I'll run into the ghost on the way, and hang my face over the sink. I pant and sweat until my terror dissolves.

Pressing a towel to my forehead, I mutter prayers to anyone who'll listen. *Please let her be gone, please let her be gone.* But when I look up, a face is in the mirror. I scream and bang my shoulder against the towel rack, and then a pair of strong arms wraps around me.

"Let me go!"

"Mica, it's okay, it's me!" Bram's deep voice cuts through layers of consciousness.

I sob against his shirt, absorbing the solidity of his body. "Bram…"

"What happened?"

"I thought… It's a woman…I don't know who she is."

"You were dreaming. That's all."

"She won't leave me alone. What time is it?"

"Six or seven, I don't know. I thought somebody was hurting you. Jeez, you scared the crap out of me."

I gaze at the shower curtain, dirty floor tiles, and mirror spattered with white dots of dried, toothpasty water. Bram's apartment. "I'm sorry. It's these night terrors."

"No, it's fine. Just…let's get you back to bed."

I let Bram lead me out of the bathroom back to his bed. Shaking, I sit and wipe away tears. Bram falls onto the bed beside me. "What's the deal, Mica?"

I sniff, pressing the knot between my eyebrows with my fingers. "I don't know."

"Do you want to talk about it?"

"It's a dream. It's always the same. A woman made of smoke without a face, wearing old-fashioned clothes. She keeps asking me to follow her. I don't know who she is or why she wants me to follow her."

"It's probably your mom."

"No." I shake my head adamantly. "I want to say she has black hair. I don't know how I know that. I just feel it. My mom's hair was brown."

"Yeah, but maybe your brain's making her look different. Maybe she still represents your mom."

"It's not her, Bram. Her voice is different. Plus, these

papers kept flying all around, like pages torn from a book, and she was holding a baby. I couldn't see it, but that's what it seemed like."

Bram ponders it all quietly. I know I must sound crazy to him. "How long has this been happening?"

"Since she died. It's been six weeks already."

His lips press together, in doubt, it seems. Maybe it *is* my mother in some other form. Especially since the woman said someone—*he*—was leaving her. "He" could mean my dad when he left her for Miami.

"Maybe you came back too soon?" Bram says. "Too many memories here or whatever."

Sobs shudder in my chest. "No, I had to come. I have to find out why she sent that note. I have to see the house with my own eyes. I almost feel like this town…pulled me here, Bram."

His eyes flare open. "That *is* weird."

Great, I'm telling him too much again. Why can't I keep the crazy-sounding bits to myself?

"Mica…" He sweeps my long bangs aside. "You were born here. You lived here most of your life. Your mom was here. Whether or not you want to admit it, this town means *something* to you."

"It does. I mean, it *did*. But I was also miserable here. How do you think I felt going around with an outgrown uniform, a backpack with broken straps, getting lunches for free? I've spent six years trying to forget that."

"So you're scared that being here will remind you."

"No, I'm scared that being here will *keep* me here. Don't you get it?"

Silence as he stares at me, contemplating. "You say that like it's a bad thing." He nods down the width of the bed. "Scoot."

I slide over for him. "Does your girlfriend know I'm here?"

He laughs. "*Ex*-girlfriend. Four weeks since the breakup. And…it doesn't matter. Lacy needs to get over it."

Still, Lacy's one more person who won't want me here, to make things even tougher. "What about your mom? I know how much she adores me." I scoff sarcastically. Bram's mother perpetuated the idea that my mom was insane, ruining my chance of making friends for years to come. Ironically, it did nothing to dissuade Bram.

"Shh." He takes my hand and rubs it between his. "Don't worry about them right now. Listen, before you start your closure stuff, I want to tell you something." He looks down at our hands, avoiding eye contact, and for a minute, I remember the old, shy Abraham, the one gathering enough courage to tell me he loved me at Kingsland Point Park. "Mica, I'm *really* sorry about everything, about your mom, and the stuff that happened between you guys."

"Thank you." I rest my head back against the headboard and sigh. "I appreciate that, more than you know."

"I mean, I'll never understand how you two could quit each other like that, but—"

I slide my hand out of his. "*She* quit *me*, Bram." This was one of my hesitations for coming here. I didn't want to have to explain myself to anybody. "Let's say your wife wants you to move to another town with her and your daughter, and you don't want to go, isn't it clear who has the problem? Besides, I was a kid!"

"But you knew your mom. You knew she'd never leave her work or anything Irving-related. Everything she was interested in was here in the Hollow."

He's right—to a point. My mother was stubborn and obsessed with her job as a tour guide at Sunnyside, Washington Irving's historic home here in Tarrytown. She was also obsessed with her dolls. Anyone who created, named, and gave personalities to inanimate playthings could not be very rational.

"Look, let's just forget it." He sighs. "You need sleep. We can talk about it again later if you want." He grabs both of my hands. "You want water? I'll go get you some."

"I'm fine. I just hope I don't bother you with any more night terrors." I drag myself to the edge of the bed. "I'll go sleep on the couch."

He climbs off and wags his finger at me. "Ah, ah. Beauties sleep on beds. Uglies stay on couches."

I force a weak smile. "You're not ugly."

He smiles, proving me right. "Snooze. You have a lot to do tomorrow." He looks at his phone and rubs his eyes. "Er…today."

I lie down again and stare at the water stain. For a minute, all I can think about is how he lay next to me and held my hand. I know he was only comforting me, but a part of my brain wonders if I could ever let myself fall for Bram—if we could ever be more. But right now, I don't know—I can't even believe I'm here again. Besides, I think I'd make for a pretty useless girlfriend, I'm so stressed.

For the rest of the early morning, I gaze at the shadows in the room as they slowly shift down the walls. I watch, contemplating, as the wheels in my brain spin full speed ahead, until the couple a few doors down starts arguing again, releasing me at last from the temptation of sleep.

CHAPTER THREE

"The whole neighborhood abounds with local tales,
haunted spots, and twilight superstitions."

*E*ventually, the smell of bacon rouses me from bed. I amble into the bathroom, trying to ignore the cracked sink and toilet seat that shifts around when I sit on it.

Entering the living/dining room, I see a bicycle in the corner that wasn't there before and someone new yet familiar sitting at the counter. In the kitchen, Bram shoots pancake batter from a pressurized can onto a rusted griddle. "Well, look who's up!"

"Hey." I give him a small wave and look at the other guy.

I almost don't recognize Jonathan Enger, if it weren't for those weird blue eyes of his. His and Bram's families, the Engers and Derants, have worked for Historic Hudson for fifty years, operating the area's historic homes and main library. Both families pride themselves on being descendants of Ebenezer Irving, brother of Washington Irving, the author who made Sleepy Hollow famous with characters like Rip Van Winkle, Ichabod Crane, and everyone's favorite, the Headless Horseman.

For nineteen years, my mother worked for Historic Hudson as an historian and tour guide at Sunnyside, and from what she claimed, *we* were directly related to Washington Irving, too. This always made the Engers and Derants laugh their heads off. They loved to remind Mami that her parents were Cuban exiles who came to the U.S. in the 1960s, so there was *no way in hell* we could be descendants of a man as American as apple pie.

For years, Historic Hudson has claimed there's a hidden fortune belonging to Washington Irving's descendants somewhere in Sleepy Hollow, but since he never had kids, said money would only belong to extended family—a.k.a. the Engers and Derants. Not that it matters. None of it. There's no proof. It's all talk, talk, and more talk. That's all this town ever does.

Jonathan stares at me, sizing me up. I do the same to him. His hair is now long and stringy. Thick mutton chop sideburns and a scruffy goatee cover half his face. He rises from the stool to greet me with a pot-smelly hug and lingering stare.

"Hey, John." I force a smile. "Thought you were… somewhere else."

His eyes drift over me. "I was, but I had to see this for myself."

"John, bro," Bram mumbles. "Don't listen to him, Mica. He's completely lacking tact."

"I never listened to him before. Why would I start now?" I smile and take a seat at a counter stool. Jonathan returns the smile warily. Creep hasn't changed a bit.

John is a year older than Bram and me, so when we were in fourth grade, John was in fifth when he suddenly developed a massive crush on me. He wrote me love notes, but I always politely wrote back, saying I didn't like him that way. The next year, he grabbed me in the hall one day and said, "Everyone's right about you." I never knew what he meant by that.

"So, Mica…" Bram breaks the awkward silence. "Guess where we got jobs this fall? John, tell her what you told me."

"Tell me what?" I grab a few pancakes and lay them on my plate.

"We're working at Ye Olde Coffee Shoppe. Me after classes, and Bram after school, if you want to join us. They're hiring extra cashiers for October. Well, you probably don't *need* to, being the daughter of a successful millionaire and all…" Resentment simmers in Jonathan's voice.

Jonathan may have started Tarrytown College last month and is dying to be on his own, but like he said, there's no reason for me to work. One, because I'm okay financially, and two, I won't be here long anyway. If it weren't for my mom's death, my only worry this year would be getting my Yale application together and finishing high school with a solid GPA. "Thanks, guys, but I won't be here long."

"Doesn't your school give you a free pass while you're here?" Bram asked.

"Yes, but the only way my dad would let me come was if I dual-enrolled temporarily. To keep me busy, I guess."

"Or out of trouble, you troublemaker." Bram laughs, sticking out his tongue at me.

I give him a flat look. He knows I'm a perfect angel.

"What she's telling us…" Jonathan's knee bounces up and down. "Is that Daddy's got it all covered. She doesn't need a crappy job at a coffeehouse, like us losers."

Silence bubbles on my skin like acid. "That's not what I said at all. Resentful much?"

Jonathan grins. "Of what exactly?"

I shoot Jonathan a look then glance at Bram for support. *Ugh, so happy to be back.*

"John," Bram warns, pointing a spatula at his nose. "Don't."

"Forget it. I didn't say anything." Jonathan holds up his hands, and I think that will be the end of that, but then he leans forward and I swear, I can almost smell his hatred through the haze of weed. "So, how about that missing Irving journal, Micaela?"

I put down my fork and cross my arms. "What missing Irving journal?"

"John..." Bram's voice darkens. "I said, cut it out."

Jonathan sniffs to conceal a smile forming on his furry face.

"What journal?" My stare shifts from Jonathan to Bram. "Can someone please answer me?"

Bram clears his throat and shrugs. "Nothing, Princess. Just a *thing* that happened over at the library a few months ago. John, she just got here, you moron. Leave her alone."

I want to ask Bram more about this half-baked insinuation, but I'll wait until Fur Face Enger is gone.

Bram does his best to defuse the situation. "Well, if you won't work at the coffee shop, you must, without question, come with us to the HollowEve meetings. John and I are head assistants for the decorations committee this year."

Jonathan plucks a mask of a bloody ghoul from a duffel bag by his feet and puts it on. He doesn't look all that different from before. "That's right. Full control of this year's thrills and chills, baby. Grrr."

"Wow. HollowEve," I murmur. "That's a name I haven't heard in years."

The annual event transforms Philipsburg Manor, another historic home in the Hollow, into an eerie landscape with more jack-o-lanterns, tombstones, and costumed characters than the world has ever seen. They also boast an annual Legend of Sleepy Hollow reenactment with an appearance by a fake Headless Horseman.

"What parts are you playing this year? Brom Bones and his *boon* companions?" I snicker. Jonathan takes off the mask and smirks at me.

Hand pressed to his chest, Bram says, "*I* am hoping for the coveted horseman's role, if you must know. I've wanted it since I first rode Apple."

Apple—I remember his grandfather's horse and how Bram would go to his ranch every weekend to ride her.

"Felix, the usual guy, just moved away, so they're looking for someone new," Bram adds.

"We'll see about that." Jonathan huffs. "A lot of people want that role. People *older* than you who've been volunteering *even longer*."

"Don't get your hopes up, buddy." Bram claps him on the shoulder. "You're too short."

"And you're too ugly."

"Dude. How does a headless horseman need to be good-looking if he doesn't have a face?"

"And how does a horseman need to be tall?"

"Guys," I interrupt, "you're still competing for the same stupid things, I see. As if HollowEve is worth fighting over."

Bram looks up at me under wilting eyebrows. "Some things are worth fighting for."

Jonathan stares ahead while cracking a knuckle. What did he mean by that? I swallow my bite of pancake slowly.

"Anyway..." Bram opens the OJ carton and begins pouring juice into three glasses. "I know you never liked the whole tourist thing, but it's the one time of year we finally get some recognition, so face it, you're a local again, which means you're trapped."

"Trapped with weirdos." I chuckle.

"Trapped with tradition!" He raises his fork. "Working might be an option for you, but HollowEve is not. You're helping us. Accept it."

Jonathan shoots Bram a knowing look. "We'll get her into a Katrina Van Tassel costume somehow." His ickiness makes me cringe.

Katrina Van Tassel, the lead damsel from "The Legend of Sleepy Hollow," probably wore a decent Dutch settler dress in the story, but nowadays, girls have turned her into a joke—bosoms overflowing from slutty corsets and bodices, sad versions of Irving's original character.

"I would never wear anything like that," I say, losing my appetite. *Especially for Jonathan.* "Anyway, nothing like a couple of festival freaks to welcome a girl back." I put down my fork and gaze out the window at the familiar treetops. I don't have time for this. There's too much to do. I need Bram to drop me off at my new townhouse. Hopefully, Nina has arrived with the key, and I can unpack my stuff, buy a few school supplies, and then visit my old house. Figure out why, if things were so urgent, couldn't Mami have done them herself?

...

*B*ram and I head into town for a few things before I meet up with Nina. After all, she wasn't in a hurry to get here for my sake, opting to spend a few days with her older sister in Brooklyn before finally arriving this morning on the same train I took last night, so why should I hurry?

I get the nicest gray wraparound sweater I can find at Dillard's and a pair of autumn boots, things I would never need in Miami. If I have to be in Sleepy Hollow, I may as well allow for some excitement over new things. At checkout, I run my debit card through the terminal. A moment later, the cashier gives me a sorry look. "That one's declined."

"What?" I say, even though I heard her. "I'll try it again." I run the card one more time, but the same thing happens.

"Are you traveling?" The older woman smiles. "Some debit cards have that problem."

It's the same card I used to check in my bags at the airport, and it worked fine there. I run my dad's credit card instead. It goes through fine. I feel Bram watching me as I take the receipt and put it in my wallet. This happened once before. Sometimes the card companies do it to safeguard you against theft when you're out of the country, and my dad is in Colombia.

As we leave the store, Bram bumps shoulders with me. "Happens to me every day, if that's any consolation." He laughs heartily. "Hey, it's only money."

We head to his car when his phone rings. He sees who's calling and sighs, debating whether or not to answer. He mouths the name *Mom*, shushes me, and plants the phone to his ear. "Hey, Mom," he says. "Yeah, I'm gonna go pick her up now. No, I don't know. Probably take her to her nanny at the new place."

"She's not my nanny," I whisper. Nina Whitman is my father's assistant. She might sometimes cook, do laundry, and pretend to keep me company while my dad is out of town, but we both know it's only a formality, since I'm eighteen.

"I don't *know*, Mom. I think he'll be here any day now. I don't know," Bram says. I can hear Mrs. Derant's voice growing agitated on the other line. Bram's knuckles turn white on the steering wheel as he backs out of the parking space. "Why don't you call her and ask her yourself? Yes, yes, whatever. Bye." He hangs up and blows out a big breath. "Holy shit."

"Someone got an earful." I laugh.

Bram shakes his head and begins imitating his mother's voice. "Why's that girl here? She needs to go back to where she came from. Blah, blah, blah."

I pick at my cuticles without comment. Some things never change. What did I ever do to that woman?

Bram stops at the parking lot exit, staring at the street signs. "Where is this place again?"

I show him the address on my iPad screen, and he takes off toward the nicer part of town. We reach a neighborhood of neatly lined-up townhouses, fresh stamped concrete driveways, and baby trees held up with sticks. Bram helps me carry my stuff, while I stomp up the steps and ring the doorbell. "Nice place," he says.

"Your mom's not happy I'm here, is she?" I scoff. "Maria Burgos's evil daughter, back in town to try and steal the imaginary family fortune." Wish they would let it go already.

"Don't worry about her. I'll fend her off." He bumps my shoulder, checking his phone. "I would stay and check out the place, Princess, but I have to get going. Work starts in fifteen minutes."

"I know. Hey, I'm glad we got to spend some time together." I give him a big hug, still not used to Bram being so much taller than me. "Thanks for taking me shopping. And for breakfast. It was awesome." It really was. He could've easily bought a box of doughnuts, but he cooked. That was really sweet of him.

"My pleasure." He taps my chin with a fingertip and stares at me a long moment. "I'll see you tomorrow morning. Call or text me when you get your schedule to see if you're in any of my classes." Slowly, he backs down the steps. "And stop looking so damn hot, Mica. Jeez."

"You stop." I laugh, feeling myself blush. I watch him get into his car, answer another phone call, and drive off. He waves out his window.

I face the house. *Here goes nothing.* I ring the doorbell again and wait. The door opens, and short, nervous, red-haired, ponytailed Nina steps back to let me through. "Micaela!" She's out of breath, stepping out of the way, so I can drag my bags into the foyer myself. "How was your flight? LaGuardia, right?"

"Good, and yes. Then, I took the train from the city late last night, only to get your text that the place wasn't ready. Thanks for letting me know sooner."

"Oh, you are so welcome," she says, completely ignoring my sarcasm. "So, which motel did you stay at?"

"I didn't. I stayed with Bram. Didn't feel like being alone at a motel. Know what I mean?" Not that Nina would care, as long as I'm alive and she's getting a paycheck.

"Oh, okay!" She fakes an interested smile, but she's doing that thing where she's not really listening to anything I'm saying. She points up the carpeted stairs. "Your room's the one on the left."

So much for pleasantries. "Is there one down here?" I

see through her intentions to keep me in the tallest tower, as per my father's orders.

"There is, but it's for your dad's office."

"My dad's not here yet," I remind her. Seeing the blank stare on Nina's face, I add, "Just stating the obvious. You can tell him I was being difficult."

"You? Difficult? Don't be silly. Fine, take it, I don't care." She flips a hand and looks around. "What was I doing? Right, phone company, rental car, refilling allergy prescription…" She disappears down a short hall, muttering, "How I'm supposed to do all that with what I'm given, I swear, I don't know…"

With what she's given. I do nothing to quiet my scoffs. Like she doesn't make enough money. Bram or Jonathan would kill for a fraction of what my dad pays her.

I find the downstairs bedroom, close the door, and plop down on a box, trying not to think about this life. I was supposed to start my senior year surrounded by friends at Carrolton, and now I'm back here, of all places. How quickly things change.

Better start unpacking. After making a decent bedroom out of this white cube of a room, I clock in some face-to-face time with Nina, but as soon as she starts on about the alarm company not receiving the deposit, how she hasn't rented a car yet because she's waiting for the transfer to go through, and more bitching, I throw on my new gray sweater and head outdoors, if only so I can breathe again.

First stop—the old house on Maple Street.

Chapter Four

"However wide awake they may have been before they entered that sleepy region, they are sure, in a little time, to inhale the witching influence of the air...grow imaginative...dream dreams, and see apparitions."

Cutting through downtown, I have to admit I'd forgotten how the Hudson Valley is its own brand of gorgeous. Treetops dance underneath clear blue skies, and the breeze coming off the river smells of sweet autumn leaves. If I hurry, I'll have time to visit both the house and Betty Anne all before the sun goes down.

See me...

I look behind me for the source of the voice.

Nobody there. As usual. It's worse when I haven't slept. "I need one decent night," I mutter to no one.

Crossing Beekman Avenue into Sleepy Hollow city limits, the street signs change from green to blue and feature the ghostly galloping horseman who rides each night in search of his head. On the corner of Broadway and College, I pause to stare at a dark bronze statue of the legendary Hessian trooper. When I was little, he gave me the creeps. I felt like he could see me, even though he had no head. Standing here facing him again, a memory filters into my mind, an exchange between my parents once, while I hid in the pantry—

"Maria, let it go. It doesn't exist. How are we supposed to ever have a life if you don't get over this?"

"I don't want to get over this, Jay. I have a life, and it's here."

"It should be wherever I am, your husband. You're killing me, I hope you know that."

Even at eleven, I could empathize. I absorbed my father's anguish as though it were my own. Yes, my mother loved the Hollow, its history, culture, everything... *but how*? How could she love it more than us?

Less than a year later, my father left. He moved to Miami to take advantage of the international market, just as a lot of people in town started investing in his medical diagnostic equipment business. The move ended my parents' marriage. Most wives would've jumped at the chance to live the good life in a beautiful tropical city by the sea, but no...not Maria Burgos. My mother had to be different.

The statue could jump off its pedestal right now from how hard I'm staring at it. I almost hear the horse neigh in ethereal protest. Across the street, church-goers gather under tents behind the chapel. Kids run amok. Then, I see someone that stops my gaze. Standing apart is a man wearing a white buttoned-down shirt, jeans, and a brown coat. Older than me by maybe four or five years. *Tall and exceedingly lanky,* Irving would've said.

Eyes solidly fixed on me.

Do I know him? Is this another childhood friend I

barely recognize? Maybe my ruffle skirt is too showy for this small town. I have to remember I'm not in South Beach anymore. I march on, taking the occasional glance back. He's still staring, only now, he smiles. Despite a towering build that should probably intimidate the hell out of me, he just seems friendly.

I barely smile back and hurry off.

At the split in the road near my old neighborhood, the chatter and smells of barbecue melt away. Here, the trees rustle, and the valley whispers breezily all around. I almost hear the voices of Dutch settlers choosing this hallowed ground as their hideaway from their homeland's troubles.

I keep my head down, just in case any of my old neighbors outside think they're seeing my mother's ghost. I do look exactly like her in the face and with hazel eyes, only younger and blond.

At the end of the street, a brown and white pit bull appears from the side of a yard and starts yammering, ramming his short snout into the chain link fence. I gasp, holding onto my heart. Suddenly, the barking dog cowers and backs off, apologetic. "Nice doggie." I scoot past him as quickly as I can.

Jeez, even the dogs hate me.

As I turn the corner, my stomach sinks like dead weight in the river. There it is—150 Maple Street. The little blue house has faded to a light gray. In my mind, I remember my parents and I standing on the front lawn years ago while Betty Anne took a photo of us for our annual Christmas card. Me in my red and black gingham dress, big bow at the waist. I remember how much I loved that dress. We stood so proudly, so united as a family. Or so I thought.

Say cheeeeese. Season's Greetings from the Burgos Family!

A FOR SALE sign droops outside of it now. My heart hurts. Something sticks in my throat. The last time I saw this house, I stood in my yellow room facing the collection of holographic stickers stuck on the wall and thanked the walls for sheltering me for twelve years. I guess it was childish, but my room *had* heard all my secrets, watched me grow, and withstood little notch marks on the doorframe. It deserved a proper good-bye.

Can I do this without unraveling? Holding it together, I cross the street. The house seems so much smaller than when I last saw it. How my father ever lived here when his tastes and dreams were so much bigger, I'll never know. The porch steps creak underneath my feet. Ginger maple leaves swish in eerie silence.

I place a hand against the front door and close my eyes, as if waiting for a pulse. *I'm home, Mami. What was so urgent? What did you need from me?* I try to remember the good times here, because there were many, and after a minute of listening to the wind whistle, the house, this porch, surges to life.

Suddenly, I'm seven again in my black cat costume my mom had sewn by hand. My father, thinner with darker hair, meticulously carves a pumpkin while Mami warms apple cider on the stove, scents of cinnamon and cloves wafting through the air. The sun melts into a tangerine glow over the river.

"Mami, when can we start trick-or-treating?"

"Just as soon as it gets dark, Lela. It has to get nice and dark."

Mami's pretty face beams through the screened window. My father concentrates on his sawing motions, carving out the intricate spider design. There's a chill in the air, shrieks of trick-or-treaters around the neighborhood, but most of all, a feeling that I'm where I belong.

When I open my eyes, the image dissolves, replaced by wooden planks of the front porch and swirling leaves. But then, another vision…Betty Anne, knocking on this same door. *"Maria?"* she says. She holds her upper lip steady while the acrid smell of death in the flaring summer heat emanates through the open window. She chokes, overwhelmed by the stench.

Forcing myself back to the present, I gasp, ripping my hand off the door. "What the hell?" Before I can analyze it, something soft brushes against my legs. I scream.

A white ball of fluffy fur, pink nose, and a sweet face peers up at me. *Meow.*

"Coco?" I steady my pounding chest and crouch down to pick up my old kitty. My God, I missed this baby kitty girl! Coconut purrs rhythmically, her wet nose pressing against my face. "You trying to kill me? Who's feeding you, *chica*?"

The cat sniffs me, purrs, and bats her eyelashes in pure bliss. It broke my heart to leave her behind, but I couldn't bring myself to ask Mami if I could take her. She was born in Sleepy Hollow and belonged here, and in a way, I wanted her to take care of my mom.

Has anyone claimed her, or has she refused to leave the house after six weeks? With a cupped hand, I block out the light and peek through the sliver of space between the window frame and the shade. Dark inside. Where's the furniture, the boxes of research, the collection of dolls? Sofia, the only one I didn't hate?

"Can we get in there?" I ask Coco. "Is that back

window still a thief's dream come true? Let's go see."

Carrying the heavy cat around the side of the house, I crunch and kick leaves. I locate the office window, the one I crawled out of at least a dozen times to go meet Bram when I was supposed to be grounded, but my mother must've had it fixed. I try the back door—locked. The side door—locked. The basement window—locked.

Coconut is fine in my arms, all happy and purring, until a twig cracks nearby. She hisses viciously, wriggles free of my hold, and bullets around the other side of the house. I glance in the direction of the noise, the far end of the porch where dark shapes flirt with the moving branches. The maples sway, casting shadows against the siding. "It's just the trees, silly."

I could try to break in, but why? The realtor must have the key. I'll simply explain who I am, show her ID, and boom, easy peasy.

I call the realtor's number on the sign. After four rings, a long tone answers followed by a short beep. "Hi, I'm inquiring about the house for sale on 150 Maple in Sleepy Hollow?" I say, not even sure it's a working voicemail. "Please call me back at..." I leave my cell number and hang up, wondering if anyone will even listen to my message.

The afternoon grows dark and cold fast. I'll be caught in this part of town at nightfall if I don't leave soon. But I need to see Betty Anne, ask her a few questions about my mom. I scuttle off the porch and head down the uneven sidewalk until I reach her yellow house five doors down. Behind me, Coco sits by my house, watching me go.

"I'll be back for you. Don't worry." I'll have to ask Bram if he can take care of the cat for now, since Nina's face will swell up like a cantaloupe if she comes into contact with any cat, cat hair, cat dander, cat anything. Hopefully, Jonathan won't mind.

Betty Anne's grass has been recently cut. There's no car in the driveway, and the porch light is on in full daylight, as though she went out and anticipated coming home late. Still, I'll ring the doorbell, just in case.

Betty Anne might know where Mami's stuff is. I swallow my nerves and walk up the porch steps, ringing the doorbell. The neighbor's dog barks at the sound. I bite my lip and wait. *Deep breath, Mica. Nothing to be nervous about.* I wait on the porch for about five minutes, but nobody comes. A voice near me whispers, *Inside.*

"Inside?" I ask, looking around. Why don't the voices ever show themselves?

Placing my hand against the window, I try to peek into the house, but all I can discern are dark shadows, a yellow light on in the back room where I used to watch TV, and lots of knickknacks on shelves. I tap the window and turn around.

When I do, there's a man standing on the sidewalk, the view of his head blocked by the edge of the porch roof. I catch my breath, my hand shaking over my brow. A car hums in the middle of the street. I never even heard anyone drive up. Unnerved, I stoop to get a better look. It's the same man from the church parking lot. The tall, skinny one who looked like a scarecrow "eloped" from a cornfield, as Irving used to say.

"Hello? Do I know you?" I steady myself against a column.

He shades his eyes. "I saw you at that house for sale and thought maybe you knew something about it." He points to my old house, then pulls a pen and business card from his pocket to jot something down.

"No, I don't," I lie.

"Are you interested in buying it, too?"

"No," I say too quickly. How absurd. Buying back what's already mine. Sort of.

"You from around here?" he asks.

"Yes. Well, no, not really." Why am I giving him information? I don't know him from a hole in the wall.

The pen and card go back into his shirt pocket. His face has a sophisticated quality to it, worldly, like he's experienced an awful lot in his life, even though he doesn't look older than a college student. His hair is dark blond and loose, and he hunches over slightly, as if uncomfortable with his height. "I just moved here this summer," he says. "My temporary lease is up, so I'm looking for a new place."

I nod, unsure what to say. Some people give up information so easily. He waits for my response, shrugs, then goes back to his car. "Guess I'll be going then. Nice meeting you."

Ugh, he's only trying to make conversation, Mica. "Welcome to the neighborhood," I blurt. There, that's something. He glances back and smiles in a way that makes my stomach tie into a knot. He's cute in a non-standard kind of way. Not conventionally gorgeous, but definitely stare-worthy.

"I'm Dane." He waves, getting into his car. He closes the door and brings down the window. "Again, it was a pleasure meeting you." He doesn't ask for my name. Maybe he figures I won't tell him anyway. I need to stop being so standoffish and remember I'm in a small town again. People are friendly. *I* used to be friendly.

He drives down Maple, elbow sticking out of his window, checking out the neighborhood. *Nice guy.*

"Nice meeting you, Dane," I mumble, watching the car until it disappears around the corner. The sunset has started, so I really need to get a move on. But it's not until I've walked halfway back, thinking about my house and the awful vision I had, Coco hissing at nothing, and the cute, tall guy who appeared out of nowhere, do I realize what Dane-lanky-guy was driving—an old blue Eclipse.

CHAPTER FIVE

"The schoolmaster is generally a man of some importance in the female circle of a rural neighborhood…of vastly superior taste and accomplishments to the rough country swains…"

The halls of Tarrytown High teem with busy, chatting students, popping in ear buds, talking about football and HollowEve a few weeks away. I recognize a bunch of them from elementary school. I tried not to wear anything showy this first morning—jeans and two thin layered T-shirts, one pink, one white, plus my new sweater, but I still manage to get stared at.

Do they recognize me? Do I remind them of that poor Hispanic girl with holes in her sneakers who they used to go to school with a long time ago? Maybe I wore these Manolo Blahnik sandals on purpose to remind myself of how far I've come. I'm not oblivious to their whispers and glances.

In fact, since realizing the blue Eclipse belonged to Dane yesterday, I'm more aware than ever before. Is he following me? Or was he another passenger who got off the train last night like I did? Maybe his was a completely different Eclipse altogether. Then again, I'm tired, and it's October in Sleepy Hollow. Spooky things just come with the territory.

Forget the staring people. Just find homeroom.

Homeroom goes without a hitch, no embarrassing introductions of the new girl. When the bell rings, I set off to find Bram in the courtyard like we agreed this morning. My heart beats like crazy as I stand around scanning for him. Whoever hasn't noticed me yet definitely will when I meet up with Bram. Finally, I spot his tall, athletic form across the courtyard. He's talking to friends and waves when he notices me. Damn, he's gotten cute.

I smile and sit on a wall to wait for him. A familiar-looking guy chewing a straw with tattoos covering his arms walks his well-used bike past me. He stops, stares at me hard. *Here we go.* "Burgos?"

"Hey." I plaster on a polite smile. Patrick Sanders? He used to be dimply and cute. What happened?

"I thought that was you. Holy shit, girl, what are *you* doing here?" He smiles, showing nicotine-stained teeth.

"School, my dad's business…stuff." *My mom died, so I came to collect her things.* "How've you been?"

"Not bad, not bad." He ogles my boobs more than my face. "Anyway…"

I cross my arms over my chest. "Yeah, anyway." I catch a glimpse of Bram, who's making his way toward us. *Save me.* Bram sneaks up behind him, puts his arm around my shoulders. "Sanderrrsss, my friend. You remember Mica, right?" Bram's easygoing smile and direct eye contact are both refreshing and a relief.

"Of course, we were just talking," I say.

"Getting reacquainted. That's awesome." He focuses back on Patrick. "And you, you're coming to HollowEve this year, right?"

"Hell, yeah, buddy, wouldn't miss it for the world!"

"Great, so you're helping us this Friday with decorations?" He vice-grips Sanders's shoulders. "We need an extra pair of hands."

"Hmm, *that* I can't promise you, sir," Sanders mutters. "But I'll try."

"All right, man."

"Take it easy. Bye, Burgos." Patrick's lecherous gaze lingers on me one last time before he rounds the corner and chains his bicycle.

I let out a breath. "Now *that* was a blast from the past. He didn't seem too happy to see me, either."

"He's an idiot." Bram greets more friends as they walk by. A whole group of seniors stares at me. "Look, some people are going to feel weird about seeing you again, that's all. You can't let it get to you. You know how this town is. Ready?" He offers me his arm. I take it, aware of how risky this move might be in front of the whole school.

Walking to class, I'm aware, more than ever, of the whispers behind my back, and I don't mean ghost voices. "Why don't *you* feel weird to see me again, the way they do?" I ask, looking away any time a pair of familiar eyes meets mine.

"You want me to feel weird?" He raises an eyebrow.

"No, I appreciate that you don't, believe me."

"Hey, I never cared what people thought of you. Why should I care now? You're still my friend, right?" He gives me a side-glance, his way of testing the waters.

I just smile. He *was* my best friend once upon a time, but high school's a whole different animal. Going against the grain by being seen with me could be a fatal flaw, especially in light of recent rumors at Historic Hudson *and* the fact that somewhere in these halls, his ex-girlfriend, Lacy, lingers. "Aren't you scared people will see you with the town weirdo's daughter and start judging you, too?"

He stops cold and turns to me. "Mica, have I ever been scared of attention?"

"Well, no, but—"

"Exactly." He tugs me along. "I mean, sure, I know a few people who'll think I'm crazy for talking to you after the stuff your mom claimed. But I don't give a shit. To me, there's only one thing wrong with this…" He lifts his arm slightly to show me my arm linked through his.

"Which is?" I ask.

He leads me through the crowds, and I can feel his hesitation. "Nothing."

"No, tell me."

"Nah, you'll take it the wrong way."

"Bram, please? Just tell me."

He sighs and shrugs. "We're only friends."

"And?"

His eyebrows slope slightly, his expression conflicted. His deep brown eyes kill me. "That's what's wrong."

Oh. I stare at him. Yeah, see, this makes me feel all sorts of indecision. On one hand, he's turned into quite the popular, hot man on campus. On the other hand, I didn't come back to complicate my life, more like simplify it. "Bram." I shake my head, breaking eye contact with him. "You know I can't start anything with you. I won't be staying long. I'll be leaving soon."

"I know. Why do you think I haven't said anything? You have a habit of leaving." His tone is dabbed with the tiniest bit of resentment. He high-fives and fist-bumps a few more people, as I slowly pull my arm out of his. Last thing I need right now are more guilt trips.

"Bram, I really appreciate you picking me up from the train station, taking me shopping, escorting me around school, but you don't have to. I'm a big girl and can handle everything on my own. I mean, if it's going to mess with your reputation…"

"That's not why I'm being nice, Mica."

"Then, why *are* you being nice?"

"Do you think anybody in this whole school has ever seen me in my Spider-Man undies like you have? I mean, come on, dude." He scoffs.

I laugh. "I remember those. They had this blue waistband and pocket thingy in the front for your—"

"Ah, shit." His voice lowers as he stares ahead. I follow his gaze down the hall to see what interrupted him. The crowd ahead of us parts like the Red Sea, allowing us a view of a pretty girl with long brown hair, talking to another girl. She looks up at us. "Great," Bram mutters.

"Let me guess. Lacy?"

"The one and only."

"Are you gonna talk to her? I'll just go. I really don't want to be in the mid—"

"No, stay with me. Keep moving." He makes a beeline for the stairs without acknowledging her. I almost feel sorry for the girl, the way he won't even stop for her. Following him, I give the girl a sorry smile to show I mean her no harm. Last thing I came back to Sleepy Hollow for was more drama. "Watch, I'm gonna get a text any minute now."

Bram climbs the stairs two at a time, now that we only have one minute left to get to class, and I do my best to keep up with him. Sure enough, Bram's phone chimes, and he shows me a text from Lacy:

You left me for that?

"See?"

What?! Screw feeling sorry for her. "What are you going to tell her?"

"Not responding. There's plenty of other guys in town." He turns down a long hall.

"Which reminds me, do you know a guy named Dane? Super tall, skinny?"

"Dane what?"

"No idea, but he drives a blue Eclipse."

"Didn't you mention a blue Eclipse the other night?"

"Yes, at the train station. He's older, maybe in college. He stopped by my mom's house while I was there yesterday. I think he's looking to buy it."

"You went by your mom's?" Bram's eyes widen.

"I said I was going to. Remember?"

"Yeah, but I thought you'd try and get the key first. How'd you get in?"

"I didn't. I never made it in. I went to visit Betty Anne, but she wasn't home, and that's when I ran into that Dane guy."

"Wow." He shakes his head. "I'm sorry to say it, Mica, but your old place looks desolate. I drove by there not too long after…you know. It looks haunted."

Haunted is a bit of a stretch, but I agree the house needs some serious TLC. "I know." I don't mention the visions I had. Considering he still pokes fun at my hearing voices, I doubt he's ready to hear about full-blown hallucinations.

"Whatever happened to her cat?" he asks.

I wince. "Oh, about that? Coconut needs a place to stay, and Nina has these really bad allergies..."

"No. Come on, Mica. Don't do this to me, dude."

"Please? I promised her I'd be back for her."

"You made a promise to a cat?" He runs down one last hallway. "Look, *I'm* fine with the fur ball, but I have to ask Jonathan. It's his apartment. If he says yes, I'll give you a key, but *you* take care of her every day. Got it?"

"Thank you!" I do a little skip that makes him laugh.

"In here." He opens a door to let me in first. The class is full, and there doesn't seem to be any teacher to care that we're late. We sit near the back, where I watch Bram greet and clasp hands with at least half the people in the room. Still everybody's main man.

The bell rings, and a round man with a trimmed brown beard, wearing a brown polo shirt and pants, walks in. He looks like a baked potato with a cane limping through the aisle. He scans the room and notices me right away like a heat-recognition robot. I've seen him before, talking to my mom at Sunnyside years ago. He nods at me. I do my best to blend in with my plastic orange chair.

"Good morning, class," he says, out of breath.

Bram leans back and whispers. "Doc Tanner."

"I gathered."

Dr. Tanner sets down a stack of papers on his desk and turns to the whiteboard, no taking of attendance, no introduction of the subject. AMERICA'S FIRST MAN OF LETTERS, he writes in purple marker. Doesn't waste time starting lessons, does he? "In the spirit of the season, anyone know who this is?"

A few students raise their hands. Bram grins over his shoulder at me.

Yes, my great-great-great-great-uncle, or so Mami fantasized. Maybe if my mother hadn't tried so hard to belong to the old Hollow families, they wouldn't have snubbed her so maliciously.

"Annette." Dr. Tanner points a fat finger at a brunette sitting in the first row.

"Washington Irving?"

Dr. Tanner recoils. "You have to ask? Everyone in this room should know this without the least bit of doubt. Our town's reputation, economy, even your parents' livelihood, all depend on this one person, so say it again...like you mean it!"

"Washington Irving!" Annette cries a little louder, giggling.

"Better." He smiles. "But did you know that Irving wrote more than just 'The Legend of Sleepy Hollow'? He penned massive biographies about Christopher Columbus, Muhammad, and George Washington, his namesake, only to be remembered for a bunch of characters he felt were silly."

Well, he got that right. Irving felt himself to be a greater writer than the stories he was famous for. I lean forward. "And I know exactly which shelf those books sit on in his study," I whisper in Bram's ear.

"Unless your mother moved them."

I dig a knuckle into his back. What does he mean by that?

The teacher puts a heavy hand on the desk to steady himself. "He was an American hero, yet he lived most of his life outside the U.S., served as ambassador to Spain, traveled the unfathomable frontier of the American West...fascinating fellow, famous for good reason."

Ah, the perfect refresher to prep me for Yale. I love

the sound of Dr. Tanner's voice and the fact that I'll be acing this class. Having spent my life listening to my mother give tours about Irving's home has its perks.

"Yes?" Dr. Tanner says.

I look up to see a guy in the middle of class holding up his hand. "Is it true that a journal of his was stolen from the Engers' library?"

My ears perk up. Slowly, I put my pen down.

The teacher cocks his head and shakes as though suppressing silent laughter. "You mean from the private collection at the Historic Hudson Library?"

"Yeah, that one."

"Eric, *stolen*..." Dr. Tanner clears his throat. "Is a harsh word, isn't it?"

I whisper in Bram's ear. "Is that what Jonathan was talking about the other day?"

Bram's face turns a hair, a *shh* at his lips. *Ugh!*

Dr. Tanner goes on. "Rumors are worthless without evidence, which is why I've brought in an expert on the subject, so good timing, Eric, good timing." Taking a quick survey of how many students there are, he passes out a stack of stapled work packets. "As you get your October unit, I'd like to introduce you to our new student teacher..."

I scan the room, not seeing anyone else who fits the description of a teacher.

"Whenever he gets here," Doc adds. "He's studying at Harvard, working on a thesis about the lives of America's earliest influential writers. This week, he'll be teaching the nineteenth century unit, while I sit on my rear and read the *Times*. If you have any questions, ask him. If you have any food to share, give it to me." Chuckles sound throughout the room.

Suddenly, the door to the room opens, and everyone glances back to look.

"You'd do well to listen to every word he says. He's quite the specialist in author biographies, especially Mr. Irving of hometown fame. Ah, here he is now. Say hello to Mr. Boracich."

I watch, in slow motion, as the spindly weathercock of a man bustles in and waves at the class. My heart races like I'm suddenly contending for the Triple Crown. Bizarre thoughts shoot through my mind—rumbling blue steel, pale hands jotting down notes, a slow and guttural voice muttering something between my ears.

"Oh my God," I say, eliciting a few wary looks from students. "That's him," I whisper.

Bram leans in to me. "Who?"

"The guy I was telling you about, the one who went to see my mother's house."

"*That* guy?" Bram sizes up the student teacher and smirks.

Dane Boracich soaks in the welcome with a happy-to-be-here smile. But just before taking his seat, he pauses. Everyone follows his gray-blue gaze as it lands on...who else? The new girl—Micaela Katerina Burgos. I glance back politely, noting Bram's baffled expression.

What? I shrug at him.

Bram faces the front again, his widely set legs bouncing nervously. I try to pretend that nothing out of the ordinary just happened, that the new teaching assistant didn't just single me out with his puppy dog stare, but it's futile. Like trying not to notice that someone's head's been shot off by a cannon.

CHAPTER SIX

"She was a blooming lass of fresh eighteen; plump as a partridge; ripe and melting and rosy cheeked as one of her father's peaches…"

"I can't believe it's him."

"So it's the same dude you saw yesterday. Big deal." In the courtyard, Bram pops open a can of Coke and sucks the rising foam noisily.

"Big deal? Bram, I saw his car at the train station, I saw him on Broadway, then I saw him at Betty Anne's house, and now I find out he's my teacher? Don't you think that's a little weird?" I rip open my spork-salt-pepper packet with so much force, the contents go flying all over our table.

"Nice." Bram picks a salt packet off his sandwich. "It's Tarrytown, remember? You see the same faces everywhere. Funny coincidence maybe, but definitely not weird. Besides, maybe you keep noticing him because you think he's hot?" His added smirk means he's fishing to see if I'll agree or not. I remember this strategy to get me to talk from our old days together.

"Maybe, but it's still weird the way he looks at me like he knows me. Then boom, he's in my neighborhood, then boom, in my classroom. Weird."

"Weird. Very weird. Now can we stop saying weird?" Bram brushes off the topic and takes a huge bite out of his sandwich.

I narrow my eyes. "You're not jealous, are you?"

"Of what?" he mutters, mouth full of food.

"I don't know." I put down my spork. My salad is old and wilted. I think about the teaching assistant staring then smiling at me in front of the whole class when Bram told me just minutes before that being "only friends" was a problem. I drop my head into my hands. Suddenly not hungry.

I feel Bram's warm guy hand rest on my arm. "Hey, you okay?"

I try rubbing my face awake. "Yeah. I just need more sleep. And to figure out what my mom wanted from me so I can go home."

"You just got here a day and a half ago, dude. Give yourself a break."

"Sorry, I just—"

"Why leave so soon?" he asks, sounding mildly offended.

"Bram, you don't understand. Right now, I'm missing my senior year at home with my friends. I'm missing Columbus football games, I'm missing Homecoming..." *I'm stuck in the town that made me want to leave in the first place.* "Can you tell me something?" I ask, dying to change the subject. Die-hard locals never understand why anyone would want to get away from here anyway. "What did you mean about my mother moving things at

Sunnyside? And tell me what Jonathan and that guy in class meant about a stolen journal."

He swallows slowly. "All right, don't get mad, *but* my mom and Aunt Janice said that just before your mom died, she would move things around Irving's study, which you know you're not supposed to do unless you're a curator. Janice had to tell her a few times to quit it."

Why would Mami purposely annoy Janice Foltz, the office manager at Sunnyside? She wouldn't want to get fired. Why would she break any rule, for that matter? "Did she get in trouble for it?"

He shakes his head. "I think they let her go with a slap on the wrist, because she was…" He glances from his food to my face, hesitant to say something.

"What? Just say it."

"Mica, you should know that by the end there, your mom wasn't the same anymore. In fact, she was considered kind of…" He points the sandwich at his head.

Oh. So that's it? Mami had gone officially nuts. That would mean that the note she sent me was merely evidence of that. I don't know how to feel about this. It's true that during my last year here, Mami had become less and less concerned with what people thought of her. She went around talking to herself. She stopped hiding her dolls in the sewing room and started putting them on display instead. Still, lots of people are eccentric without actually having a mental illness.

"Hey." Bram looks up into my eyes. "I'm not saying she was. I'm just letting you know what others said about her. She rarely talked to anyone much after you left. Only Ellen at work and that neighbor lady of yours, so it was easy for people to think that."

"She was just passionate about her interests. A bit of a

loner. But she wasn't crazy."

Then again, I remember times when I went into the basement to say good night to Mami and found her at the sewing machine, whispering to herself. She'd pause, whisper again, as if having a conversation with nobody. Didn't I talk aloud to the voices yesterday, too?

The thought of becoming like my mom makes me shiver. Another reason I need to get out of Sleepy Hollow—ASAP. This town will suck you in and not let you go.

"I didn't think she was," he says. "Just felt maybe she was kind of...obsessed."

Obsessed. Mami, living alone, distraught, only Coco to keep her company, moving items around Sunnyside like a madwoman. Not to be mean, but she brought it upon herself. She could've joined us in Miami instead of staying with the very people who hated her.

Bram reaches out and swipes a thumb across my eye, then the other one. He dries it on his napkin. "I shouldn't have said anything. I'm sorry."

"It's okay. I haven't really thought of these things until I got here, so I guess it's all kind of hitting me. So, tell me about the missing journal." I fold my hands on the table and regain my composure. "Please."

"Don't worry about it."

"No, I need to know."

Bram extends his legs, bouncing his knee nervously. "You know how, for years, people have talked about Irving and his private journal?"

"Yeah, so? All the great authors of the time kept them. His journal is totally public and easy to find online. His private writings are even on display."

He scoots closer to the table and whispers, "Not

those. A different one. At the Engers' library, in the rare collection. Not *even* the rare collection, more like the never-to-be-*shared* collection. Not-even-with-an-appointment collection. It's all hearsay, Princess. For all we know, it doesn't even exist. I know I've never seen it."

"Seriously? I think I would know about this. My mom would've talked about it incessantly. What does it say?"

"Well, assuming it wasn't staged, like the fake stuff he knew everyone would read and analyze about him after he died, it would contain real bits about him, things we never knew—the dirt. That's all. You know how locals here feel about their Irving history."

"Yes, but I still don't see why it would be a big deal. So we'd learn he really liked brunettes instead of blondes. Wow, call the *New York Times*." I shake my head, glancing at my phone. Lunch is almost over.

"I agree. He's long dead, and that's why I told you don't worry about it. Hey, can I ask you something?" He takes a big sip from his soda. "Are you coming with me to the meeting Friday? I need someone to spray paint the oversize door knockers."

I stare at him. How can he think about HollowEve when I'm asking about a missing Irving journal and why it was important enough for Jonathan to insinuate I'd know anything about it? Is he that insensitive or brushing me off? "Way to change the subject, Bram."

He smiles sheepishly.

"Fine, I'll help you at HollowEve." I watch him carefully. Being around him and Jonathan and other locals might clue me in more if he won't be straight up with me.

His dark eyes flare. "Yeah?"

"But only if you help me get to the bottom of my mom's issues. Anytime I need it. Until it's done. Deal?"

He clucks his tongue, impressed by my persuasive skills. "Deal." He winks, and a lingering smile slides across his face, making me fight some unexpected tummy butterflies. Two seconds later, he throws his charm into high gear as I watch him recruit three more volunteers for HollowEve right there in the courtyard.

Everyone's obsessed with something, Bram. Even you.

After school, I rush out, eager for fresh air. I book it toward the police department and call the realtor again. I get the same annoying voicemail beep without a greeting. What kind of realtor doesn't want to talk to a potential client? "Hi, this is the second time I've called about the house on 150 Maple Street. Please call me back as soon as you can."

I hang up and take two shortcuts, but I'm still out of breath by the time I get to the Tarrytown Village Police Department. Inside, the station is empty, except for a receptionist playing a word game on her computer. She has brown hair and bored eyes. "May I help you?"

"I need to speak with someone about my mother's death in August, whoever dealt with it, I guess." On a bulletin board beside me, a posted flyer reads: *Historic Hudson Theft TIPS? Contact Officer Stanton,* along with a number and extension.

"Nobody's in. Come by in the morning." Word Puzzle Girl focuses back on her screen.

"But this is the only time I can come. I'm in school in the morning."

"I understand, but you need to talk to Officer Stanton,

and he's only here in the mornings. Who was your mother? I'll make a note." Reluctantly, she picks up an actual pen.

I clasp my hands in a tight grip. "Maria Burgos."

Her lazy eyes pause on me. She places a notepad and the pen on the counter. "Leave your information here. I'll have someone contact you."

I stare at the pen a moment, wondering if I should go Miami diva on her and demand to speak with someone immediately or play by small town rules. I decide to go with sugar over vinegar. I write my name and number, underlining them twice. "Thanks. It's important." I tap the notepad.

"Mm-hmm." She places the note on a pile of papers. Then, without even looking at me, she returns to her screen and clicks on letters and blank squares. Really? Miami Beach Police would've been buzzing like a beehive already *and* offering me a mango soy latte.

I drum my fingers on the smooth counter. "Thanks so much. You've been a super huge help." I turn on my heels, wondering how long "mm-hmm" really means, assuming they even get the message. Right before exiting, I pause at the Historic Hudson Theft poster, swipe my camera phone on, and snap a pic of it.

On the way home, I make use of my long walk and bring up the poster photo, dialing the number shown. Of course, I don't expect Officer Stanton to actually answer if he's only there mornings, but there's no harm in trying. The line rings four times before voicemail picks up.

"Thank you for calling Historic Hudson Theft Tips Hotline," a gruff voice announces. He sounds like the cop who called me in Miami after my mother died. "Please leave any information you wish, anonymously or not. If you leave a phone number, we will call you back. Thank you in advance."

I prepare my chirpiest voice while waiting. *Beeeep.*

"Hi, Officer Stanton? My name is Micaela Burgos. Could you please call me, like, when you're actually in the office, or...whenever? Thanks." I sound so stupid, but I leave my phone number, then hang up, satisfied that I did everything I could to get through to the guy.

Entering the townhouse, I hand Nina the thick, customary packet of parent paperwork. She drops her head in exasperation, then I head back to my room for a quick recharging nap before moving on to Plan B. No such luck. Petticoat ghost woman is back. She doesn't speak this time, only stares ahead with her smoky face. In the corner of a dark room, she sits in a rocking chair, rocking back and forth absentmindedly.

Micaela, she finally says, turning her face toward me. *I'm so incredibly sad.*

I'm sorry, I tell her, *but I can't help you...*

I can't. I truly, honestly cannot help the dead, nor do I want to. I'm not in deep sleep yet, so luckily, I'm able to rip myself right out of the dream and sit up in bed, sweating.

Bare white walls of my temporary abode remind me of everything I don't have right now—the salty ocean breezes, my bike rides on Ocean Drive, my friends... Same as has been happening since I was little, I get that familiar feeling the phone is about to ring. A moment later, it's a text from Emily—a kissy face emoji:

So? How's it being back?

Weird. Familiar. Distant

Bram treating you ok?

Yes tho I think he's getting heat
for being around me.
Anyway he's not the prob

What is the prob? Mica u gotta
open ur chakra

Em, chakra-opening doesn't work
with me. I'm in a stress fog all the
time. I desperately need sleep.

Ru breathing? Be aware of ur
breath

I try but it's hard to tell when I'm
awake and asleep sometimes

Turn inwards, Mica. If you tune
out ur brain, u will fall asleep

I wish it were that easy. But I hear
voices whispering around me. I
can't see anyone but I hear them
warning me.

Like with ur mom's note?

I stare at her words for a long time. I appreciate her
concern and willingness to help me, but her yoga chakra
breathing stuff has never solved my problems. I feel
perpetually worried. Her speech bubble waits expectantly.
With Emily, I can't really tell her everything. I decide on
giving her what she wants, finally typing:

Exactly.

•••

After another few chapters of *Wuthering Heights*, I head
out to clear my head. I cut through the college at the
heart of town on a gorgeous moonlit night, enjoying the
cold air over my nose and mouth, the lake, brick buildings,
iron benches, ornate lampposts, and other things I'd
missed while living in Miami. Above the trees, the full
moon is just visible, creating shadows along the cracked
sidewalks.

Can you see me?

I rush past a couple sitting on a bench, canoodling
and whispering closely. Conceivably, the voice could be
coming from their quiet conversation, except...I know it's
not them. "I need sleep, I need sleep, I need sleep," I chant
in rhythm with my footsteps. "Go away, go away, go away."

I turn onto University Avenue where Ye Olde Coffee
Shoppe glows like a beacon of caffeine for the under-
rested. At least six bikes are parked outside. I pull on the
wooden handle, the chimes sound, and the aromas of fresh
brewed coffee and baked goodies kiss me hello. I slip into
the warmth and spot Jonathan in the back, wiping down a
counter. "I see you're quite the cashier."

He stares at my boobs and body then back to my eyes
for a fraction of a second before looking away. "I'm not on
register tonight. He has me slaving away."

"Well, you have to jump on the corporate ladder
somewhere," I joke.

"Or, you could just have it handed to you."

I ignore his jab. "Is Bram here?"

"Should be soon. You want me to tell Sir Fudge you're
here to see him?"

"Who?"

"The manager. He's always saying 'fudge' instead of 'fuck,' so that's his nickname. You sure you don't want to work here? It was always your dream. The benefits are awesome…free skinny lattes." He slaps on a fake smile.

I don't know why he feels so compelled to force work on me. Did he not hear the part when I said I wasn't staying in town for very long? "No, thanks, John. You know I'm here to settle my mom's stuff. But I appreciate your looking out for me and all."

"Suit yourself." He shrugs and returns to counter-wiping.

What's his problem? I get in line to order, and a girl's voice speaks next to me. "Micaela?" I turn and find Natalee Torino from middle school, mouth agape, green eyes blasted right open. "Oh. My. God!"

"Hey, Natalee, how's it going?" I give her a quick hug. She's still short and pretty, a little taller than when I last saw her. An aura of vanilla-smelling body spray surrounds her.

"Good! Really good! Was that you with Bram in Dr. Tanner's class? Were you the one the new assistant kept staring at? I knew it! Well, that would make sense." She rolls her eyes.

"Wow, you were there? I was so nervous. I'm sorry, what would make sense?"

"Just, you. You know…Micaela, blond, pretty, hooked to Bram's hip." Natalee's smile fades slightly like she might have said too much.

When we were in elementary school, some kids had a hard time understanding that Bram and I were just friends. They'd say that boys and girls who were friends as kids would one day end up married. It was an innocent assumption at the time, but some girls really like him. My being back in town could possibly be a threat to girls like Natalee and Lacy.

"He wasn't looking at me. It was something behind me." I clear my throat uncomfortably, order a latte and an oatmeal raisin cookie, and then step aside to let Natalee order. "What did you think of the class?" I ask just to change the subject.

"Welllll, it's Doc Tanner." Natalee raises an eyebrow. "So we're gonna have to work really hard. I'm kind of glad Mr. Boracich is there to buffer things, though."

I can't say I agree. For me, the literature class would have been easier without Dane Boracich. Having him stealing glances at me when he's as cute as he is will make it exponentially harder for me to concentrate.

Natalee pays the cashier, then scoots past me. "Well, good seeing you."

"Yeah, same here. Nice to see you, too." I smile and wave good-bye. I let out a quiet, nervous breath. At least she was nice to me.

From behind the counter, Jonathan keeps a close watch. I'm not sure what to make of it. He could just be getting used to the sight of me again. Or plotting to kill me. Or staring at my breasts. It's hard to tell. I sneer at him and go find a seat.

There's one by the big front window, so I head over with my coffee and cookie, pulling out a fresh, clean notepad and pen. Taking in a deep, cleansing breath, I begin to write:

HOLLOW TO-DO LIST

1. Go back to house and get Coco.

2. Ask Betty Anne about Mami's things.

3. Call Officer Stanton again.

4. Get house key from realtor OR break in.

5. Try not to break in. Try to use actual key.

The chimes sound, and a moment later, Natalee's vanilla bean cloud whooshes back to my side. "Speaking of the devil…" Her sights land somewhere by the ordering counter. "Super tall, isn't he? And kind of adorable, right?"

It's Dane, unwrapping a dark gray scarf from his neck, checking out the menu. "Yeah." Since he's not looking straight at me, for once, I take advantage and check him out. Handsome in a non-traditional way, pale chiseled face, soft, wide smile when he talks to the cashier. Not bad for a stalker. I run my fingers through my hair. Maybe Bram is right. Maybe I *do* find him attractive.

"He's not like firefighter-hot"—Natalee giggles—"but there's something about him. Am I right?"

Definitely. I don't think it's so much about physical appearance, though. I think it's because he's older, goes to Harvard, plus he's teaching my favorite subject. A college man…nothing like the boys in this town. As if that weren't enough, he's new here, kind of like me.

"I guess so," I reply, as blasé as possible. I don't need to express how hot I find my literature teacher and give people more fodder for rumors.

Dane takes another step in line, and I notice how he watches everyone in the shop. Silently, carefully. His eyes are clear and beautiful, steel blue and powerful. I often wonder what mysteries lie behind people's facades, and this guy is a prime example.

I sip my coffee, trying to focus on my to-do list, but I'm keenly aware that he's already spotted me. When I finally gather enough courage to look up again, I'm not surprised to find him studying me. My heart races.

I smile politely and catch Natalee eyeing the whole wordless exchange with a goofy grin. Dane orders then waits by the counter while I, for the life of me, cannot think of the next item for my to-do list. I tap, tap, tap my pen, as he stares. *Stay focused, Mica.* A moment later, I feel someone crouch by my table. "Hey, there."

My stomach knots. I act surprised. "Ah, the other newbie in town."

"Micaela, right?"

My smile softens a bit. "How did you know my name?" I didn't give it to him at the house yesterday.

"Dr. Tanner's attendance sheet?"

"Ah." *Derp.* But then I remember… "You didn't take attendance today."

Dane's eyes flit side to side across mine, then he glances down in shame. "Okay, you got me. I asked someone. But you told a little lie yourself. You said you weren't from around here."

"I'm not. I mean, not anymore. I used to live here six years ago. So, technically, it was the truth." I feel bad that he's still crouching. Should I invite him to sit? Even though I'm eighteen, he's my teacher. Won't that be, like, taboo?

He peeks at me sideways. "I see. I don't suppose you're related to the Maria Burgos who owned the house we were looking at yesterday, are you?"

My fingers tighten around my ceramic mug. It's probably all public information, but it still stuns me to hear my mother's name from the lips of this guy, someone even newer to Sleepy Hollow than I am. "I, uh…"

"Sorry, that was personal." He stands and glances around. "I was only wondering if that was your house. If it is, I didn't mean to make you feel like I was intruding yesterday."

"No, it's just...that *was* my mother's house. But I just don't see it as a house for sale yet."

"I completely empathize. Again, I'm sorry."

I notice his retro black-and-white-checkered sneakers. *Nice.* "Have you called to see it yet? The realtor doesn't get back to me." Nobody gets back to me.

"Not yet, but I'd like to get inside soon, maybe take a look around."

It's odd to think that he wants to see the very room where I used to dance and twirl, even see my growth chart and stickers. Assuming my mom kept it all there and didn't erase the memory of her betraying daughter by painting over them, that is.

"I'm sorry to ask...I mean, I know the circumstances by which your house was made available..."

"My mother's house."

"Your mother's house." He clears his throat. "It seems like a nice enough place, but I'm wondering if there are any structural problems with it, anything I should know, or..."

"I wouldn't know. You have to call the realtor."

He points at me. "The one that doesn't answer."

"Right."

"Right." He smiles, and we both chuckle. "Sorry to ask."

"It's okay," I say. But if he wants to be nosy, two can play the same game. In fact... "I feel bad you're standing there. Want to sit?" I gesture to the chair opposite me.

"Oh..." Dane checks the time on his phone, like maybe he has somewhere he needs to be, then looks at my to-do list. "You sure? You look like you're working on something."

"I was, but it's okay. Two more minutes won't kill me." *I have questions of my own.*

He nods and takes the seat. "Thanks."

"No problem." Whoa. Nerves and excitement course through me at the same time. "So, why are you teaching at Tarrytown High as opposed to a college somewhere?"

"Well, I'm still a student myself, just started out teaching. And your high school is in a literary town." He pauses as if judging to see how receptive I might be to an expanded answer.

I don't encourage him, but I don't discourage him, either.

"See, I'm writing my practicum, which covers Irving, Hawthorne, Longfellow, Poe. I'm interested in how their literary choices paved the way for postmodernism."

Ah. Now he's starting to speak my language. "That's one of my favorite topics."

"No way." His light blue eyes disappear into a crinkly smile. I know I shouldn't be staring right at him this way, but he doesn't seem like a teacher to me. He seems like just another student.

"Yes way. They led fascinating lives, didn't they? So secretive and tragic. I could read about them for days. It's what I want to study when I get to Yale." I toast my coffee cup at him.

He taps my cup with his. "Good for you. And great school. You got in?"

"Not yet. Hoping to."

"You will." He takes a sip of his coffee. His demeanor is so easygoing, I'm starting to feel like he's someone I've known my whole life. "So I'm touring their hometowns, trying to get a feel for what they experienced when they lived...where they lived. Well, at the time anyway."

I never heard of anyone touring historic homes while writing a practicum before. What a great gig. Except he's forgetting one thing... "But Irving wasn't very secretive." I study his face closely. Surely, he must know this. "He wrote everything in his diary. Anyone can read it online."

I know I'm giving him a hard time, but it's true—Irving's life was an open book. Every little thing from what he had for breakfast to the people he met throughout the day for years and years. As a teacher on the subject, shouldn't he know that?

"Impressive." His clear eyes hold my gaze. I find it difficult to look away from them. He sits back, clasps his hands. "I guess all the locals are just as familiar with his life as you are?"

"Not all of them, but some." I sip my coffee, noticing the shape of his lips. Full but not too full. "My mom was an Irving historian." I realize I haven't spoken openly about her to anyone but Bram in a long time. Without warning, I find myself wanting to tell him everything—how I spent half my life at Irving's home, read his works right from his very own leather-bound copies at the library, how my mom believed we were related to him, how Coconut was born from one of Sunnyside's resident cats...

I could go on and on.

"Not that you're from around here or anything." He winks, then we both see it at the same time—Bram bustling up to the coffee house, cold hands shoved in jacket pockets. "Thanks for the chat, but I have to go now." He stands suddenly, smiling. "Lesson plans, things like that. I'll see you in class tomorrow, Micaela." He pronounces my name correctly, the way people do when they make an effort to say the soft Spanish L, the way my mother used to.

I twiddle my fingers, try to hide a coy smile. "Bye, Mr. Boracich." Sweet Jesus in Heaven, I am flirting with an older man. A teacher! He can't be more than twenty-two or three. But still!

He dawdles a moment longer to get his scarf on right and collect his things, then he smiles at me one last time. The door chimes tinkle, and Bram plows into the shop, unbuttoning his jacket and blowing out harried puffs of air. His eyes capture me and Dane together, and for a second, he seems thrown. He stops short of my table. "There you are, Micaela."

"Hey, *Abraham*." I widen my eyes at him. *Someone's acting weird.*

"What's up, teach?" He gives Dane a momentary nod.

Dane points at him. "Bram, right?"

"The one and only." Bram takes on a stronger, tough guy stance.

Dane nods, and I'm embarrassed by Bram's little show of bravado. "Have a wonderful evening, you two."

"You too, teach." Bram's eyes could shoot lasers as he takes the chair opposite me and follows Dane's movements all the way out of the coffeehouse.

Dane pauses at the door, preparing his scarf for the cold. He glances back at me, a silent apology in his eyes. Not that he did anything wrong. Then, he spills through the chiming door into the night with his coffee.

I smile at Bram sitting across from me. "Hi. Did you need me for something?"

"Flirting with a teacher, huh?" He laughs, folding and unfolding a napkin.

"Who says I was flirting?" I cock an eyebrow at him.

He taps the table with nothing else to say, then gets up. "I'll see you later, Mica. Gotta get to work."

"But you said, 'there you are,' like you were looking for me. What's up?"

"Nothing. Don't worry about it. You look awesome, by the way." He winks then rushes to the back, grabs his apron off the wall, and claps hands with Jonathan.

What just happened? It's not like I was on a date with Dane. Is Bram still sore? I know I rejected him, but I was only twelve at the time. If I wasn't here on a mission, I might be interested, but… Wait, what am I talking about? I shake my head and stare at my list.

6. Stay focused on what you came to do. No thinking of Bram Derant OR Dane Boracich.

7. Because the Hollow knows how to push your buttons. It knows how to lull you back into its dreamy hold, Mica. And once it does, it'll never let you go home.

CHAPTER SEVEN

"...the more bashful country bumpkins hung sheepishly
back, envying his superior elegance and address."

Turns out I have a rotating block schedule, so it's
three classes one day, then three the next. Rinse
and repeat. So I have to wait until Wednesday to have
American Literature again.

On Wednesday, I watch Dane from my seat behind
Bram. I'm beginning to internalize things about him, like
the length of his loose blond hair and the way he nods
every time Dr. Tanner says something. The way he scans
everything going on in the room when he thinks nobody
is watching him, and the way he covers his mouth with his
fist when he's listening.

I have to say, even if my dad wasn't making me stay
in school while visiting Sleepy Hollow, I'd probably attend
anyway, just to watch him. He's completely fascinating.
However, I'm careful. Every time Bram looks back to see
what I'm doing, I pretend to be absorbed by my literature
book. I know we're not together, but something definitely

simmers just underneath his surface.

"And now, ladies and gentlemen, I'm handing it over to Mr. Boracich for the start of the new unit," Doc Tanner says, putting up his feet on a plastic chair.

Dane stands at the front of the class, and he and Doc Tanner fall into a deep discussion over something, as though agreeing first on the material to be presented.

Dane claps once to get everyone's attention. "All right everybody, here's my big debut." Chuckles echo throughout the room. "I'd like to begin by asking…how many of you have secrets?" He raises his hand to get us to do the same.

Half the room raises theirs. I don't, even though I have plenty of dreams, visions, and voices nobody knows about.

"Right, most of us do." Dane paces around slowly. "But would you ever tell anyone your secret?" Quiet laughter and *hell no*'s resound. "No, because then it wouldn't be a secret anymore, right? But what if you were a writer—any writers in the room?" He raises his hand suggestively again. A few lift into the air.

Aside from a research paper I wrote last year, I'm not much of a writer.

"Well, what if you were compelled to write everything down? Whether for posterity or because you're just cursed with the need to record every thought, emotion, plan you've ever had? Would that be a great testament to your existence, or would that be…say…shooting yourself in the foot?"

"Shooting yourself in the foot," Bram offers, eliciting chuckles around the room.

"Could be." Dane holds eye contact with Bram for what feels like an eternity. "And that's why primary documents—journals, birth certificates, notes, letters—

are so important to historians. Because long after we're dead, everyone will read them and know more about us. Especially the dirt."

Bram taps his pen on the desk repeatedly. I nudge his shoulder to get him to stop.

Dane goes on. "It's interesting to discover that people we regarded so highly were just like you and me, people who made mistakes."

"I never make mistakes," Bram mumbles, and his buddies erupt in laughter.

Ugh. Bram is in a dork mood. "Let the man speak," I whisper.

"Of course not, Bram. Not you." Dane grins.

Muffled *oohs* resound around the room. I want to hide under a rock.

Dane uncaps a marker and writes two names on the board. All the awkwardness suddenly melts away, replaced by the sound of scribbling pencils:

Washington Irving & Mary Shelley

"So when we find out more than basic facts about a person, like where they lived, when they were born, what books they published, you start getting clues, and these clues make you wonder where the truth really lies."

I've seen those two names together before, but it's all suspect. What does Dane think he knows about it? A hand goes up in the front. "Who's Mary Shelley?"

Seriously? Come on, people.

Dane holds his arms out. "Anyone want to answer that?" Nobody raises their hand. I want to, but I'm scared of looking like the teacher's pet. "Nobody knows this author's most famous piece of Gothic romantic literature?"

"Micaela knows," Bram declares.

I almost smack him over the head with my binder. "Instigator."

Bram snickers.

"Micaela?" Dane raises his eyebrows at me.

"*Frankenstein*," I say. I can't believe nobody else knew that.

"Correct." He smiles.

Natalee raises her hand. "I thought the author of *Frankenstein* was British, but isn't this American Literature?"

"She was, very good. But Irving was barely American himself, for all the time he spent on the other side of the Atlantic Ocean. The reason I wrote their names up there is because a lot of people believe that these two..." He gestures to both names with his dry-erase marker. "Were hooking up."

Giggles erupt through the room. One guy loudly yells, "Yeah!"

I've heard of this, but it's pure rumor. Behind Bram, I mutter to myself. "Shelley wanted Irving to want her. I'd hardly call that hooking up." I heard my mother talk about this to guests at Sunnyside before. Irving and Shelley were briefly a couple after her husband died—the famous poet, Percy Bysshe Shelley—but the romance lasted less than a year and didn't really amount to anything. He must be bringing this up because it's October and fun to think about.

"Can you imagine if these two would've married and had kids?" Dane raises an eyebrow. "Two major celebrities having a baby. Not that different from today's famous stars getting together."

Natalee raises her hand again. "But Irving never had children. Didn't his fiancée die when he was like nineteen?" *Ding, ding, ding! Go, Natalee!*

"Yes, but he could've been with another woman after that," Dane says, and a few guys chuckle knowingly. "I'm not saying they *did* have a child. I'm saying *if* they did, that child would've been a famous kid back then."

"My mom said he was probably gay," Natalee adds. "Never married, never had kids…"

"…Was a world traveler, yes, I've heard those, too." Dane sits on the edge of the desk. "And it could be true. But he still could've had a child. Many gay men in the nineteenth century were fathers and husbands. Things weren't as out in the open then as they are now."

Everyone's taking notes while I just sit back. I don't know. I don't buy it.

"But as I discussed with some of you…" His eyes land squarely on me now. "Irving wrote everything down. His diaries were extremely detailed. Miss Burgos, why don't you tell them? You've had an interesting perspective considering where you spent a lot of time growing up."

Ground, swallow me. The stares at me range from envy to genuine curiosity. If anyone had missed the return of Micaela Burgos earlier this week, they definitely caught it now. I clear my throat. "You pretty much hit on everything. But um…he wrote about things like music and language lessons, the friends who came to call each day, what he ate for supper…daily, boring stuff like that."

"Everything, exactly. Thanks." He uncaps his marker again and writes on the board: *1825–1826.* "Yet the year he spent with Ms. Shelley went undocumented. Only his recorded meals and visits with fellow authors take precedence during this time. No details about their relationship."

All is quiet, except for Bram, who nervously taps his foot against the floor.

"Odd, right?" Dane cocks his head. "That Irving should so deliberately skip over the time he spent with Ms. Shelley? But then, the years that followed while he was in Spain spoke vaguely of something he brought with him from London. *The double creation,* he wrote." Dane pauses for huge dramatic effect. "Twins maybe?"

What? *Oh my God, please, Dane, this is so silly.* I never read anything about Irving bringing something from London, double creations, or any babies for that matter. What would make him say something like that?

Bram raises his hand. "Wouldn't people have known if she was pregnant with twins? That's not exactly easy to hide."

Dane shrugs. "Depends. If you were Mary Shelley, a woman shunned by a society that already hated her, who spent all her time trying to have her husband's works posthumously published, living with her only surviving child in a run-down apartment because she wasn't making any cash from her books—not really. She wasn't in the limelight like Irving was. In fact, she was considered crazy and a leech to rich and famous Washington Irving. Not the type of woman he would ever mention in his journal. I mean, God forbid anyone reads the embarrassing stuff about him." He pauses. "Would you record it?"

"I wouldn't write anything," Eric says.

"But Irving couldn't help it," Dane says. "He left a paper trail everywhere he went, which means that *somewhere*, he must have written about his involvement with this young woman who was only nineteen when she wrote her most famous novel. And it'd be interesting to imagine what happened between them. I mean, we're talking the authors of 'The Legend of Sleepy Hollow' and *Frankenstein* having a romance together. That's pretty freakin' cool."

The class laughs, while I keep my eyes down before he calls on me again.

"Two legendary characters of Gothic and post-Gothic literature, the brainchildren of two amazing people," he says, his words lingering in silence. Doc Tanner is taking mental notes of all our reactions. "Anyway, just something you all might not have known about your *town hero*."

Bram leans back and stretches. "That would be one awesome monster movie right there. *Spawn of the Headless Horseman and Frankenstein*! Grrr!"

I roll my eyes. "They're both boys, stupid."

Our eyes meet, and he gives me a mock shocked look. "Stupid, huh?"

How incredible would it be to prove Dane's theory correct? The truth is, nobody will ever know. Any diaries of Irving's not housed at the various universities around the country are at the Historic Hudson Library, the Engers' library. And my mother read them all. She would've known about any kids the two authors might've had, and she didn't.

Dr. Tanner discusses something with Dane, but I can't hear them since the rest of the class is talking about Bram's suggested new horror movie. In the midst of this, Dane looks over at me protectively, as if I'm surrounded by wolves.

As crazy as this idea sounds, I'm liking Dane Boracich for his creative theory. Dane and I are so much alike. He's a mature man of Harvard, whereas I've applied to Yale, and he knows his history of literature, and I'm going to study literature as a precursor for law school. And lastly, whenever he's around, he watches me like a hawk.

Which is sexy, albeit borderline stalker-ish.

But strangely reassuring.

And nothing to do with being two peas in a pod. But I like it.

Chapter Eight

"But all these were nothing to the tales of ghosts and apparitions that succeeded."

After school, I check my messages, hoping the police department called me back, but only Emily did to see how I'm doing. I head to the townhouse to drop off my backpack and books, determined to scratch items off my to-do list. Nina is in her room on the phone, whiny voice rising and falling between what sounds like whimpers.

I knock lightly on the door. "Nina? You okay?"

The whimpering stops. "I'm fine, Mica. How was school?"

"Same as always. I'm going for a walk. I'll be back later." I don't know what's going on with her, but I sneak out to give her privacy. Once outside, I focus on Item 1 on my list—*Go back and get Coco.*

From the top of the hill, I gaze down on a rustling blanket of orange and gold. The air smells of matted leaves and browning foliage. Red brick buildings sit on gray country roads, and the whole thing makes me smile.

Fine, maybe I did miss Sleepy Hollow a little.

Though I used to hate the droves of tourists passing through to check out the changing leaves and the field trips full of kids learning about the area's history and famous resident author, one thing I always loved were the Halloween decorations. On my walk, I note all the cool stuff on porches everywhere—stretchy webs, giant spiders, tombstones, carved pumpkins, painted pumpkins...more pumpkins than you can count.

I make my way down the slope, opting for a shortcut to my old house through a row of yellow birch trees. It's a quiet route I used to ride my bike on with Bram a long time ago, with a bubbling brook that parallels the foot-drawn path. As water glides over the smooth rocks, I don't know what I love more, its bubbly sound or the biting cold air sending fresh puffs of leaves raining into the brook.

One lands by my feet, beautifully intact and orange, and I bend to pick it up. I'll take it back to show Emily. She was so envious I'd be seeing the change in seasons.

Fallen branches crackle underneath my feet.

Lela...

A shape of a person to my left catches my eye. But when I look straight at it, it's nothing more than some birch trees outside the barren backyard of an old house, its chain link fence sagging in the middle. Who the hell is talking to me?

"Mami?" I call into the empty path.

Nearby open windows emit fragments of conversations from within houses and other sounds filtering through the screens. Pots and pans clanking, clothes dryers running, even the smell of lavender static sheets in the musty air, but no one is here with me.

To my right, I catch another glimpse of a grayish

shape, but when I stare straight at it, it's just the trunk of an old maple tree. "Jesus," I mutter, keeping my eyes focused on the end of the path.

I hurry toward it, almost there when another sound joins the hubbub that is my crazy mind, a sound completely unlike the din of domestic household noises. I stop and strain my ears. Rhythmic pulse of footsteps. Running? Coming down the shortcut? Leaves crunch somewhere behind me—choppy, in a hurry, and...headed in my direction. Human or animal, I'm not sure. I whirl around to face it, hoping it's a dog trotting or a jogger charging through the woods.

But there's no one there.

"Uh, okay..." My whisper forms a warm cloud in the chilly afternoon air. A cold sweat breaks out on my forehead as my heart begins pounding hard. My hands turn clammy. I wipe them on my jeans.

The golden path is as empty as when I walked through it. But something ran through here, I know it did—I heard it. Turning back around, I break into a sprint. At the end of the shortcut, I push through an opening in the trees on the east end of Maple Street. Four older boys are there, circling on their bikes. Was one of them in the woods just now, and I just didn't see him? One boy plants his feet on the ground to stop his bike and gapes at me openmouthed, as if he's seen the headless horseman himself.

I wave at him to show it's only me, and he resumes riding. "I'm losing it," I mutter.

Collectively, the boys ride to the opposite end of the block. I'm alone again on the empty street. Panting, I hustle onto the sidewalk and make my way back to my old blue-gray house. When I finally arrive, I stop to catch my breath and take in the scene again. The house's faded exterior, sagging front porch, and tall, thin, dry grass all around makes my heart ache.

"Coco," I call out. "Cocoooo."

No kitty to be seen. She must be getting her food from somewhere else.

I try the realtor again but get the same stupid voicemail beep. "Hello? Can someone please call me back?" I leave my number yet again then hang up. Then, I do the same with Officer Stanton's information number and leave a message there, too, when no one answers. What is going on with these people? Exactly how hot is a hotline number that no one picks up?

Taking slow, deliberate steps, I head up Mami's steps and knock on the door. All is still. Even the trees have stopped moving. Slowly, I press down on the handle. Locked.

"Coco?"

Ambient sounds calm me—distant cars humming, a horn blasting on the river, squeaking of the porch planks. Every time I try calming myself through breathing, like Emily suggested, the action triggers a memory. I hear my parents—

"How long has this been going on, Maria?"

"I don't know what you're talking about."

"You know exactly what I'm talking about!"

"Let go of my wrist, Jay. I swear, you're more like your father every day, imagining things that aren't there."

"You calling me stupid?"

"I'm calling you delusional."

"Interesting, Maria, when you're the one who talks to people who aren't there. Maybe if you'd pay more attention to me—to her..." Though I was hiding in the pantry, I

could tell he was pointing at me. So much for my secret location.

A surge of sadness rises in my chest. I choke with the unexpectedness of it. Why couldn't we make it as a family? Swallowing back tears, I fight the urge to leave. I must stick this out. The side yard is overgrown with weeds, and the crawl space lattice is broken, exposing the underside of the house and a spot matted with white fur. "So that's where you've been sleeping, Coco?"

Lela, go.

I freeze then turn around slowly, straining to listen. As usual, nobody's there. All I hear are birds chirping, a screen door slamming somewhere, and my own punctuated laugh. "Mami?"

No answer. It must be my mom if she says Lela. Why is she telling me to go, though? I pinch the bridge of my nose. This is what it feels like to go crazy, isn't it? When nothing makes sense, but everything feels so real.

The windows and doors to the house are still locked. Though I checked all ways in last time I was here, I'll try them again. When I crouch to the basement window, something's changed. The window is broken now, the pane completely gone except for a few jagged edges. Someone broke in since I last came by. I hit the cold ground on my stomach and slide in. Hopefully, someone will suspect me of being another burglar and call the police. Then I'll finally get to talk to them.

Inside the basement, I choke on the pungent smell of dried urine. How could the realtor not do something about this? In the murkiness, I make out the old Berber carpet, the scratched walls in need of paint.

Holy crap. Look at this place.

Where sewing machines and craft tables used to stand.

Where I colored and played with Barbies while Mami crafted dresses for each of her beloved creations. Why didn't she ever take a break and sit on the floor to play with me?

Heading up the stairs, I realize the basement door might be locked, but when I try it, it gives way. Quiet space looms ahead—

...not here...

Not here? Who's not here? Whispers flicker in my mind again, most of them indiscernible. And then I realize I have a choice—to either shut my brain against them or open myself up. Thing is, I know that once I do, I might unlock more voices. What if doing that starts a flood of voices and visions, opening a portal or something? Am I ready for that?

Voices can't hurt me, I tell myself. *Just do it. Talk to them.* "What was that?" I ask the emptiness bravely. "What do you mean 'not here'?"

Cold silence this time.

My presence has stirred up the stagnant air. Vertical strips of light filter through the blinds like ghostly sheets hung up to dry. Illuminated dust vortices swirl between them. To my left is the office once used for paying bills and storing boxes of papers—articles my mother had researched, all by hand, never with a computer, books about the region, Irving, the Rockefellers, political histories of Spain and Portugal, whatever. Now it sits empty, two wire hangers in the closet.

"Shh, stop shouting, Maria. She'll hear you."

"She's asleep!"

"She's not, she's listening…you don't even know your own daughter!"

I fight back tears, picking up more of the argument,

but I can't tell anymore where my thoughts begin and end. The wind is back, softly rattling the living room window panes. I stop at the bottom of the stairs, foot poised on the first step, staring up into the darkness.

Gripping the railing, I gradually edge my way up. Regret, like a thick, heavy fog, settles over me. The whole separation began as whispers behind closed doors when I was six or seven until finally one day, my parents were yelling right in front of me. I reach the landing and pause. "Hello?"

Ridiculous. This house is nothing but musty and empty. I aim toward my old bedroom. The door is closed. I brace myself, hand on the doorknob. It'll be completely painted over, I know it. Any mother who barely spoke to her daughter over the years would have removed all traces of the little girl who once lived here, the little girl who abandoned her. I'm going to find storage boxes, a bigger office, or worst of all—more dolls.

I turn the knob and let the door fly open.

Shiny silver stickers flicker at me, still stuck to the wall, which is still yellow, though more pale than I remembered. I cover my gasp with my hands, and the tears come. The mark on the wall from using my bed as a trampoline is there, too. In the closet, the board games are gone; clean white rectangles on dusty shelves remain. They sat there until recently. I move to the spot where my bed had been, where my little night table with the ballerina lamp used to be.

"Night-night, Mami."

"Night-night, my little Lela."

Huge, fat tears slip out and fall. I make no effort to wipe them. This room is used to tears anyway. I back out into the hallway. To the left, my mother's bedroom looms in the dark.

...was an accident...

I stare at the master bedroom. Again, I try talking back to the voice instead of ignoring it. "What was an accident?" Or was that *wasn't* an accident?

The voices are muddled, or maybe I'm not letting them in right. I take two tentative steps toward the room. *"What is it, Lela? Come in already,"* my mother's sniffling voice said to me one night, as I lurked just outside her door. All I'd wanted was to say good night to her.

Now, I step into the master bedroom. Moss green walls, drab and dusty beige curtains surround me. I cross the vacant space, pausing outside the bathroom door, pulse pounding in my ears. The little orange tiles, still here, still old and dirty. I force my eyes toward the tub, cracked and rusted around the faucet, dull metal coated with soap residue. A cruel image flashes against my mind like the glint of silent lightning—brown hair streaked with gray, pale expressionless face pressed against porcelain, blood running into the drain.

My limbs begin shaking, but I can't leave. Not until I know. "How did it happen, Mami? Tell me." My voice shakes in my throat.

Suddenly, a coppery taste laces my tongue. I swipe it with my thumb. Blood. In the rusted mirror, the girl staring back is almost not me, standing here so goddamn heartbroken. Is it me, or my mother? Something scuttles behind me. I spin around, dropping my leaf. "Hello?"

The tree outside the window scratches against the pane.

What are you doing here? Get out.

"Mami? But you asked me to come…"

No answer. Only my heartbeat pounding between my ears, the whoosh of blood flowing through the capillaries in my head. In the distance, the faraway sound of a boat's horn blasting. "Mami? I'm not going. Not yet."

Silence.

Six weeks. Six short weeks ago, Mami was still here, a living, breathing person—the woman who brought me into this world and loved me despite her obsessions, a woman I once loved, *still* love, even though she did nothing to stop me from leaving...gave me no reason to stay.

Had she tried, had she *told* me how much she loved me, that she would change, pay more attention, I might've never left. Instead, I tested her. Because I was twelve and just as stubborn as she was. The blank space ahead of me feels crackly and charged with energy. I reach out my hand.

Mami, my flesh and blood. No reason to be afraid of her, if she's here. Even though I can tell. I can tell that I'm not alone.

That she *is* here.

Right now.

Watching.

LELA, GO!

I bolt away, plummet down the stairs to the dining room, fleeing the voice, crystal clear and right in front of me. That one was *not* in my mind. It's one thing to imagine you're not alone and another to hear someone in the hanging stillness, a voice not your own and yet so familiar. Or was it me who spoke aloud?

Scratches mark the wooden floor where the dense dining chairs had been—my mother's chair more than the others. The smell of dying lavender returns, a reminder of all things withered in this house, but it's only my brain playing tricks on me, like everything else.

"Run, like your father."

"No," I say, shaking the memory. That can't be her now. That voice is a memory. I remember her saying that. It's connected to the dining table. The day my mother sat on one end, me at the other, and she forced me to decide. "You made me choose."

"Me or Dad. Who's it going to be?"

I couldn't take the neglect anymore—the nights at the library, the incessant sewing and research, having to make my own meals or go to Betty Anne for food. Somehow, I had to show her the damage she'd caused me. So I chose my dad. Because that would *hurt her* and make her change. But it backfired—*I* changed.

Balled fists at my side, I yell, "Do you hear me? I was twelve! A child should *not* have to choose!"

All is still, except for my heaving chest. Slowly, a chilly breeze wafts its way in and wraps its icy tendrils around me. My own cloudy breath hangs suspended in the air. Then I hear it. The sickening sound of shoes dragging—*foom-foom-foom*—from somewhere upstairs.

"Who's there?" It's hard to think rationally, but maybe the realtor's been in the attic all this time? I'm not about to find out.

When I spin around for the front door, it's wide open, as if someone has just dashed off in a hurry without bothering to close up. I have to run through there? *No.* I don't feel like trailing behind a ghost, if that's what opened the door. But it's the only way out. I barrel straight for it, stomach in my throat. I can't help but feel like I'm in one of my own dreams.

Two steps onto the porch, I slam into a live, warm body. A woman cries out and falls against the railing. "Ma-Maria?" She stands there ashen, shaking hands at her mouth.

"What?" I pant and double over to suck in a breath.

Betty Anne's mouth moves as if to say something, but no sound comes out. She looks the same as the last time I saw her, except grayer, a few more crow's feet around her eyes, horror splashed across her face. "Who are you?"

I realize the terrible thing it was to come here and dredge up the past, scare the crap out of myself and the neighbor, too. I should've gone to her first. "It's me, Micaela." I force out my dimples. Betty Anne always loved them, said she could hide inside them, they were so deep.

She shakes her head. Little by little, her face changes as she realizes who I am. Then, her arms stretch out. "Mica? You're finally home. Oh, come here, honey. You scared the living shit out of me."

I fall into her arms, half laughing, choking back tears. "I'm so sorry."

"Are you okay? You didn't go in there alone, did you?"

I nod.

"Lord Almighty. How could you?" She pats my back.

I want to sob all over her shoulder. I want to tell Betty Anne everything, how I was overcome with a need to see the house, to know and understand, but all I can do is stand here in her arms, remembering. Dinners after her husband died, after Dad had already left. I was on the fence about whether to stay or go. We consoled each other, the two of us sitting in her kitchen like old ladies.

"How did you get in? You have a key?" Her big green eyes question me. She steps into the foyer and surveys the empty house.

"Through the basement. Through—"

"The loose window?"

I nod.

She sighs. "I've been meaning to take care of that." She runs a hand over her silver hair. "But this door was open. I thought you had a key."

"I thought *you* opened it," I say.

"I didn't." We look at each other. Betty Anne doesn't seem as shocked as I expect her to be, as if she were used to doors opening all by themselves. "I found her, you know."

I swallow hard. "Yes. That must have sucked."

"I won't tell you about it."

I already know. I think back to Sunday when I stood on the porch and felt the horrific vision overtake me. Betty Anne stares at me with an expression I can't quite decipher. I guess it must be weird seeing me six years later, no longer a little girl. "I was wondering when you'd visit. I have something for you."

For me? Finally.

"Yes," she says, as though she heard my thoughts. "We need to leave. We shouldn't be here. It's too soon. Come." She tugs me by the hand. I let her. It's nice to have someone treating me like a daughter again.

I peer back into the lonely house. Some movement, some twist of smoke catches my eye. Something is still there, but I'm not going back in again. "Wait. Please," I tell Betty Anne, pausing to soak in the house one last time, because I will not be coming back. *I'm leaving now, Mami.* I wait for the voices, fragments of thoughts, anything.

My mother doesn't answer. I can't tell if I'm relieved or disappointed.

I step aside to let Betty Anne back out, and a flurry of movement from the stairs catches my eye again. I turn my head. Call it stress or lack of sleep, but right as the old woman mumbles something about finding the right key on her key chain, for one fleeting moment, I see her—gaunt and wispy on the stairs.

In a nightdress. Blood spattered on her shoulder.

Twirling my fallen maple leaf.

CHAPTER NINE

"All these, however, were mere terrors of the night, phantoms of the mind that walk in darkness."

Maybe it's pent-up wishes or regrets forming before my very eyes, but I still reel at my first sight of my mother since the day I left. Clinging to the doorframe, I stare at her, not knowing what to do, but she dissipates as quickly as she materialized. I might not have really seen her at all.

If Betty Anne notices my troubled expression, she doesn't show it. "Come on." She urges me out of the house then locks it. "You look like you could use some tea. I have chamomile, orange spice, Earl Grey…want some?"

"Coco," I mumble, dumbstruck. Did I imagine the whole thing?

"Yes, I've been leaving food out for her, but I haven't seen her since yesterday. Wonder where that kitty cat's been. Mica, you all right?"

The blood on her shoulder…it was spattered.

...

*F*ive doors down, Betty Anne's house is filled with antique furniture, framed photos of her late husband, grown children, and seven grandkids, all boys, all with the same round face and high forehead as Betty Anne. Figurines of owls and frogs in funny poses fill the shelves. These things were a part of my life for so long, yet all it took were some palm trees and ocean views to eradicate them from my memory.

I plop onto the couch in the back room, needing a moment to myself to think about all that happened.

"I'll be right back. Or would you prefer coffee?" she asks.

"On second thought, just water, please." My mouth is parched.

Is that...

"Is that what?" I whisper.

"Is what what?" Betty Anne asks.

"Nothing," I say. Wonderful. She probably sees my mother in me, talking to myself.

On a shelf behind her, dwarfing the knickknacks, is one of my mother's dolls—a little Dutch girl with a blue and white satin dress and coif, wide blue eyes with small black pupils, and a tiny, awkward pale pink mouth. Her skin is spongy and horrible. The more I gaze at her, the more it seems like she'll come alive at any moment. At least Betty Anne appreciated my mother's handiwork.

She returns with a small manila envelope in one hand and a glass of water in the other. "Here you go."

I take the glass and down a long chug, letting the water soothe my throat. "I see you have one of my evil stepsisters," I say between breaths.

She follows my gaze behind her. "Oh, don't say that about Diana!" She lovingly caresses the hem of Diana's dress. "She's so pretty. They all are."

"They're wretched." I hear the twinge of jealousy in my voice, my ten-year-old self creeping out to say hello.

"Well. I can see how a child might not appreciate them. They are sort of peculiar."

I want to retort with the fact that I'm now an adult and still not anywhere near appreciative of the dolls. She flips the manila envelope over and over in her hands. "Why did you take so long to come?"

She was your mother... I can almost hear her say it.

The unspoken words make me wince. It's not like I meant to take so long. "There was a bad storm in Miami. My dad kept leaving town. I couldn't find a moment to make him talk to me about coming here. It was like he was trying to avoid it. He's not the easiest person to talk to about my mother."

"Yes, I know. Don't forget I knew your father. Your mother still talked about him," she says, looking away. "It's been hard because nobody's been able to get a hold of you."

My eyebrows crunch together. "What do you mean? My mom had my number. She even had my email if she'd bothered to use a computer. It's not like I lived on another planet."

Worry lines on Betty Anne's face tell me something's not right. "Oh, honey, I don't think so. I'm pretty sure she tried to get in touch with you but couldn't."

Is that true? If it is, then my dad has some explaining to do. Knowing my mother, though, she probably just said that to vilify my dad or twist the story around. I glance at the envelope in Betty Anne's hand.

Her expression dampens. "She gave me this a couple of months ago. Said to give it to you in case there was ever an emergency. I never thought for one second I'd actually be doing it." Her voice breaks, but she quickly recovers.

I swallow hard and take the envelope. It feels light in my hand. *MICAELA (MY DAUGHTER WHO LIVES WITH HER FATHER)* is written on it, underlined twice. *Ugh, guilt trip even now.* I unclasp the metal brad and peek inside to find a folded piece of paper. I slide out a small, lone key.

...yes...

"Originally, her attorney had it, a Riley-someone. But a couple weeks before she passed, she said she couldn't trust him or anyone, so she gave it to me." Betty Anne wrings her hands. "Looks like a safe deposit box key."

"Where's the rest of her stuff? Furniture, her papers, all her things?" I ask. "I tried going by the police station yesterday. I even left them a message, but nobody calls back."

"I believe it's all in storage."

"How can I get it?"

"Honey, you'd have to call the police or the state attorney's office. I do know that if nobody claims her stuff within a certain amount of time, the house and everything else goes to auction. So you'd better hurry."

"Then I have to find out where that storage is. She should've left the key to that, too." I shake my head. Had I stayed with her, this would be easier to handle. I have to get out of here.

Betty Anne takes my hand. "Mica, I know this can't be easy."

I stare at the key and envelope. "No, it's not. So is this

it? Did she give you anything else?"

"That and the house key are all I have. Your mother made me a copy when she changed the locks."

"She changed the locks?"

Betty Anne shifts in her seat. "Well, yes. Someone broke in a few weeks before she died. I suppose you didn't know that, either."

My heartbeat pounds in my ear. *Lela, please come home. It's urgent.*

"Did they take anything? Was she okay?"

Betty Anne sighs. "She was at work at the time. All the drawers had been pulled out. The closet floorboards cut up. Yet they left her jewelry box full of jewelry. Strange."

Yes, strange. Why would they go to all that trouble and not take anything of value? Mami had some nice pieces of jewelry my father had given her. He'd tried so hard.

I drop my head into my hands. "She could've called to tell me. I was available. She just wanted everyone to think it was our fault."

"I'm so sorry for everything, Mica. You know, even though your mother was a wonderful friend and neighbor, I always thought she was hiding something."

I pull out the piece of paper in the envelope. Maybe whatever she was hiding is here. "Where's South River Bank?"

"In White Plains. I would run over as soon as possible, see if that's where the key fits." She looks at her watch. "Darn, they're already closed for the day. You might need documents from her attorney, though." I fight back a wall of tears. Betty Anne pats my hand. "I know you two didn't end on the best terms, but you were all she had left. I know she would've wanted you to have her things."

Betty Anne might mean well, but she didn't see

Mami's face at the train station like I did—the anger lines, the determination to punish me for leaving.

"A mother never stops loving her child. Ever." Her words force me to tear up again. "I just can't believe your father didn't let you come to the funeral."

"What? What do you mean?" I stare at her. "She was cremated."

A long, uncomfortable pause. Then, "If she were cremated, then Ellen and I were at the wrong funeral. And I've been laying flowers at the grave of a different Maria Burgos all month." She shakes her head.

I can hardly breathe. Why would my dad lie to me?

Big green eyes bore right through me. "I think you need to speak with your father."

No shit. "Where is she buried?"

"Where else?" Tired, ironic smile. *Sleepy Hollow Cemetery.*

"I appreciate all your help," I tell her. And now, I'm dying to get out of here. When the sky begins darkening, Betty Anne offers me a ride home, and I'm too mentally drained to decline. I poke my head back through her car window as she's dropping me off. "If Coco comes back, please call me. I'd like to keep her."

"I'll do that." She smiles warmly then drives into the darkness.

In the chilly night, I lean against the railing of our back porch, overhearing Nina in the upstairs bedroom talking to her boyfriend on Skype. She sounds upset, though I can't pick up exactly what she's saying. Then it all goes quiet, and I'm left with the sounds of crickets.

They cut up the floor. What were they looking for? And could Dad and Nina *both* have forgotten to give me my mother's messages when she supposedly called? I can understand once, twice maybe, but for years? How could my father not know she'd had a funeral?

I breathe deeply to calm my nerves before popping in my ear buds. *You can do this. Just ask him straight out.* I call Dad three times, but the call drops every time. Finally, on the fourth try, his phone starts ringing.

He picks up immediately. "How's my beautiful girl?" The usual, bubbly voice.

"Good." I can't show him I'm pissed, or he'll shut down. "Dad, when are you coming up? Nina sounds worried."

"Ah, that. I've had some trouble, had to wait for a big deal to come through before sending money for the rent and the car. But it's coming in the next couple of weeks. Any minute now."

"A couple of weeks? Is everything okay? You've been going to Bogotá a lot."

"Damage control, baby. Things you needn't worry about. Just get your mother's things. Tell them who you are. Come home, okay?"

"But you said you'd be here soon." *Living with Nina is like living on my own.* I know my father is doing his best for me, and traveling is the sacrifice he pays to be able to do so. "I went to the old house today…"

Long pause on his end. "That must have been something."

"It was." I don't mention the vision on the stairs. "And, Dad?" I have to know the truth about the cremation…

"Mica?" His slow drawl comes out a warning. Yes, I

may be in Sleepy Hollow, but that doesn't mean I'm free to excavate the past and drag it out into the open. Coming here was my idea, not his, so he doesn't want to talk about it. When *he* left, he left for good.

I know he wouldn't lie to me. Maybe they buried her ashes. Still, I would've liked to know about it. "I just wanted to say…" *Say it. Ask.* "Did Mom have a funeral? You told me she was cremated."

"That's what they told me, Mica."

"It is?"

"Yes."

"Okay." I sigh. "I love you." I hate sounding like I'm accusing him of lying. The last thing I want is to ruin another relationship.

"Love you, too. Call me if you need anything." I hear him zipping up his suitcase in the background.

I need a lot, actually. I need all these problems solved, preferably by him instead of me, but I can do it. I'll figure this out. "I will. Bye, Daddy."

CHAPTER TEN

*"I profess not to know how women's hearts
are woo'd and won."*

On Thursday morning, I open Nina's door and shuffle up to her bedside, determined. She's sleeping with one arm over her face. "Can you rent me a car?" I ask. "I have to get to a bank far from here."

She mumbles then stirs and rolls over onto her other side. "If I could…would've gotten car…ready…to get the hell away from here…" Two seconds later, she's snoring again into the tangled sheets.

Okay. So much for that. I close her door, grab a banana off the counter, and take off for another enlightening day at Tarrytown High. After school, I call Bram, begging if he can please take me to the bank in White Plains.

"I work, Mica, but I can go with you on Friday. You can wait 'til Friday, can't you?"

"Not really. What about tomorrow?"

"Come on, dude. Your dad wouldn't have set you up in

a townhouse if he expected you to settle everything in one week. Stay a while. Chill. Come by the apartment. I have something for you."

"What is it?" My stomach tightens at the thought of what it might be.

"Just come. I'm here now."

I don't argue, hoping that when I reach his place, he'll let me use his car anyway. I could always drop him off at work and borrow it. I'm surprised to find the door unlocked. Gently, I push it open, tiptoeing in. A hodgepodge of things invaded since I was last here. Vampire masks, cauldrons, chandeliers, and giant metal chains.

Bram lies napping on the sofa. He's wearing his uniform pants but no shirt. His body is lean, arms and chest muscular, and as my mother used to say, *Ay, Dios mío.* Softly, I close the door to not wake him.

I'm so enraptured with the sight of him that I almost don't notice another prop, tucked between his feet and the side of the sofa. A white cat, super real looking. It blinks at me. *No way!* "Coco?" I whisper, so excited to see her, I almost break into cartwheels.

Coco yawns and stretches her paw, laying it possessively on top of Bram's foot, like she's saying, *I see you checking him out, but he's mine.*

"I can stare at him if I want." I pet her soft fluffiness.

She surveys the floor before hopping off the couch and sashaying over to me.

"I didn't hear that. At all," Bram says, stirring, cracking open an eye.

"You better not have. I can't believe you got Coco. Thank you so much!"

"You're welcome. The moment she starts scratching

shit, she's out of here."

"I'll make sure to get her a scratching post." I pick up the big ball of white fur and hug her close.

"I'll make you a key to the place, so you can feed her."

"When did you get her?"

"Late last night after work. Your mom's house was so dark, dude. I had to go around with a flashlight searching for her."

Late last night. That was after I was there, so he couldn't have broken the basement window. "You wouldn't know why the basement window was broken, do you?"

He shakes his head. "But I did hear a noise inside, almost crapped my pants."

So eloquent, Bram is. "What kind of noise?"

"I don't know. Raccoons maybe. They didn't even bother letting the realtor know." He laughs at his own joke. "Smelled like piss around there."

I recall the strong smell of urine in the basement. Were raccoons capable of smashing windows? "Great, my mom's house will be a haven for woodland creatures if it doesn't sell soon. Well, we just missed each other then. I was there after school looking for Coco."

"You mean I didn't have to go through the trouble and scare myself shitless? Thanks."

"Thank *you*, Bram, for getting my sweet Coco kitty." I bend to give him a quick kiss on the cheek, but he holds onto my arm, keeping me near. His breath falters lightly against my skin. I swallow gently.

"You're welcome," he whispers. His soulful dark eyes study my mouth, his hand sliding down until it's in mine.

For a moment, I love the way it feels. But then slowly, I slide my fingers out of his. *Don't complicate matters,* my eyes do their best to say. Though, honestly, how horrible would it be to just surrender and indulge in happy feelings? Something to counter all the anxiety.

"I'm, uh...going to get some water," I say, narrowly escaping the intimate moment. I head to the kitchen, trying not to show him how badly I'm swooning.

"So you like my armada of decorations?" Bram says from the couch. "It's all stuff to take to the meeting Friday night."

"I saw. Amazing." I grab a glass of water and fill it, standing at the refrigerator door, reviewing in my mind what just happened. "What do you do when Halloween is over? Your purpose in life ends?"

"Start on next year, of course." I hear him yawn and shift around on the couch.

"So you're like Jack Skellington when he discovers Christmas, all excited."

"Only if you'll be my Sally." He gives me a wide smile. "They're gonna post parts on Friday, for the show. I can't wait!"

"Ah, yes, the Headless Horseman might be yours." I chug back half the water. If he comes close to kissing me again, will I let him?

"And if I get it, all the girls will be after me. Even you. You won't be able to resist me. You won't even remember who Mr. Boracich is."

"Wait, what?" I set down the glass and gawk at him. "You really think I'm interested in Mr. Boracich?" I smirk at him. "And a guy without a head, sexy?"

"He doesn't need one. That's how good he is." Bram laughs, getting up to sit at the counter. Still shirtless. Still the proud owner of an amazing body that I am *so* not staring at. "What did you think about his theory?" he asks.

"Who? My teacher crush? I think it's insanely interesting," I say, if only to drive him crazy. By now, I'm sure he hates Dane for the way he looks at me.

Bram laughs in a forced way. "He's full of shit."

"Really? You liked the idea of Shelley and Irving having a kid together. You were all 'ohh, the horseman versus Frankenstein,' and all that."

He shrugs. "Because it *sounds* interesting, but I don't believe it for a second. Boracich's just another tourist in search of treasure that doesn't really exist. Next he'll be saying he found the Headless Horseman's bones at the Dutch Burying Ground. *Pfft*, whatever."

"Bram." I wash the cup in the sink and set it in the drying rack. "After the dreams I've been having, the voices I've been hearing, I honestly don't know what's real anymore. But please stop acting weird about Mr. Boracich. Just because he's sexy, smart, *and* intelligent, that's no reason to be jealous." I bite my lip. I love messing with him.

"Ha-ha, very funny." His lips press into a thin line. "People aren't what they seem. He might not be the gentlemanly scholar you think he is. In fact, he seems like the type of guy who wouldn't think twice about stealing someone else's property." He scoffs and grabs a banana.

Where's this coming from? "Who you calling *property*?"

He stops mid-peel and cocks an eyebrow at me. "Who said I was talking about you? You give yourself away, Princess."

"If you think Mr. Boracich is here to steal something, you're as paranoid as the rest of Historic Hudson."

"I'm just saying…stranger comes from out of town, starts talking about a weird theory in class, riles everybody up, and now he thinks he's hot shit. That dude doesn't know anything." And I would say that Bram is acting just like Brom Bones did after Ichabod Crane arrived in town. He eyes me sideways. "Would you go out with him?"

I poke my head around the column leading to the dining area. "What kind of question is that?"

"The perfectly normal kind. What? I'm just asking. He's not that old."

"He's our teacher, Bram."

"After graduation then?"

I shrug. "I won't even be here."

"Irrelevant. Would you?" His eyes darken with a tiny hint of menace, and his jaw tenses as he awaits my answer.

He asked for it. I shrug and play the coquette. "Sure, why not? I mean, he's a nice guy who also happens to have a functioning brain, *and* he reads the same authors I do. Plus, he's got great eyes."

He waits a moment, probably gauging how serious I am. "Hmm, gotcha." He picks up his phone and starts tapping on it.

Seriously? I laugh, shaking my head. "Bram, why don't you tell me what you really want to say, instead of dogging on poor Mr. Boracich?" Bram pretends to become really absorbed by his phone. "Hello, that was a question?"

"Huh?" He looks at me as if he completely forgot what we were talking about. "Oh, I was just kidding, Mica. You can have your rubber band, lightning rod, air traffic control tower, whatever. It's cool." A flicker of laughter shakes through his chest.

I remember these games. He's trying to get *me* to show that I care.

"He's not *that* tall," I mutter, refusing to fall for

his ploy. Coco pads into the kitchen and rubs her body against my legs. I crouch down to pet her and plant a kiss on her nose before I leave. "Love you, girly."

From behind his phone screen, Bram looks up at me. What is he thinking? Ever since he told me that being friends might be a problem, when I told him I wouldn't be here long enough for us to hook up, he's seemed to hold back on his feelings. If only he'd tell me, I might know. And then, I can decide, too.

"Thanks for picking up Coco." I collect my purse from the coffee table and walk over to him. His face is full of something I can't decipher. He's all talk and showy in front of his friends, but with me, he becomes a little kid again.

"Not a problem, Princess." He smiles and reaches out to *boop* my nose.

"See you at the coffee shop later," I tell him.

"If I'm lucky."

I head out and close the door, exhaling on the other side. As much as he's trying to show that nothing bothers him, I think I know the problem. He's still wondering if we'll ever have a chance. He told me he loved me before I left six years ago. Does first love ever die? He probably still feels the same.

Maybe, like an eager jockey, Bram's just waiting for his horse to fly out of the gate, waiting for the signal—*my* signal to tell him that I want him. And all I have to do is open the gate and watch him become a knight-errant of yore. Which I might want to, actually, especially after how sweet he's been to me.

Except I'm supposed to leave soon. And when I do, I'll be hurting him again.

Unless…I choose not to leave.

...

At Ye Olde Coffee Shoppe, finishing Math homework, I hear Sir Fudge in the back, yelling at Jonathan. "For fudge's sake, keep the scones wrapped or they'll dry out!"

I giggle to myself. Good. Someone needs to yell at him.

I'm polishing off my coffee when I feel the air displaced next to me. "You know, at first I was threatened by you," a girl's voice says. I look up and see Lacy, Bram's ex, hands in the pockets of her puffy parka. She's even prettier up close with her small nose, sharp cheekbones and chin, and honey brown eyes. Way behind her, I spot Bram looking on.

"What do you mean?" I ask, glancing up at her.

"Don't take this the wrong way, but now I'm just relieved he has someone *else* to obsess over." Lacy laughs a short, weary laugh. "Just watch out for those outbursts of his. Let me know if you need my help setting him straight."

"Lacy, I'm not with Bram."

She scoffs gently. "But you will be." She flips the furry hood of her jacket over her head and walks off.

I watch her leave the shop, chimes tinkling at the door, wondering what the hell that was all about. In the back, Bram just rolls his eyes and goes back to stocking the sugar counter. Finishing up my homework, who should stroll in but Dane again. Right away, his gaze finds me.

Did he come looking for me? I like to think that he did. Satisfying. Very satisfying. As I put away my homework and pull out *Wuthering Heights* to decompress, Dane picks up his coffee order and comes over to my table. "Is this seat taken?" He smiles.

"No, go ahead, *Mr. Boracich*," I say, just to see him smile. I know Bram is probably having a hissy fit in the back, but it's not like Dane isn't allowed to talk to me.

"Mica, I'm not that much older than you, I don't think."

"How old would that be anyway?" I ask.

"Twenty-two. You?"

"Eighteen." Well, now that we have that out of the way, we can both sigh and feel better about this coffee talk. "Interesting theory in class yesterday."

"Ah, you liked that? I thought it was fascinating when I read it."

"Where'd you read it?" I ask.

"Local articles. It has a lot of people talking. Surely you've seen the posters around town about the theft at the Hudson Library. Thought you'd know that."

I stare at his clear eyes, the way they seem to know so much about me when we only recently met, the way he tests me to see how much I know. "I've been sort of in my own world this week. Sorry."

"No need to apologize. I know what it's like being new in town and having everyone question your reasons for being here. Speaking of my reasons, you said you grew up at Sunnyside, right?"

"That's right. Why?"

"Do you still have connections there? I would love to go visit. I mean, I'm dying to see where Washington Irving worked and slept. You wouldn't mind being my tour guide, would you?"

I'm taken aback by the request. I haven't been to Sunnyside in six years, but I could probably still recite my mother's historical facts and ramblings. The bad part, though, is that the old house brings back memories. "I don't know, Dane. Sunnyside is the reason my mother stayed in Sleepy Hollow. Going there will stir up old memories."

"Ah. I get it. I'm sorry about that. I'll go on my own then. I heard there's lots of activities this time of year."

"There are. Literary festivals and stuff. You should look into it."

He smiles, wide and winsome. "Well, I won't keep you. I see you're busy."

I'm so not busy, I want to tell him. *Stay and talk to me some more.* He has a soft, reassuring way about him, and I just know we could probably sit in silence and not have to speak. But I'm sure he doesn't want to give people fodder to talk about any more than I do. He tips an invisible hat on his head. "Have a good evening, Micaela. See you in class on Friday."

"Good night." *Dane.* I smile and watch him go.

No sooner than a minute after he leaves, Jonathan is by my side, restocking the coffee stirrers. "Jeez, Mica, I didn't know you had a bodyguard. I better be on my best behavior." He chuckles his lecherous old man laugh, and I toss three crumpled napkins on the floor just to make him pick them up.

CHAPTER ELEVEN

"He was always ready for either a fight or a frolic; but had more mischief than ill-will in his composition..."

Things are crankin' along. Now I have a key belonging to a bank and a ride there, and it's only Friday. At this rate, I'll have my answers before the police ever call back.

As I wait for Bram downstairs by his car under cloudy skies and dense humidity, I think about what I'll find at the bank. During sixth period Economics today, I fell asleep and dreamed about shadowy people cutting up my mother's floor and the persistent thought that whatever is in the safe deposit box today is what they were looking for.

Bram locks up the house and comes down, opening my car door before rounding the back and slipping into the driver's seat. "All right, ready? Let's go."

"I can't thank you enough for taking me," I say.

"You're welcome. I had to postpone my pizza and beer hangout this afternoon with Jonathan to take you to this place," he laughs.

I shake my jazz hands. "Ooo, first Coconut, now this. I owe you my life, Bram."

He smirks at me. "Sassy girl. You got your mother's key?"

"Got it."

"Then let's do this."

When we arrive at South River Bank south of Tarrytown, I write my name on the waiting list and sink into a plushy seat. What could it be? Research? Jewelry? A flaming bag of poop?

I imagine finally opening the safe deposit box, and inside—a note: *Here you go, selfish daughter of mine, this is what I leave you—nothing.*

"You okay?" Bram takes my hand.

I stare at its smoothness, his skin tone slightly darker than mine. It should feel awkward that he's holding it, but it doesn't. I need the comfort right now. "Just nervous." With everything going on, I worry about what could be inside her safe deposit box. And if anyone else is dying to know, too—townspeople, Historic Hudson people, police people...

I close my eyes. At least I'm not alone.

After a while, a nicely dressed man comes to the waiting area. "Miss Burgos?"

"Yes." I give Bram a parting look and follow the man over soft carpeting into a little office overlooking the parking lot. There are potted plants, framed certificates, and pictures of family on a file cabinet behind his desk. *Theo Hertz* is engraved on a nameplate in front of me.

"What can I help you with today, Miss Burgos?" He smiles, sitting down.

I take the tiny key from my backpack. "I need to know if this opens a safe deposit box here, or something." I sound so childish even to my own ears. Now I realize how many things my dad has always taken care of for me.

"Do you have an account here?" he asks.

I flip the key over in my hand. "It would be my mother's. She passed away this summer. It might be in her name or mine."

"I'm very sorry to hear that. What about her other possessions? Did she leave you in charge of them as well? Was there a will?"

His questions feel like sandpaper against my ears. Why didn't Mami take care of these things? Why was she so hell-bent on making my life as difficult as possible? "I don't know anything. I'm hoping this key will give me some answers."

Mr. Hertz has a friendly smile. He holds out a hand. "May I see?" I hand him the key to examine. "This does look like one of ours, one of the older ones. The new ones are card keys. But unless you have probate documents allowing you to use it, I won't be able to help you."

Probate documents. Wonderful. "What if I don't have any? Does her stuff just sit here forever?"

"Not forever, but for a while. It goes to the state's unclaimed property office."

"But I don't have any documents." Bitter resentment swells in my chest. Why would my mother go and put a single unidentified key in an empty envelope like that without any other instructions, or even send a short message in the mail? Unless she was in a hurry.

My eyes burn with fresh tears. Mr. Hertz plucks a tissue and hands it to me with a sympathetic nod. "Here you go."

I press it to my eyes. "Can you at least confirm that the box belonged to her? If it was in her name? I just, I don't have anything else."

"I understand. Believe me, this sort of thing happens a lot." He types on his computer. "Her name?"

"Maria Burgos." I look out the window. In a way, I hope the key doesn't belong to this bank, that it doesn't belong to anything. A childish part of me wants to be absolved of any responsibilities my mother might have left me. "150 Maple Street, Sleepy Hollow," I add.

The keyboard and mouse make soft clicking noises. "Let me just see something…" His fingers fly over the keyboard. He stops typing. "Yes, she had a safe deposit box here. And you're…Micaela?"

"Yes." My heartbeat picks up speed.

He swivels his chair to face me. "Good. Because your name's there, too." He smiles. All I can do is stare at him. "Are you all right, Miss Burgos?"

My chest feels like it's lifting, expanding. My name is on the account? So she *did* love me enough to trust me with something. "You said my name is there?"

"She just added you recently but couldn't get your signature. It says here you were unavailable."

Lela, please come home.

"I…I live in Florida, but I don't understand; she knew where to find me." Each time I checked the mailbox the week Mami's letter came to Emily's, it had already been emptied. Were they keeping my mail?

No… Lies…

I can't listen now. I rub my temples and try to mute the voice.

Mr. Hertz looks at me funny. "I'm instructed to call a William Riley for the probate docs. Was that her lawyer?"

"I…I think so." Though I remember Betty Anne saying that Mami no longer trusted him.

"Give me a minute." Mr. Hertz gets up and holds out his hand. "I'll need two forms of ID."

I pull out my Florida driver's license and social security card then hand them both to Mr. Hertz, praying it'll be good enough. He glances at my license. "Nice photo. Oh, and you're going to need the password, so think about that while I'm gone. Be right back."

The lighthearted feeling I had a moment ago deflates. Password? What could that even be? Outside, a silver car pulls into a disabled parking space. A moment later, a pair of thick legs clambers out of the driver's seat along with a walking stick. My brain leaps to attention when I see the familiar bearded face. Immediately, I text Bram:

> *Doc T to your left.*

He uses the same bank as my mother forty minutes away? First, someone arrived at my mother's basement before I got there. Now, someone's at her safe deposit bank when I'm at her safe deposit bank. Am I being followed? I want to cower, as if he can see me through the bright reflection outside the bank window. I watch him pull a black leather book from the backseat. Slowly, he heads for the front door.

My phone chimes. Bram texts back:

> *Dude, wtf???*

> *IDK!!*

I start to reply, but then Mr. Hertz is back, flustered. "Okay, I'm going to need you to sign this, so we can fax it to Mr. Riley. Then he can send a power of attorney, which you'll also need to sign, and we can get this all taken care of. Usually, this takes a while, but he seemed to be in a rush." He waits, fingers poised on the fax, as a document comes through. He takes it and places two papers in front of me, indicating where to sign.

I swipe his pen and sign my name, hoping to get through this without any further red tape. He takes them back and enters them one at a time through the fax. "We needed your signature to assign you as a co-applicant, but now it should be quick and easy."

"Sorry about all this." I try to smile.

"Not at all." Mr. Hertz reaches into a drawer and pulls out a set of keys. "Would you follow me, please?" I trail behind him down a brown and beige hallway lit with pretty, antique-looking lamps. He uses a card key in another door and lets me through. My phone buzzes again.

> *Went back to his car...think he forgot something*

> *If he comes back, stall him please.*

It makes no sense, but I feel the need to buy time. Mr. Hertz makes small talk along the way, stuff about his daughter getting braces today, but I cannot focus on a single thing this man is saying. We reach a wooden cabinet where he opens a drawer and begins searching. Then he pulls out a key identical to mine and moves a tablet with an electronic pen over to me. "Sign here."

I force another scrawl out of the pen.

"This way." He leads me straight to the middle of the left wall where the boxes are slightly bigger than the ones to the right. "She rented out a medium-sized safe," he explains then stops in front of the box marked 512 with a little keypad next to it. "Four to six letters or numbers. But Miss Burgos"—his expression changes—"if it doesn't open, I can't help you anymore."

"How many chances do I get?"

"Let's say three," he says then politely turns away.

My heart pumps blood faster and faster through my body, adrenaline spiking. What if I get it wrong? What if my three chances get me nothing? I insert the key and a little red light blinks. *What is it? God, help me, what is it...*

Sunnyside? No, too long. Coconut? Seven digits. No. Wait...Coco?

Slowly, I enter 2-6-2-6, but the red light remains fixed. Damn it. What else mattered to my mother? Sleepy Hollow? Irving? Yes, of course. Irving, Irving—the Earth, Sun, and Moon all revolved around Irving. "Please, please..." My fingertip presses 4-7-8-4-6-4. I cover my eyes then slowly peek between my fingers. The light remains red.

"No." Tears threaten to spill right here in front of Mr. Hertz. God! Where are the voices when I actually need them? What mattered most to my mother? Maple Street? The Hollow? Yes, it has to be.

My finger lightly touches the pad without pressing down. Something doesn't feel right. *No, that's not it.* Mr. Hertz leans against the wall of boxes, allowing me room to breathe. I press my forehead against the cool metal.

My brain screams a million thoughts.

Inhaling deeply, I reach as far back into my mind as I can for the happiest time I could ever remember. It was Christmas. I was little, in bed with the blankets up to my chin. My new doll, so pretty and perfect, tucked under my arm. My mother had finally made one for *me*—a special doll that even looked like me with blond hair and hazel eyes. Mami sat on the edge of the bed, her pretty face aglow from the little ballerina lamp on my nightstand.

"Isn't she pretty, Lela? You like Sofia?"

"Yes, Mami, I love her!"

My eyes fly open, and swiftly, I punch in the password, like I've known it my whole life. *If it's HOLLOW, may you forgive me, Mami.* 7-6-3-4-2—SOFIA. The green light switches on. I cover my face, and the tears flow freely.

Mr. Hertz moves in to open the second lock with the guard key, and then steps aside. "Lucky guess, I take it?"

Wiping my eyes, I peer into the safe deposit box. There's a large folded manila envelope stuffed with papers, a thick rubber band wrapped around it. I reach in and pull it out. The box could easily hold more stuff. A yellow note is tucked under the rubber band. My mother's handwriting no longer seems weak or maniacal, as I originally suspected. It looks…

Lela, I should've

told you while

you were still here.

Take it and run.

…as if she'd been in a hurry.

Mami's words slice through layers of ether, like a knight's sword through tangles of thorn-infested vines from another dimension. I slam the empty box shut, turn on my heels, and for once in my life, do exactly as my mother tells me.

CHAPTER TWELVE

"Away then they dashed, through thick and thin; stones flying, and sparks flashing at every bound."

Down the corridor and past file-carrying bank employees, I run. Through the lobby, slowing down once to shove Bram's arm holding up his head. "Let's go." In the parking lot, I hear the shouts of "Miss, come back, you have to sign out!" Bram opens the driver's side door then reaches across to open mine for a speedy departure.

"I hope you have a good reason for this," he says, the old Accord ripping into action. "Just tell me you didn't kill anybody."

"I did not kill anybody." I get in and slam the door shut.

Bram backs out of the space, then rockets out of the parking lot, tires screeching against the asphalt. I check for any followers. "Then why are we running? What did you steal?" He readjusts his rearview mirror.

"Nothing." I stare at the windshield. "But I think someone might be after this stuff."

Bram speeds through three yellow lights and a red one at an empty intersection. I check the side mirrors, even though I haven't done anything wrong except not sign out. The box was in my name, the password was Sofia... My mother couldn't have left me stolen property, could she?

"I take it the key worked." Bram eyes the package. "You gonna open that?"

"As soon as we get back. I have to be alone."

He opens his mouth to speak.

"No questions. Just drive."

Once we're back on Route 9 with no traffic lights to slow us down, I breathe a little easier. Sundown's light creates deep shadows on the roadside trees. Bram glances at my mother's hastily written note. *I should've told you while you were still here.*

What does that mean?

Questions whirl in my mind. None turn into solid answers. My mother left this package, yet barely talked to me? Fresh tears rise into my eyes. Was Dad really keeping us apart?

"Are you okay?" Bram asks.

"I don't know. I just don't understand why my mom barely called me, and then this."

"Are you sure she wasn't trying?"

I look at him. "You think she did everything she could to reach me, don't you?" Same as Betty Anne.

He shrugs. "If she'd been able to, you wouldn't be in the situation you're in now."

"Which is?" I eye him sharply.

He turns to me, lips slightly apart. "Mica, look at you, getting weird notes and keys from your mom, important things from safe deposit boxes. I mean, I know you love your dad, but you realize everyone knows he's had you living in a bubble, right?" His voice takes on a crazed undertone.

"How would you know how I've been living?" I snap.

He's quiet, staring at the road ahead.

If my dad has me living in a bubble, would he have let me come back to Sleepy Hollow despite his hating it? "My dad," I say carefully, "would've told me if my mom had called or mailed me anything. He had no reason to keep us apart."

But...even as I say it, I don't believe it.

Bram cocks his head uncomfortably. "Unless he didn't want you to be involved."

"Ugh." I drop my head into my hands. God, I didn't want to think that. "Just stop."

"Maybe your mom was dealing with forces outside her control. Maybe your dad doesn't want you in the middle, maybe he has his own private shit going on, you know, that's all I'm saying."

"I said stop! This is not happening..." Have I really been this blind?

"Or maybe..." He shrugs. "I'm full of shit. It's just a feeling based on the way things ended for her, Mica. All alone, you know. Hopefully, whatever's in that envelope will explain it. I'll shut up now. Your place or mine with that stuff?" he asks, resigned.

"Mine." I don't want my personal things anywhere near Jonathan Enger.

He nods and takes my hand. I let him. I need calm and peace. As we re-enter Tarrytown, I revel in these last few minutes of normalcy, knowing that whatever my mother left inside this package will probably change my life forever.

•••

Inside the townhouse, I lock the front door quietly. Bram stands there, holding my backpack.

"Wait here a minute," I instruct and go knock on Nina's door. The light is on in the space between the door's bottom edge and the floor.

"Open," she mutters. I crack the door to find her shoving her things into a bag. Her eyes are pink and puffy. "Have you talked to your father today? He's not answering my calls."

"He's in Bogotá, remember?"

"I know where he is," she snaps. "That's not what I asked."

Whoa. "No, I haven't talked to him."

Her shoulders slide downward. "Mica, I'm going to visit my sister in Brooklyn for a couple of days. Do you think you'll be all right?"

"I guess so. Is everything okay?"

She shakes her head angrily at a shirt in her clutches. "I just need some time. I don't know what I'm doing here." Pressing a ratty, crumpled tissue to her nose, she sniffs.

"Is it me? I know I haven't been around as much as I should. There's a lot going on. I'm sorry."

"No, no. It's not you. I'll be back, okay? Three days, tops."

"Sure."

Her face is so red from crying. I stand back with a sinking feeling as Nina moves past me and quietly lays her key on the foyer table, looking at me one more time before shutting the front door.

...

In the living room, I unwind my scarf from my neck, toss it onto the couch, and plop my tired ass down. The silence between Bram and me is deafening. I pluck off the rubber band from around the folded envelope. This better be worth it. Bram leans against the doorframe to my room, running a hand through his hair, looking unsure what to do. I stare at him, not about to browse anything until he makes himself scarce. I appreciate him taking me and everything, but I need to do this alone.

He takes the hint and turns in to my bedroom. "I'll be in…this room…if you need me."

The bed's springs creak under his weight, and I know it's safe to open the envelope. I unclasp and remove a massive block of papers, some white, some yellowed with age, the corners of old photos poking out the sides.

"What should you have told me while I was still here, Mami?" I whisper.

At the top of the thick pile is a visitor's pass to Historic Hudson Library, rare collections by appointment, where everything requires supervision. Last I remember, Jonathan's grandfather, Benjamin Enger, has been head librarian there. I stare at my mother's photo ID lanyard. Amazing how much I look like her. There's another lanyard to some place called NDCC.

Next are faded photos of my mom as a little girl, plus older black and white ones from Cuba. Her parents fled Castro's regime in the 1960s, which makes me side with the locals sometimes—why would Mami say we're related to Irving? Did she just love this town so much, she wanted nothing other than to fit in? Is that what she wants to confess? That we're really just children of political refugees with no relation whatsoever?

It'd be disappointing, but at least it'd be the truth.

I pause to admire a lovely sepia-toned photo of a man dressed in a white suit seated with a small guitar. Smooth and shiny black hair, thick mustache, surrounded by three children, two in dresses, one in a linen suit. The two girls are identical twins with curly blond hair. Next to him sits an even older gentleman, also in a white suit. On the back, the year 1911—Enrique Salazar Vasquez and Pablo Vasquez Medina. A sticky note with my mother's handwriting reads:

> Your great-great-grandfather—
> Enrique, Pepe's dad, (Pepe was Pablo, my grandfather)

In his eyes, I detect the same mixed expression my mother always wore—obsessed, pained, never happy about anything, yet patient, meticulous, and loving. Yes, loving. She may not have been the sweetest woman on Earth, but it wasn't because she lacked affection. Life had just hardened her.

The next paper is folded, thin, yellow, and brownish in spots with cracked edges split in places. Another sticky note is attached, and I silently thank my mom for having thought to label everything for this posthumous tutorial:

> This managed to leave Cuba safely.
> DO NOT lose it, whatever you do. IT's very old and now, very yours.

Very mine?

Carefully, I unfold the decaying sheet until it's spread open wide in front of me. It's a family tree composed of different handwriting over the years, outlining a complicated web of lines and circles. Hundreds of dates and names cover the page, beginning in the late 1700s on one end and spanning across two centuries in every direction. Family members born in Spain, Portugal, Cuba, even the U.S.—the most recent.

A recent entry belongs to Patricio Vasquez Rodrigo, born in 1947. His daughter, Maria Pilar Vasquez Salazar, was born in 1971. In 1997, she married Omar Jaysen Burgos. My parents. My grandfather, Pablo, died when Mami was two years old. I remember a story about how he left Cuba with his wife, Ofelia, my grandmother, in the sixties.

Related. Yeah, okay. My family was as Cuban as rum and cigars. The last entry, written in by Mami herself, is for me—Micaela Katerina Burgos.

What's so horrible about all this?

I trace the long family names back in time all the way to the first documented ones in Spain. Madrid 1826, Juan Cristóbal de Medina, underlined twice. And in small faded print, so much so that I might have missed it if I wasn't straining my brain to make sense of it all, the Spanish word *adoptado*. Next to it, two more names—Hernán Juan de Medina and María Teresa de la Cruz. Above that, instead of two parents—only one.

I stare at it, my pulse quickening. Next to it, another of my mother's sticky notes with nothing but a big bold arrow pointing to it.

There is no way.

The parchment shakes in my grip, and I set it flat on the table. I can't touch it anymore. The handwriting is small, the ink faded. I would accuse my mother of writing it in herself, but it's not her handwriting. I pluck off the note with the big arrow and gaze at the name—

Washington Irving of New York, United States of America. 1783.

"Holy shit." My breath catches in my throat.

But Irving never married, never had children of his own, only nephews and nieces back at Sunnyside. Maybe this is another Washington Irving, and my mom just assumed it was the author? Is this thing for real?

I hear Bram's voice from the other room. "Is it a big deal?"

"Yeah."

I stare at the glaring, empty line in place of a mother's name. If Irving had a Spanish baby born in Madrid in 1826, the mother could've been anybody. He was fascinated by Spain, the Spanish language, even lived there a while after London. He also served as U.S. Ambassador to Spain later on.

A child.

A Spanish child.

I stare at the paper a long time. So I really am related? As a great-great-great-granddaughter? I rub my eyes and try to absorb it all. Why didn't she show me this before? Was she trying to confirm it before she suddenly died?

Lela, please come home. It's urgent.

Yes, there has to be more. *What is it, Mami?*

Quickly, I riffle through more photos for something— anything that might validate, separate fact from fiction. I almost flip right past it. A folded piece of white copy paper—a piece of modernity tucked right into the middle of decaying evidence. Unfolding it, I spot the familiar typeset I internalized after so many hours in the Sunnyside gift shop, looking through Irving's published journals. Phrases strung together with long dashes—the words doused in yellow highlighter—

> I could not allow that to happen;
> already frowned upon as she is; it
> would be the end of her—so I convinced
> her I would take him, and so he is
> here, as is the double creation, and we
> are in Madrid where I am ambitiously
> translating some works into English.

Then the words:

> El niño se llamará Cristóbal—the boy
> will be named Christopher, in honor of
> my fascination. Madrid, Sept. 1826.

Juan Cristóbal de Medina was Irving's flesh and blood son, named after the subject of his greatest work—a biography about Christopher Columbus. Fitting, that he should name his son after one of history's biggest names, as his own father named him after the great American general.

I sink back into the sofa and let out a long breath. *Whoa. Stay calm.*

Yes, it's shocking that I might be a direct descendant of *the* Washington Irving, but was it worth Mami staying in the Hollow and ruining her marriage, never seeing me again, just to show me?

I look at the typeset on the page. *The double creation.* Dane mentioned that in class. Has he seen this journal page, too? Who else has seen it? The top edge of the page appears to be the photocopied words of a label—*property of Historic Hudson Library Services.* This must be part of that rare journal. Jonathan's grandfather must know about this, which means so does Jonathan, and probably everyone from Historic Hudson.

I'm the odd man out.

"Mica?" Bram calls from the bedroom.

"Just a minute."

The last item in the pile is another old photo—a woman—black hair pinned into a loose knot. Dark dress and petticoats. A boy of about six or seven stands next to her in knickerbockers and a dark vest. In the woman's arms is a bundled baby. Her eyes are familiar—dark, pained—misunderstood—a visage that comes to me every other night since my mother died, though how I know this, I'm not sure. I've never seen her face.

But my mind spins. I almost throw up when I realize who it is.

On the back, one last sticky note from my mother—

Follow her, Lela. She will guide you.

CHAPTER THIRTEEN

"Oh these women! These women!"

It's her. The woman who haunts my dreams. Except
her face is so clear and before my very eyes, I feel
I've always been able to see it. My stomach hurts like I
swallowed ten pounds of pure sugar.

"Bram?"

"Yeah?"

"Can you stay here with me tonight?"

He pokes his head out the doorway. "Mica, don't mess
with me."

"I'm not messing. I'm scared!" I slam down the packet
on the couch and bury my face in my hands. I hate the
thought of being alone in a house I barely know after my
mom told me to run and run fast with these papers. God
only knows who might be after them...and me. "If Nina's
not going to be here, I don't want to stay alone with all
this." I gesture to the strewn pile of papers.

"Is it bad?"

Don't tell him yet. "It's important."

"Then stay with me at my apartment. Bring all this and enough clothes for a few days. I can't bail on Jonathan again after I postponed the beer and pizza thing. We're supposed to work on decorations before our HollowEve meeting. Come on, I'll make dinner."

I really don't like the thought of taking these things around a real, live Enger, but I guess I can hide it all. He'll never know the difference. "Okay." I breathe in and let it out slowly. "Let's get the hell out of here."

*D*ragging myself into Bram's apartment, the first thing I notice is it's piled with more Halloween decorations than ever before. Coconut jumps off the couch and stretches, digging her claws into the carpet. I also notice Jonathan's glare from the kitchen as I walk in with my weekend bag, my backpack, and a few things shoved into grocery bags, as if to say, *What, you live here now?*

I spend the day on Bram's bed, away from Jonathan and Bram's beer and pizza hangout, trying to recuperate from the blow my mother dealt me. I keep it all to myself, not ready to share any of it. Occasionally, Bram comes in to make sure I haven't died, offering beer, soda, and homemade pizza that's actually not half bad.

In isolation, I try to understand how any of this is even possible. How did my mother know about the ghost woman haunting me, enough to say, *follow her, Lela?* How did she happen to have a photo of her? I think back to when I first saw her in my dreams. It was the night after Mami died.

Could she have been Mami's spirit guide who moved

on to me once she died? Emily has mentioned spirit guides before, when talking about chakras and new age stuff, how they sometimes stay within the same families.

At night, the ghost woman filters into my dreams. Cross-legged, she sits quietly in the corner, seething, wondering how to talk to me to make me listen. Her face is a tiny bit more visible this time, and her attitude more impatient as she rocks in the corner. Finally, she floats up, muttering the house, the garden, the river... And her eyes. Her eyes are frantic, demanding, vacant.

Leave me alone, I yell, though I realize now I should listen to her. She's trying to tell me something, and like an idiot, I'm ignoring her. But *maybe* if she wouldn't stare at me that way or hover in my face, I wouldn't be so damned scared of her. I wake up sweating, stare at the walls and ceiling for a good two hours, while Bram and Jonathan snore in the other room, then turn off my alarm before it has the chance to wake me up for school.

In the morning, I don't dress for school. I need sleep and to figure all this out. Sitting on the bed with Coconut curled up against me, I absorb every photo, every scrap of paper, every sticky note, over and over again, until I can see everything in my mind by heart.

At three p.m., an email zings in from Dane: **Hi Micaela, didn't see you in class today. Hope you're all right. Dane.**

For the first time since yesterday, a smile materializes on my face. Thin smile, but I'll take it. I hit reply and think about what to say. *The house, the garden, the river,* the ghost woman said to me last night. The only place I know of where those three intersect is Sunnyside. I type: **Hi Dane, sorry I missed your class. I have a lot to sort out. You said you wanted to visit Sunnyside. I think**

I'm gonna take a trip down there tomorrow...

I stare at the cursor blinking on the screen. *Shit, what am I about to do... Here goes nothing.*

Care to come along?

I wait, obsessively refreshing my email over and over again. Finally after a few minutes, his reply arrives: **That would be fantastic! I'll pick you up. What time and where?**

I shove all my papers back into the envelope, bury it under Bram's mattress, and tag along with him and Jonathan to Philipsburg Manor for the HollowEve meeting. It's the least I can do after he searched for and found Coconut, drove me to the bank, and took mc in like another stray.

While the boys unpack the car loaded with decorations, I stand by a column and attempt calling my dad again, but he doesn't pick up. His voicemail beeps. "Dad, call me when you can. I need to talk to you." I hang up, about to call again, when Jonathan walks by, carrying a big black box that says *ProFogger* on the side. He sees me, shakes his head, and mutters something.

Pfft, what's his problem?

Inside a big ballroom, I help by painting a giant chandelier made out of plaster to look like dark iron and twisted metal. I add light silver streaks to create the appearance of highlights. Halloween is all about illusions. Not unlike the lies my mother was probably feeding Betty Anne about trying hard to contact me in Miami. Or the ones my father seems to be feeding me. Who's telling the truth?

I spot Bram at the end of a hall supervising a giant spider decoration workgroup. He catches my stare and smiles that boyish-man smile I love. I have to say, it's been nice having one solid friend by my side throughout this, even if he is a little crazy.

I smile back.

At the end of the night, when the volunteers go home, I wait by the car for Bram while he finishes up inside the ballroom. I try calling my dad again and get his voicemail. Again. "Dad, please call me. I need to talk to you." I hang up and smack the car's trunk. "Ugh!"

Suddenly, the scent of weed wafts in on the breeze, and someone sneaks up behind me. "So..." John is there, folded arms over scrawny chest. "Your dad out of the country again, huh?"

"Yeah, so?" I recoil, eyebrows drawn together. "He has clients in South America." Not that I have to explain anything to Jonathan. How my father chooses to handle his business is none of his concern.

"You know, he owes my parents a visit real soon."

I stare at him. What does he mean? "He's coming. He has new contacts here."

"Is that what he told you?" Jonathan half laughs, mostly a huge scoff.

"Yes, that's what he said. Is there a problem?"

"He hasn't mentioned his *existing* investors here? People getting a little sick of trying to track him down?" He shakes his head. "Man, you've really been living in a freakin' golden tower, haven't you?" He walks off toward the bushes to light a cigarette.

I can't even speak. So that's it? He thinks I'm naive? So my father has always taken care of me. So I don't have to struggle for a paycheck. How is that a bad thing?

"Asshole," I mumble. Still, I can't help but feel like I'm taking some kind of unfair treatment on behalf of my dad's business dealings here.

Bram comes out of the ballroom, talking on the phone through his ear buds, flustered and annoyed. He carries a box piled with more Halloween decor, sees the look on my face, and stops next to me to open his trunk. "Fine, fine, let me go. I gotta go." Hanging up, he looks at me. "What happened? You okay?"

"I'm fine," I say, chewing on the edge of my nail, looking away. From the way he sets his box on the ground and holds onto my upper arms, I know he's not buying it.

"That's bull, Princess. Tell me what's wrong."

"Nothing. It's...just John." I sneer in the direction of the smelliest Enger across the parking lot. He looks at me over his shoulder, like he can hear me talking about him. I shake out of Bram's hold. "And please stop calling me Princess. I'm not a princess."

"Ouch. Okay, okay... What did he do?" Bram puts himself between me and John, his back to his friend. The concern in his face is overwhelming, like he might just go and beat Jonathan up if I give him the go-ahead.

"Nothing. Forget it."

"Listen, Mica..." He tries again to hold my arms. I let him. Only because he used my real name. And because he genuinely cares about me. "You know how stupid John can be. He's a grump, all because you dissed him in fourth grade. Besides, you've always liked me better." He tries getting me to smile, peering down into my face. "Am I right?"

I bend down to pick up a dirty rag that fell out of his pocket, trying not to let him see my smile.

He drops to help me, taking my hand again. "It's true,

though, right? You do like me, Mica?" He cups my face, the touch of his hand sending shivers into my body.

"Of course I do," I whisper. I do love the warmth his hand transfers to mine in the cold night. "I always have."

"You have?"

"Well, Bram, you're my best Hollow friend. I mean, the circumstances that brought us together this time sucked, but if things were normal right now...if my mom hadn't died, if I'd never left..." I trail off, not knowing exactly how I want to end that statement.

"Yes?"

I sigh. "We'd probably be together now," I finish. It's true. All those people who said we'd end up together were probably right. There's no reason not to give Bram the benefit of the doubt. He's made himself available for me. No, he's not the only guy I find attractive. Dane Boracich watches me in that compelling, protective way, but he's older, more of a fantasy. Bram is the real deal, the one who's known me most of my life.

He stands slowly, hoisting me up with him. "Good, because I want to tell you something."

"What is it?"

"I've been arguing half the night with my mom, Lacy, you name it. Maybe it's the full moon, I don't know, but everyone's on my case tonight. But I'm ignoring them. You know why?"

I shake my head. "Why?"

His finger slides along the underside of my chin. "Because. Damn, I don't know how to say this. I'll just come right out and say it." His deep brown eyes gaze at me, his fingers paused on my cheek. "Because I don't care what they say. Not my mom, not Lacy, not the people who talk shit. Since you called me last month, you opened something up inside of me."

"A wound, probably."

He lets loose a relieved, rough chuckle. "No. Well, maybe a little. The thing is, Mica, I've always cared about you. Now, seeing you here is doing strange things to my brain. You're stirring me up, and…well, I'm excited again for the first time in a long time. I care about you. I really do."

"I care about you, too." I can say that much and mean it. There's too much going on to know whether or not Bram and I will ever turn into love, but I know I've always cared about him. I close my eyes, fighting back tears. His face is an inch from mine. *Don't think, Mica. Whatever happens, it's just Bram.* "I just…"

It's the timing of the situation. Maybe if I weren't dealing with the loss of my mother…

"You don't have to say anything." He leans in gently. I don't mind it. At all. "I just wanted you to know how I feel." His lips press against my cheek, nothing more, nothing less. He leaves a kiss—a tingling, cooling signature—where my dimple is. Not quite where my body wanted it, expected it, but not where a best friend dares to linger either.

Chapter Fourteen

*"To look upon its grass-grown yard, where the sunbeams
seem to sleep so quietly, one would think that there
at least the dead might rest in peace."*

I don't know if Bram is playing his cards right or what,
but he doesn't push for more physical contact the rest
of the night. In fact, he lets me retreat into his room again,
where I check the mattress's underside to make sure my
things are still there, which they are.

I slide into bed with a sigh.

If the ghost woman tortures me again, I will lose my
shit. I breathe deep, letting the oxygen relax my muscles,
and hope for a good night's sleep. No such luck. This time,
she slips into my dream and begins pacing, muttering,
desperate. She says "garden" and "river" again, wringing
her hands. The Hudson River is the only river near me,
and I'm going to Sunnyside tomorrow, which is right on it.

I'm hit with a moment of clarity. If I go to Sunnyside,
to the river, the house, the garden, like she wants, maybe
she'll leave me alone. "I'll go," I tell her calmly, swallowing

back my fear. "Then will you leave me alone? I need sleep."

She backs away, ghostly eyes fading through her countenance-less expression. And I get to sleep. Accompanied and under surveillance, maybe, but it's sleep nonetheless.

In the morning, Bram and Jonathan leave early for the last days of HollowEve prep before rehearsals begin. I dress quickly, down a simple breakfast of OJ and a granola bar, then stand outside on the balcony to wait for Dane. We still communicate through email, as if texting is just one layer too intimate. I finally get a message saying he's on his way.

I'm excited beyond belief. I don't know why. Maybe because, for once, I get to be the expert. I know Sunnyside like the back of my hand and will get to show Dane, Harvard scholar, a thing or two. When I see his car roll around the corner, I tighten the belt on my gray sweater and head downstairs.

"Hey, thanks for picking me up." I slide into the front leather seat, cold even through my jeans.

"Thanks for inviting me. I've been looking forward to this." He smiles wide, throwing the transmission into first gear. "Do you miss it?"

"Actually," I say, staring straight ahead, the nostalgia starting to hit me. "I do."

After a few minutes down Route 9, Dane slows and makes a quick right into the familiar snaky road that slithers through trees all the way to the riverbank. My hands begin to sweat. Who will be there who might remember me? Ellen, the other tour guide my mother shared shifts with? Janice, Bram's aunt, who was a bitch to everyone?

The Hudson's gray surface reflecting ashen sky slowly comes into view. Slow-moving boats and a sense of isolated tranquility brings a smile to my face I haven't felt in weeks. Above the gentle hillside, the red roofs of Sunnyside peek out at me.

The parking lot is full of cars. "They're probably having their shadow puppet performance, a tradition here." I can still see it fresh in my mind—black cardboard cutouts silhouetted against a lit background, depicting "The Legend of Sleepy Hollow." My heart starts a little dance of excitement.

"Sounds lovely already." Dane pulls into a parking spot and cuts the engine.

Most boys I know would never use the word "lovely." There's something so refined and mature about Dane Boracich that I adore. No leering glances at my body, no dorky sexual innuendos. I feel safe around him.

The sound of our car doors shutting is out of sync with the surrounding woodsy silence. To my right is the little garden house on the property. To my left, the walkway down the grassy knoll to the courtyard and gift shop where tour tickets are sold. Dane offers me his arm with a gentlemanly stance. "My lady?"

"Thank you, sir." I giggle, taking his arm.

Dane's chest swells with pride. "I've always wanted to see where Washington Irving wrote 'The Legend of Sleepy Hollow.'"

I recoil, scoffing. "Mr. Boracich," I say in my most ladylike voice, "as a literature student of Harvard, you should know that Irving actually wrote 'The Legend' while living in London, not here in Sleepy Hollow." I honestly can't believe he didn't know that one.

He eyes me sideways. "You really know your stuff, girl."

"Don't mess with the best," I say, and he laughs.

We clomp down the curved path toward the white tent where the month-long literary festival and puppet show are taking place. Families are buying books, making colorful crafts, learning about the famous resident author of long ago. Dane lets go of my arm to pull open the wooden door to the gift shop, and I'm smacked with scents of cinnamon and apple, candle wax, and old paper—an immediate trip back in time.

"Welcome to Sunnyside," a familiar voice says. Behind the counter, someone is crouched over a box of books. "Next tour starts at ten." A small face with thin-rimmed glasses and a wary expression peers over the counter.

"Hi, Ellen." I give the woman a small wave, praying she's not mad at me, too.

She stands, a short, thin woman wearing a white sweater hugging her petite frame. More gray than I last saw her. She takes one look at me and smiles. "Nooo. Micaela? Lord, look at you!"

"Yay, you remember me." I smile.

"Of course I do. I'm so sorry to hear about your mother, dear. I was very fond of her."

"That makes one of us," another voice mutters from the storage room. My smile disappears. Janice Foltz appears, tall and burly with thick brown hair that looks like tumbleweeds. "Oh, look who finally made it back!" she says, totally facetious.

"Give her a break, Jan," Ellen says.

"Don't let her into the house alone." Janice returns to

the storage room. "She'll only take things, like her mother did."

"What am I going to do, steal the fake gelatin?" I do everything in my power not to spew expletives. I feel like I've been dragged through snow that's been pissed on. Dane squeezes my arm. I fight back the trembling in my voice. "I loved my mother," I tell Ellen, pressing my fingertips against my eyes. "She made things difficult at times, but I loved her."

"Of course you did, Mica. Don't listen to her," she whispers. Ellen reaches under the counter and comes back up with a tissue for me. "Here you go." She cranes her neck back to peer into the storage room.

"Not even for one minute?" I press my palms together in prayer.

Ellen checks to see if Janice is looking. "The guard's on break, but he'll be back in time for the next tour," she says dramatically. Then she reaches behind her and pulls a big key ring off a giant nail on the wall. "So you may as well come back later." She winks and shoos me away with a flick of her hand.

"Okay, then I guess we'll do that," I stage-whisper, taking the key and sliding it into my pocket. "Thanks, Ellen. It was nice to see you. *Only you*," I say loud enough for Janice to hear.

Outside the gift shop, Dane draws in a fist. "Yes! Perfect comeback, Mica. Witty and well-deserved. But uh…fake gelatin?"

"You'll see. It's a prop dessert in the dining room. Bram and I used to take turns hiding it in the house. It used to drive Janice insane."

"So, you and Bram have known each other quite some time, huh?"

"Since before Pre-K." I lead him down the footpath to the front of the little romantic cottage. "We were best friends, but then I left, and things got weird. People talked about my mom and my dad…I don't really want to rehash it all right now." Not knowing Dane that well, I feel strange telling him that my mother was considered the town crazy. Then what would he think of me?

"It's okay. I understand." He stops and looks up at the house, snapping a few pics on his phone. The vines on the outer walls of the house have grown more expansive since the last time I was here, but everything else is still the same—green shutters, wrought iron benches outside, green front door… "So this is where Irving called home once he finally settled back in the States."

"That's right. Good job, you." I laugh, and he elbows me with a playful, sour face. Below me, I hear a meow. A big orange tabby who, eight years ago, gave birth to Coconut looks up at me with one green eye, one blue eye. "Pumpkin! Getting big, old girl!" I squat to pet her, and her body yields to my hand. Her awesome purring begins. "Wow, she's getting old." Standing, I push in the key like I've done a million times and pop open the front door to reveal checkered tile in the front patio.

Like coming home.

The house is simple and clean. Irving's study to the right, dining room to the left. "See? There's the fake amber gelatin, still on the dining table."

"That"—Dane laughs—"is just awful."

"It really is. So unappetizing, isn't it?" I laugh, leading him farther inside. The white lace curtains still hang in the windows. Years ago, one could walk a certain distance into each of the rooms, but now a velvet rope is set at the doorway. "Wow, this is different."

"What is?"

"Security has gotten tighter around here." I think about how much I want to tell Dane about the papers my mother left me. Yes, his theory about a missing journal from Historic Hudson was interesting, but it was also way out there, and I don't know that I can trust him. Trust anybody.

"I'm sure it has to do with the recent theft," he says, not pushing and questioning about my mom, and I'm grateful.

Dane peers into Irving's office. "Whoa." Leather-bound books on the back shelf, desk, lamp, little bench where he slept…it's all still there.

"He used to take naps right here," I say, pointing to the bench.

"This is completely fascinating." His fingers lightly brush the stair handrail, the walls, the solid wooden furniture.

I smile. "I remember a run-in with a tourist one time in this very hallway when I was about seven. I was wearing the old-fashioned period dress my mother made for all us tour guides. 'Aw, are you Washington Irving's daughter?' some guy said. 'Can I take your picture?' I looked at him and said, 'He didn't have a daughter,' in this totally flat voice."

Dane chuckles. "He must've been scared of you."

"You should've seen his wife. She looked at me like I was pure evil, took her snapshot, and walked away." I never minded the photos. I kind of liked my mom and I in matching old-fashioned dresses, lace collars, and coifs on our heads.

"You are anything but, Micaela." Dane follows me through the kitchen into the courtyard. I smile to myself.

By the old apple tree, a flurry of movement on the lawn catches my eye. Dane tosses me an apple at the same time I look away, and it hits my shoulder then falls to the floor.

"What's the matter?" he asks.

"I thought I saw someone."

The wind swirls long blades of grass into big, circular patterns, but otherwise the grounds are empty. A bird chases another off the power lines and into a tree. Just past the apple tree, on a little bench under a maple, sits an older man, smoking a cigarette.

"Must've been that guy over there," Dane says.

"It wasn't. It was something else." I scan the landscape again. "Dane...sometimes I hear voices, see people out of the corner of my eye. People who aren't there." I look at him warily. Most people think I'm crazy once they know this about me, but for some reason, I think Dane will react differently. We've had so many other things in common.

"Ghosts? Visions?" His face doesn't reflect any accusations or mockery. God, I hope I'm right about him.

"I think so, yes."

"That used to happen to me when I was younger."

I exhale, parting with a tired smile. "It did? But not anymore?"

He shakes his head, staring out toward the river. "No. I think I've seen too much. My brain's closed off to it now. It's awesome that you can still do it."

"It's not awesome, trust me. Most of the time, I wish it would never happen." I walk toward the big grassy area and plop down in the long blades, taking in the landscape. If I blur my vision against the power lines, train tracks, and Tappan Zee Bridge, I can see why Irving chose this cozy spot as his permanent residence.

Dane sits next to me, elbows over his knees, plucking blades of grass. "What's that over there?" I see he's pointing across the grass toward the flowery fields.

"The English garden and shed," I tell him. "Irving was fond of gardens."

There...

I squint, shading my eyes from the morning sun. "Did you hear that?"

"Hear what?"

"Someone said 'there.'" My heart pounds. "This is what I'm talking about."

"No, I didn't hear it." He doesn't give me doubtful looks the way Bram used to. He only cocks his head, as if trying to hear the voices, too. "You don't know who's talking to you?"

"I'm not sure." Though I could probably guess.

Suddenly, Ellen is standing near us, making us crane our necks back to see her. Against the sky, she looks bigger than her usual self. "Time to go, kids," she says, holding out her hand for the key. I give it to her and she turns and walks off over a grassy knoll. "Come on. Before the big bad wolf sees you here."

"Thanks for letting us in. We'll go now." I scramble to my feet, but something catches my attention again. A flash in the far left recesses of my vision. I try focusing on the area between us and the garden. Something's there.

Dane tries following my gaze. "Micaela?" His voice sounds far away, like he's talking through a tunnel.

A figure. Standing in the field, and yet...it could be anything. Like the walk in the woods a week ago, when I thought I saw someone, but then...no one. Is it a mirage on the water's reflection? A stray cobweb floating on the river's breeze?

Suddenly, feathery wisps of light coalesce to slowly form an image, and the same paralysis that grips me in my sleep seizes me. I recognize her—the woman from my dreams, from Mami's photo. Standing in the field.

"Mica?" Dane's voice sounds miles away.

I want to scream, but I can only watch as her eyes slowly appear—urgent, wounded, framed by dark, sloping eyebrows. That's her. Her hand lifts slowly then points in the direction of the garden house.

I'm imagining this. She can't hurt you, Mica. I push my body forward to break free of the paralysis's lock on me, but it's like my own aura has formed a straitjacket around me. I push again, until finally, I surge forward, barreling into Dane's arms.

He catches me, his pale blue eyes full of concern.

"Get me out of here, please." I fight for each breath. When I glance back, the woman is gone. "They're appearing in real life now. I can't take this."

"Real life? As opposed to..." Poor Dane is trying so hard to understand, and great, I just showed him a glimpse of the unstable girl everyone expects me to be.

"My dreams," I try explaining. "That's where I usually see her. Now she's here."

"I see," he says, but it's not condescending. He just doesn't know what to do. "Why don't we get you home? Come on, I'll help you." Dane tugs me by the hand. I let him lead me toward the gift shop, past the worried faces of tourists who think I've fallen sick and Ellen, and up the winding path into the parking lot.

I succumb to his movements like a rag doll as he works me into his car. When he closes the door, I drop my head into my hands. I'm losing it so bad...

Dane gets into the driver's seat and starts the engine.

Then he looks at me helplessly. Quiet. Suspended breath. "It's okay, Micaela. How can I help you? What can I do?"

"Just get me home, please. Back to Bram's, I mean." I sob into my hands.

Driving back onto Route 9, I try to thrust the mental image from my mind—the woman's horrible look of desperation. She pointed to the garden, the shed, or Lyndhurst, the castle adjacent to the property, I'm not sure which.

What does she want with me, Mami?

"I have to figure out what she wants," I whisper, staring at the blur of trees flying by my window. "So I can help her. So she'll leave me alone. I think my mother sent her."

"What if you talk to them?" Dane suggests. "I know that's easier said than done, but maybe they want to tell you more."

I nod, pressing my hands against my eyes. Yes, I have to *try* to be more receptive to the ghosts from now on. I was hoping not to, but now it appears I have no choice. *Great.* Any sense of normalcy I might've started feeling since I came to town suddenly crashed out on that field. I was actually beginning to settle into the valley again, like a lost child in her mother's arms. But Sleepy Hollow excels at casting spells like that. It pulls you, draws you in, it lulls you.

But now I either need to wake up from the valley's charms…

Or give in to them completely.

CHAPTER FIFTEEN

"It was the very witching time of night."

At Bram's, I stumble in just as he's stumbling out again with more decorations piled in his arms. He spots the blue Eclipse driving out of the parking lot and makes a series of sarcastic expressions. "Nice."

"What do you mean by 'nice'?" I'm not in the mood for an argument or any immature comments.

"Nothing."

"Nothing?" I throw my purse down on the couch and face him.

"Yes, nothing, oh, lover of literature. Don't worry about it."

I let loose a sarcastic laugh. "Whatever. Don't tell me how you really feel. It's fine."

He sets down his box on the couch's armrest. "Oh, you want to know how I really feel? Okay. Maybe I'm getting a little nauseous over your sentiments for a certain teaching assistant."

"Ugh, I knew you'd get like this. First of all, the word

is *nauseated*, and no, I don't have *sentiments* for him. I just think he's fascinating." He wants to be jealous? I'll give him a reason to be jealous then.

"Princess, not only do you have sentiments for him, but you drool down my neck during class, and not because of my charming good looks."

I can't contain my laugh. "Wow. Keep going. You're on a roll. Listen, if I like Dane, it's in a kind of unattainable way."

"Aha, which means if you could attain him, you would. Am I right?" He raises an eyebrow at me. "All I want is the truth. Why can't you just be honest with me, Mica?"

"You know what?" I throw my hands up and head into his room. "I just had something disturbing happen to me, and the last thing I wanted was to come home to an inquisition."

"I haven't asked you a single question about where you went with that guy." He follows me into his bedroom, pulls me toward him, and spins me around. My mind reels from the roughness of his face and how close he suddenly is. "All I care about is you. Tell me what happened."

Gently, I push him away. "Bram…"

His warm breath on my cheek sends shivers up my arm. "I haven't stopped thinking about last night, after the meeting. Did you feel anything at all?"

I nod. "I did. But I have a million things going on in my head right now, and I'm trying to sort them out."

"Like what? Just tell me."

I know he'll mock me for telling him what happened out on that Sunnyside field, but what kind of friend would I be if I trusted Dane with my secrets but not Bram? Bram may not be perfect, but he's my oldest friend. *Sigh.* "Fine, I saw the same ghost woman from my dreams.

Except I saw her in front of me."

"Does Dane know you saw her?"

"What difference does it make if he does or doesn't?" I scoff. "I can't believe that's your question. After you told me to confide in you, too."

"I'm sorry, Mica." He grips the sides of his head like he's trying to banish all jealous thoughts from his brain. "I'm so, so sorry. What I meant to say is, holy crap, that's scary. Maybe it wasn't a ghost, though. You know? Like, maybe it's your brain making pictures. Making you see whatever your subconscious wants you to see. Matrixing." He snaps his fingers. "I'm pretty sure that's what it's called."

"I wasn't imagining her," I snap, cringing at how insane I sound just by saying that. "It was a *person*. The woman from my nightmares. I *saw* her," I say through gritted teeth. "Not a shadow. Not the wind. I am *not* crazy."

I am definitely crazy!

"I'm not saying you are!" He blows out a breath. "I'm just trying to help... Forget it."

Yes, I know people sometimes see faces and shapes in shadows and patterns, like seeing a pair of eyes, nose, and mouth on the face of the moon. But this is not matrixing, and if it is, then I've been matrixing all around town for the last week.

By his silence, I realize I'm leaving Bram far behind in another reality. I feel myself shutting down, unable to share anymore. He wouldn't understand anyway.

"Look, let's talk about it later tonight. They're posting parts for the show in a few minutes, and I don't want to be late. But when I come back, let's sit down when we're both calm. Okay?"

I nod. "Sure," I say, but I know that, unless Bram tries

to understand what I'm going through, I won't be telling him about the voices and visions again.

I dial my dad's number and wait. No fear. But he doesn't pick up. 11:06 p.m. and busy in Bogotá? He must know I'm working to find answers to my mom's issues. His voicemail picks up. "Dad, I need to talk to you about Mami. Call me."

To avoid falling asleep and seeing the ghost woman in period dress again, I pore over my mom's papers for the hundredth time. I've created sticky notes of my own and a list of questions. On the bed, Coconut clings to my side. Poor thing is recuperating from years of neglect. *I understand the feeling, Coco, I do. But, maybe...Mami had good reason.*

After the HollowEve meeting, Bram and Jonathan return with more masks, ropes, chains, a leather saddle, and several bolts of white fabric. Jonathan grunts as he plops the last box in the corner by his bed. "Getting down to the wire."

I stare at my papers. I don't really care. Plus, Jonathan can go eat shit and die anyway.

"I can't believe they didn't post parts tonight," Bram mumbles.

"Yeah, it doesn't exactly give us much time to practice." Jonathan stares at me again for good measure then walks out of the bedroom. "Later, freaks." The door slams, and then it's just me and Bram.

"Where's he going?" I ask.

"I told him to leave us alone."

"He can be here. It's his apartment."

"Mica, after today, you need time alone." Leaning over me, he moves stray hairs from my face. "I wanted you to have some space."

Eyes closed, I give in to the gesture. He sits on the edge of the bed. "Feeling better?"

I shake my head, rubbing Coconut's ears. "No. I need sleep. Will you watch me while I sleep?" *In case the woman comes back,* I want to add. If only I could trust him not to laugh.

"I'll watch over you. I'll kick the ass of any ghost that tries to haunt you, all right? Promise." He presses a palm to his heart. I smile. At least he didn't mock me. He gives me a quick kiss on the cheek then lies back on Jonathan's bed. "Go to sleep. I'll stay out here watching…whatever."

"Thank you." I stand and start picking up all my stuff. Bram tries to get a sneak peek at the papers, but that's one thing I can't share right now. I pack it all up and slide it underneath the mattress again when he starts fiddling with his phone.

Despite my efforts to fall asleep, all I can do is think about my mother's envelope, its messed-up contents, and my lady ghost standing in the field. I open Bram's night table drawer where I keep the one photo of her and stare at it.

That's her all right. Mami said to follow her.

Take it and run.

But where?

• • •

The woman glides through the wall, hands over her face, and right away, I know I'm in for it. She sobs uncontrollably and trembles. Though I've never had a child, I can feel with inexplicable empathy her anguish over having lost her baby—a blunt, soaring pain that rips a gaping cavity where a soul had been.

In the rocking chair is a squirming bundle. I approach it and reach out to pull the blanket away. Tiny arms and legs pump underneath the sheath. Slowly, I peel back one corner, and...blond hair, face too soft to be real, big hazel eyes that sway open and closed. *Sofia?*

My ghost appears next to me, dark eyes floating in the middle of her face. I can almost see them completely now. *Do I know you? I saw you today by the river.*

Please follow me!

Not this again. But this time, instead of avoiding her...I close my eyes and imagine myself following her. The walls dissolve, and suddenly, we're outside under a blazing, sunny hillside. We glide over old wooden train tracks. In the distance, a steam train is fast approaching through the hills.

The smoky specter stops on the tracks and holds up her hands, like trying to stop the oncoming train. *Move!* I shout, my words lost under the chugging of the engine. *Move!* I scream again. The train screeches louder— rhythmic metal on metal—as the old locomotive speeds toward us. The woman holds fast, determined to stop it. Then, just as I'm about to recoil in horror at the inevitable bloody mess, she turns to mist as the train surges right through her, chugging on to its unknown destination.

Keep him safe, I beg of you...

She's inches from my face. Soft, pleading, tearing eyes. Something's familiar about them. I can't make sense of it,

though. It's as if our souls are connected, or had been, for
some time. Then, I hear my mother again...

...was my father's guide, then mine...now yours...

follow her...

As much as I try to do as she tells me, panic strikes me
again. I fight it with a strong lunge forward, and it works.
I break away, hurtling toward the ghost woman with
outstretched hands. Solid iciness grips me and tugs hard.
Suddenly, we're flying above the chugging steam train, and
I'm following her down the grassy landscape. When she
glances over her shoulder at me, her face is clearer. Eyes,
nose, mouth, for a fraction of a second. *I know you.*

Micaela...

What is it?

Find it.

Find what?

Proof.

Of what? My God, what does she want?

Of us! The woman shouts, her mouth opening into a
gaping black hole.

I scream. *Wake up! Wake up!* My own voice shrieks in
my ears, drowned out against the screeching of the steam
engine.

"Wake up!"

Something holds me down. The paralysis. The woman.
I can't tell... Rock-solid hands grip my arms, too strong to
be a frail, grieving wraith. Finally, I let out a shrill cry and
force my eyes open. Dark, except for the white blinds over
the open window tapping lightly against the sides.

Bram hovers over me in bed, struggling with my
flailing arms, using his knee to block my kicks. "Mica,
stop! You're dreaming." But I keep fighting. Is he
attacking me? Was he snooping in my mom's envelope?

Where *is* the envelope? Then I focus on Bram's face, and reality swerves in. He's just consoling me. "Oh my God. I can't take this anymore. I swear, I can't."

"That's it. I'm calling a doctor for you."

"No!" I cry against his shirtless chest, his smooth skin warm against my face. "I don't want doctors. They wouldn't understand. I just want…"

I don't know what I want, but it's definitely not a psychotherapist telling me I'm delusional. I want someone I can trust near me at all times. I need Bram here, just like this. Every night. I can't sleep alone anymore. That way, if I do fall into the sleepless abyss again, he'll be here to yank me free.

"Want what?" His confused eyes search mine, heavy breath from the struggle of waking me still on his lips. The air between us, electric. I'm falling from all things sensible, like dreams blending with reality, except reality keeps changing with every passing day.

Bram's face is inches from mine as he tries to focus in the dark.

I hear his heartbeat.

Lacing my hands around his neck, I raise myself to meet him, but it's his expression that kills me. Weak, defeated, trying to convince himself that the best thing right now would be to just leave the room and give me space. But I don't want him to go. Gently, I pull him down and press my lips against his.

How? How did I manage to wait so long for this? What was I afraid of? This is Bram, the same boy who rode his bike to my house every day for seven years. Who sat with me without a word the night I left and watched my tears fall. Who held me and told me he would miss me, promised me everything would be all right.

I pull away from him. "I'm sorry."

Deep, airy breaths. "For what?"

"For not telling you everything before." I cry freely now. "It's hard knowing who to trust. Your family hates me. Your friends hate me. Feels like the whole town hates me. I just want to feel safe."

"You talk like someone's after you."

"There will be soon." I have too many important possessions.

"Well, you're fine. You're with me. You're safe."

"No, Bram. Something's happening. First the dreams, then voices, now visions. I wanted to tell you all about it, but when I left, you stopped talking to me. I figured you took their side. How do I know you won't do it again?"

"I was a stupid kid. Let's forget about it. We can make it work." He brushes my hair away from my face, swipes his thumb across my lips. "You're battling something fierce. I don't know what it is, but I'm here. We're all here."

I know I'm giving up what little control I have left by opening up to him, but if a ghost woman wants to send me cryptic messages via dreams, and my mother wants to materialize as mist and voices in my head, if people around town are really accusing my dead mother of stealing important documents, and if I am losing my mind, there's not a damn thing I can do to stop it anyway.

"Who's *we*, Bram?"

He nods toward Coconut sleeping at the foot of the bed. "The fur ball, me, you? Who else do you need?"

"My mother," I say to my own surprise. "My mother. She had things to tell me, and I didn't want to hear them. I wasn't *here* to hear them. Now she's gone, and I'm ready to listen. That's nuts, isn't it?"

"You didn't know any better. We'll figure it out. But

you have to talk to me."

My sobs catch in my throat. How can he be so understanding? And what's wrong with me for mistrusting him? It's hard to judge his intentions with his face so close to mine, his lips parted and aching for another kiss. I rise up to kiss him again, but he pulls back.

"I have to tell you, though, if you keep doing that, there's no way you're safe with me. Not crying, kissing me, wearing that..." He takes in the sight of me in a thin T-shirt and no bra. "You're making me crazy." He lies down, his warm body stretching alongside mine. His mouth takes in my neck, jawline, lips. There won't be any more talking. I reach over and pull up the flannel sheet, enclosing us in a tight, warm space.

This is how things should be. Normal, not piecing together bits of my troubled past. Not warding off ghosts. No more voices, either. I close my eyes, my mind, focusing only on myself and Bram's arms around me. So by the time we've fallen asleep tangled in each other's arms, layers and years of doubt and mistrust lifted off of us, there's nothing left to stop us.

In the morning, he kisses my cheek, slips out of bed, and the warmth between us is replaced by cold air from the windows. The memor few hours before lingers fresh in my mind. But thoughts of the ghost woman come barreling into my brain, too. Her pleading eyes. What proof does she expect me to find? I pull her photo from the night table drawer and look at it again.

Bram returns from the bathroom fully dressed, ready

in his Ye Olde Coffee Shoppe polo and jacket. "I need to go put in a few hours." He sits on the edge of the bed and plays with my hair. "After work, we're meeting to finalize the activity schedule. Want to come? It might help get your mind off stuff."

I can't stop staring at the photo. "I would, but I have to keep researching."

You sound like me now, I hear my mother's soft laugh from somewhere.

I remember my promise to include him in everything from now on. "My mom left me photos, a family tree…I'll show it to you when you get back. And this." I turn around the photo of my nightly visitor to face him.

Bram's eyes narrow at the picture. "That's her?"

I nod. "Yes, from my dreams *and* the field. I think she used to appear to my mom, too, and my grandfather before her. Do you think people can become psychic later in life, or do you think you have to have it from birth?"

Bram doesn't answer. He cocks his head. "Are you sure that's her?"

I flip the photo back around. Yes, those are definitely the same dark eyes, the same pleading look of urgency that started the night after Mami died. "Why?"

"You didn't see it in our Lit book?" He grabs the photo for a closer look, and a puff of air escapes his lips. He lets the photo flutter onto the bed. "That's Mary Shelley."

CHAPTER SIXTEEN

"To have taken the field openly against his rival would have been madness…"

It's freezing and windy when I arrive at the college campus. After Bram left for work, I verified what Mary Shelley looked like on a few websites, then emailed Dane to ask if he could meet me. He suggested the college courtyard at noon, since not too many people would be there on a Sunday.

Nervously, I wait behind a giant oak tree.

It may be Sunday, but there's plenty of students here, reading and lazing about. Even my school's color guard is practicing on the football field. I honestly don't want people around when I tell him about the evidence I have. This morning, it hit me just how much I'm in possession of secret information and I would much prefer to meet in an isolated area.

I'm about to email Dane from my phone to ask if we can meet somewhere else when I spot his tall form emerging from the parking lot, keys hanging from his jeans' belt loop. My pulse quickens. Am I really going to tell him about my mom's confidential papers? I have to. This is his area of expertise.

He stops in front of me, blowing out a chilly breath. "Hi. You okay?"

"Not really." I cling to my backpack straps tightly. "Where can we go?"

"What about the lake?"

"Where's that?"

"Over here. It's quieter. Where did all these people come from?" He looks around, leading me as he walks.

I keep up with his long strides, trying to control my breathing. We stroll down a sidewalk between two glass buildings, and for one split second, I note how nice we look together. But just as quickly, I shake the thought from my brain. I kissed Bram last night.

"You want something to eat?" He points out a sandwich cart by the lake.

"No, thanks. Actually, maybe just coffee." Something to ward off the cold. Dane orders a panini with two coffees. I try to pay, but he pulls out his wallet and hands the lady cash. "Thank you. You didn't need to do that."

"You're welcome. How does this look to you?" He points to an iron bench by the water. We make our way over and sit down. "So tell me what's up." He takes a cautious sip of his hot coffee.

I let out a slow breath, holding tight to my warm paper cup. "Every time I think things can't get more complicated, they do. I learned a thing or two over the last week, and…I need to know what you think about it."

"About?"

"The Washington Irving–Mary Shelley hookup you mentioned."

He smiles. "You liked that, huh? I thought that was interesting, too."

How can I find out more without giving him too much of my own personal information? *Delicately.* "You know my mom passed away. You told me you knew why her house was for sale."

Dane stares back at the lake. "Yes, and again, I'm very sorry to hear that. You know, my father passed away suddenly, too. Three years ago. I hadn't spoken to him in a few years, either, so I know what you're going through."

I don't think I ever told him that my mom and I weren't on speaking terms, but by now, it doesn't surprise me. Small town. Everyone talks. "I'm sorry to hear that, too," I tell him. "Do you ever think about how things might've turned out differently had you stayed in contact with him?"

"Every day," he says, his mouth turning into a hard line. "Not a day goes by when I don't. But tell me about what you've learned." He focuses on me and bites into his sandwich.

"Okay...so my mom left me some papers..." I hesitate. Whatever I say, I can't un-say, so I should probably think this through carefully.

He squints. "Papers?"

"How can I put this?" I play with my coffee cup, spinning it a quarter turn at a time over my lap. "I have some evidence that might support your theory." I watch him sip his coffee, then set it down. I expected at least raised eyebrows from him or any other clue of interest, but he's so calm.

He leans forward. "What kind of evidence?"

"A photocopied page from a journal. It doesn't mention Mary Shelley, but I think there has to be more."

"There might be. The page you're talking about is from a private, longer journal of Irving's. Supposedly, it fills in the gap in the timeline without ever actually mentioning Ms. Shelley."

"That's the one you mentioned in class."

"Yes. I've seen it, too. Does it mention a double creation?"

A flush fills my cheeks. *So, it's not that secret anymore?*

He continues without waiting for my answer. "Pretty much the whole Historic Hudson group your mother worked for has seen it. It definitely has a lot of people talking."

"That's only one of the papers. You know, it's weird to hear you talk about my mother, like you knew her." I suddenly hate how famous she'd become for all the wrong reasons.

"People talk, Micaela." He raises an eyebrow, letting that one sink right in. "And I believe you used to have a doll named Sofia, too, right? And a cat named Coco?" His gray-blue gaze pierces right through me. How did he know all that? My brain reels, but I will it to calm down. I have to keep reminding myself that in small towns, info gets around fast.

A tingling iciness races through me as I remember the bank's password. "Point taken." Talk with enough people in this town, and anyone would learn those facts. If he knows them, so could Dr. Tanner or anyone my mother collaborated with. Is that why Doc Tanner was at South River Bank? To try his hand at the safe deposit box with my password? "What else do you know about my mother, the secret journal…anything. I want to know everything."

"Why? How will it help you?"

"Because I deserve to know. I need to understand

what happened to my mom," I snap, staring at him. "I spent too long without her. I need to know what drove her, what she was doing with all that research. I need to know what was so important about it that she couldn't move to Miami with me and my dad. There's forces not letting me leave until I do."

"The ghosts you've been seeing?"

My mother's voice, the flash of white nightgown, Mary Shelley's faceless spirit begging me for help, the snippets of voices and images flitting through my mind. *Forces*, telling me what to do. "Yes. I feel like I'm going to lose my mind, Dane. I just...I have to see this private journal at the Engers' library. Can you help me? Don't you get special privileges as a researcher?"

He chuckles under his breath. "I wish it were that easy. Don't you get special privileges as family of an Historic Hudson employee?"

"No. They would never let me in anyway, now that everyone thinks my mom stole that journal. You saw how that lady, Janice, treated me at Sunnyside. I only just learned about it when Bram mentioned it and then I saw a flyer at the police station."

"You were at the police station?" He raises an eyebrow.

Finally, a surprised reaction from him. "Yes, last week when nobody would help me. Remember I told you I couldn't get into my mom's house, and the realtor wouldn't answer? I don't know where her belongings are. All I have are the papers she left me." I fight off the pressure building behind my eyes.

"I remember now. Even if I *could* get you into the rare collections, you'd have a hard time finding that journal. Few people know this, but it was sent to a private lab in

Andover, Massachusetts, called the Northeast Document Conservation Center, to be authenticated."

My brain racks itself for a moment, then I remember—my mother's ID lanyard. "NDCC?"

"Yes, even the Smithsonian uses them. All they do is authenticate old documents using a video spectral comparator, paleography, IR spectroscopy, other forensic methods. And that page, the one about the double creations, leaked and has been circulating the literary community. That's how I know about it. Problem is, the original journal never made it *back* to the library. It's been missing since May. And the last person to view it..." He watches me carefully. "Was your mother."

I can't move. My mouth solidifies to stone. I knew everyone thought it was her, but I hadn't known she was literally the last person to see it. "What would she have been doing at NDCC?"

He shrugs. "No clue. Maybe she had special permission to view?"

I stare at him. Cold dust devils swirl near our bench. My mother was the last to see it. Who would Mami have known at NDCC? *Special privileges.* Another displaced vision attacks me—wooden floorboards, ripped and splintered. I rub my eyes.

Dane rests a hand on my shoulder. "Are you all right?"

"She didn't take it." A group of ducks waddles our way. One of them is yellow, while the rest are black. He straggles behind the others and reminds me of my mom, different from everyone else.

"*I'm* not saying she did. But she's a suspect."

"It's ridiculous. My mother might have been flaky, but she wasn't a thief." I snatch up pieces of Dane's sandwich that have fallen on the bench and pelt the other ducks with it. "If she stole it, she would've left it for me, like she left the other things. But she didn't."

His face lights up with interest. "Other things?" He blinks slowly, smoothing each of his fingernails patiently.

"Yes, the reason I'm meeting you. I want to tell you about them, but I'm scared to. I'm not sure I can trust you. Or anyone."

"Smart, but I'm not looking to take things that don't belong to me, if that's what you're thinking. If anything..." He pauses, giving his paper cup a turn. "It's others you shouldn't trust. People you know better than you know me."

"Who?" The only other people I even speak to are Bram, Jonathan, my mother's co-workers, and Betty Anne. *They cut up the floorboards...*

"Think, Micaela."

"You don't mean the Derants or Engers, do you?"

He might not think twice about stealing someone else's property. Bram's words from the day he brought home Coco seep out of my consciousness to warn me.

My face twists into a knot.

"You don't believe me?" He shifts on the bench, then takes my hands gently. "Where have their families worked for the last sixty years?"

"Historic Hudson."

"And what are they missing that originally belonged to them?"

The journal.

All this makes me wonder how much Bram and Jonathan know. Do they know my mom had access to the authentication lab in Andover? All of a sudden, I'm dying to question them. And to think I've been staying at

Bram's place, even showed him the photo of Mary Shelley. He *assured* me I could trust him, but one meeting with Dane, and suddenly I'm filled with doubt.

Dane shakes my hands with emphasis on every word. "Let me be clear. I'm not blaming anyone. I'm only saying, be aware of your surroundings."

The ducks fight for the last crumb on the ground. One pecks the other hard in the neck, and it runs off squawking. Dane goes on while all I can do is stare at them. "That journal was found in the walls of Sunnyside in 1952, a few years after the Sealantic Fund bought the house. Washington's brother, Ebenezer, didn't want anyone to see it, because it would tarnish his brother's good name."

"So, he hid it," I say, turning to him. His steel gaze is reaffirming.

He taps my hand softly. "Yep. But then the house sold, and the journal was found years later. They moved to Historic Hudson's Special Collections where only longtime employees of the organization could see it, like..."

"Benjamin Enger."

"That's right. And?"

"His family."

"And?"

"The Derants." I stare right past him.

"Rumor has it there's a note inside the front cover. Something about keeping it private until his own flesh-and-blood children claim it. They all figured he meant 'when pigs fly,' because everyone knew he didn't have children."

"Why didn't they just display it? It's been more than a hundred and fifty years since Irving died. No one would care about this anymore. What's the big deal?"

"The *big deal* is that the old families rooted here live and breathe to preserve his good name. It's their bread and butter. He was pretty much a hero in those times."

"But nobody would *care* now if he had an illegitimate child!" I cry.

"I agree, which is why I believe there has to be more. A better reason why they'd go to these lengths. If he really did have an illegitimate kid, then, on the contrary, I think he was quite the father to set him up with a good family, even visit him for years. Some men wouldn't have bothered. People dealt with problems differently back then, but they still had them."

So that was why Irving became Ambassador to Spain.

So he could visit his son.

"Mary Shelley didn't have the best reputation. There was no way he was gonna marry her. Can you imagine superstar Irving and his family, and desperate, widowed Shelley, who everyone saw as crazy, living at Sunnyside together? Or the alternative…raising a baby alone in London in 1826 when everyone knew her husband, Percy Bysshe Shelley, was too dead to be the father?"

Yes. I recall the words from the photocopied page — *already frowned upon as she is; it would mean the end of her.* "So instead of leaving her high and dry" — I stare ahead — "he took the child and gave him a good life."

"An anonymous good life, yes. The best thing for a kid in his position during those times. He probably even supported the child financially."

"Child support?"

"Exactly. So he's still a hero, as far as I'm concerned." Dane looks off across the lake.

That's all good and fine for Irving, but what about the

grieving mother? The troubling image of Mary Shelley's spirit desperately chasing down a train comes back to haunt me. "The baby was on the train," I whisper.

"It probably did go by train, yeah," he replies, oblivious to the fact that I know.

Other than the journal and the genealogical map my mother left me, there's no proof that their relationship even existed. All it ever says in biographies and history books is that they had a brief romantic liaison. How glossed-over is that? No wonder her poor spirit can't rest.

Until flesh and blood claims it. That would mean Mami, and now…me. Why didn't she tell me all this sooner? It might've made understanding her a bit easier. "I have more…" I begin to say, though Bram's voice filters into my mind. *Don't tell him anything, Mica.* But I need Dane's help. I swallow hard and stare into his clear blue-gray eyes. "A family tree. It mentions Washington Irving with a son named Cristóbal born in 1826."

Dane listens, but it almost seems like he already knows, even though he can't possibly. I just acquired that document myself straight from a safe deposit box. "What else does it mention?"

"That the baby was adopted. The rest of the names are his descendants, from Spain all the way to Cuba." I leave out the part about how the whole family had come full circle from Spain, to Cuba, to New York, and how it appears as though I'm directly related to Irving.

"And it didn't say who the mother was, did it?" Dane runs his thumb over his lips. "That's quite an artifact. What are you going to do with it, if you don't mind my asking?"

I've said enough. "Even if I knew, I wouldn't tell you."

He smiles. Few of my answers ever surprise him. Like

he knows it all, has seen it all, and is anticipating my every move. "Good girl."

I narrow my eyes at him. "Dane, are you sure you're in town just to tour literary America, and nothing else?"

"What do you mean?"

"There's something you're not telling me."

"I could say the same about you."

I chew the inside of my lip. Clearly, he's better at mind games than I am. He props his elbows up on his knees and presses his face into his hands. "Like I said, I'm not here to take anything that doesn't belong to me. Your instincts are good, but..." He taps me on the knee. "Don't give anyone else the info you just gave me. That's all you need to know for now."

So there *is* more to him than meets the eye. Who is he?

"Micaela, let me just add this, because I really care about you. You're smart, curious, and all..." His eyes rove over my face gently—experienced, unfazed, protective.

"But what?"

"You *are* being watched," he whispers. My stomach twists into a dreadful knot when he says it. "So be careful. If I were you, I'd make sure whatever your mother left you is in a safe place. I hope it's well protected."

Holy shit. I knew it. I knew someone's been following me, and it's not just voices and visions. "How do you know this?"

"I just do."

"That doesn't exactly make me feel better." And now I'm back to trusting no one.

"No, but it sure as hell will make you more cautious, won't it?"

Crap. My papers are all at Bram and Jonathan's

apartment. Assuming they're still there, I have to hurry over, grab everything, then move it all back to a new safe deposit box with an entirely new password. I stand, almost tripping over my feet. "I'm sorry, I need to go."

He takes my hand suddenly. "I know this is a lot to process, and it must sound strange coming from me, but just trust me."

I don't know what it is about Dane, but he calms my soul. I don't know what to believe, who to believe, or anything else at this point. The pressure of tears forms behind my eyes again. I want to trust him. I do. Where this leap of faith is coming from, I don't know, but I nod.

"Good." He stands, and I wish I didn't have to let go of his hand yet. But I do, and he pulls a card from his wallet for me. His name, Dane Boracich, and his phone number. "Here. If you need me again, call me. It's a lot faster than email."

Chapter Seventeen

"…what chance was there of escaping ghost or goblin, if such it was, which could ride upon the wings of the wind?"

I rush down University Avenue. I've never seen anyone's head explode before, but I imagine it might resemble something like the conversation I just had with Dane. What did I gain from telling him about the very documents my mother dodged danger trying to protect? Information about where the journal was last seen, for one. Confirmation that my mother was the last to see it, which puts me in direct danger, for two.

Mami slipped in the bathtub? Accident? I think not. My mother might have had some help slipping. But what if Dane is just as interested in finding the journal as the Derants and Engers are? What if he has his own agenda of fame and glory? The journal is still out there somewhere and could be worth a lot of money.

I sprint through all my shortcuts, hurrying.

At the apartment building, I fly up the steps to the second floor. When I reach the apartment, out of breath,

I turn my key in the keyhole and pause. Someone left the screened window open. *Shit.* "Coco?" I call, waiting for her to come running like she usually does.

A quick scan of the apartment tells me that nobody is home. Quickly, I search the entire apartment, anywhere Coco might hide—in the living room, both beds, the couch, under the bed. I even check the kitty litter in the kitchen, then realize she probably... I fly to the open window and tug on the screen frame. Loose in the lower right-hand corner. "Damn it." I throw down my purse and run outside. "Coco!" The outer veranda is empty.

Coco will have to wait until I handle my original purpose first. I dart into the apartment again, then the bedroom, and shove my hand underneath Bram's mattress—the envelope is still there. *Thank God!* And its contents? I flip the envelope open and riffle through it, looking for the most important pieces. All there. On Bram's bed, I rock back and forth, hugging the envelope.

I have to move these items out of here, take it all back to the townhouse. I doubt Nina is coming back anyway—it's been four days. But for now, because I need to go find Coco, I'll keep it somewhere safer than the mattress, long enough to search for Coco. "Damn it, cat." I run into the walk-in closet, reach behind a pile of sweaters on a shelf, and place the envelope way behind them.

But then, imagining the worst will happen while I'm gone, I quickly pull the envelope back out and take it with me, stuffing it in my purse, locking the front window tightly and leaving the apartment. I search the parking lot, the surrounding woods, and dumpster. Maybe she tried making her way back to my old house. I once read about a cat who walked ninety miles home after accidentally crawling into a neighbor's moving box.

Mami's house is less than two miles.

Taking the main street into the heart of town, I stop often to ask if anyone has seen a fluffy white cat. Nothing. After a while, my thoughts turn to Mary Shelley. Is she really my ancestor and spirit guide? I recall the dark look, the tormented face in the photo. *Find the proof.*

But how do I do that? Is the journal enough to prove a relationship? What were the results of the authentication in Andover, I wonder? I don't know that finding the journal again would prove anything, but it *would* make me the possessor of a very sought-after document.

But I don't want fame or glory. I just want to make things right with my mom. Irving asked that only flesh and blood see the document. If I can manage that, Mary Shelley's spirit might move on to a more peaceful place than where she is now.

I reach North Broadway completely out of breath. At the fork in the road, I hear the voices. Not the house. It sounds like Mami, but so faint. I close my eyes to listen. We're not there.

"We," I whisper. "Who's we?"

All of a sudden, I'm hit with a strong urge to follow the road down to the one place in Sleepy Hollow I haven't visited yet since I arrived, the one place I've been scared to go, because seeing her name on a stone will drive it home—the cemetery. It's the familiar tug from my dreams, only I'm awake and being drawn, just like at Sunnyside. I follow the curved road down Route 9 until finally I reach the cemetery gates next to the Old Dutch Church.

Grabbing a tourist map from the gates, I cut through the parking lot. The cemetery may have been mentioned in Irving's tale, but it's not fiction. It's as real as the death it contains. Thirty-nine thousand souls lie here. The cemetery stretches for eighty-five acres over rolling hills, knolls, and cliffs. I doubt that Coco is here, but I let the voices guide me.

The Irving family plot *is* here—Washington Irving, Ebenezer, and other family members. Not a grand mausoleum either, like William Rockefeller's, Andrew Carnegie's, or Leona Helmsley's. It's as simple a grave as they come. A short, round stone in a small, fenced-in space.

Great elms and oaks shade the plots, and perilous, narrow roads snake throughout. On more than one occasion, I've seen cars trying to make their way around the plots, come face to face on a narrow path, only for one of them to back up with limited visibility and nearly clip a headstone with its back bumper.

Come...

"Where?" I whisper, reveling in the beauty all around me. Aging tombstones adorned with crosses, stars of David; kneeling, praying angels surrounding me for acres and acres. I pass one angel statue whose arms are draped around the tombstone as if mourning whoever lies beneath, crying silver tears.

The trees rustle, the wind croons. Houses dot the hillside below me, and the Hudson shines in the distance. When I die, I want to be buried here.

Perhaps you will, a dark voice creeps in from somewhere. I look behind me. "Hello?"

Nothing here but tombstones and tire-worn grassy paths. Then comes the sound of bubbling water. I must be nearing the Pocantico River, more like a stream. Something flashes in the grass ahead of me. I sprint toward it, checking the ground, but from this angle, it's so difficult to tell. I jog back to where I'd originally stood and sway back and forth slowly, waiting to catch the same angle of the reflection once again.

There. Next to that stone. I run up to the same spot again and look down. A small metal disc, half-caked with moist dirt, lies on the ground. I crouch low to pick it up and flip the disc over:

COCONUT

(914) 555-3746

Heaviness washes over me in a hulking wave. I scan the area. "Coco?" Why is she here of all places? I look up, praying I won't find my cat hanging off a branch from her collar. I bought her one of those breakaway collars for that very reason, yet only the tag has come off.

Twigs crackle nearby. "Coco? Here, Coco." I blow kisses and yell, "COCO!" listening to my cries echo all around me.

Leave, or you're next.

I whirl around.

The trees rustle again. "Mami, what's going on?" I wait for the ethereal replies I've gotten used to, but it's only my own voice that rings in my ears. I walk faster, checking between the stones, searching for white fur on the green grass. "Co-cooo!"

As I whistle and call, I venture deeper into the cemetery. Up ahead are the banks of the river. Farther down, a rickety covered wooden bridge about twenty feet long—the very one some say the legendary Headless Horseman is said to cross each night. My dragging feet swish over piles of fallen leaves to get to it.

It doesn't look very sturdy, but there doesn't seem to be another way to get to the other side, either. The wind picks up, sending a fresh burst of golden leaves raining to the ground and water. I start crossing the bridge, my eyes adjusting to the darkness within.

Go...

"Mami, I don't know if that's you," I whisper, hurrying through the tunnel. "But I'm not leaving until I talk to you. Where's Coco?"

Exiting the tunnel, the trees almost look as though they're leaning, whispering into one another. I hear what sounds like mumbling up ahead. I strain to see who might be there. More trees and headstones.

The mumbling comes again, but I can't decipher it. I walk on for another minute, then stop cold. Breathing. Someone is near me. Just like the night at the train station. Or is that my own breath, suspended in the air in front of me? My heart beats loudly against my ears. At least I think it's *my* heart...

Lela.

"Mami?" I shout, fists rigid at my sides.

Leave now.

She answers me. My mom is answering me. "No! I'm tired of running. Tell me what's going on!"

A low snicker comes through just then, not in the cemetery, not in my mind, either. I freeze and listen for it again. It starts low, then grows louder. Is someone laughing? "Bram, is that you, because if it is, it's NOT funny!" I yell, echoes resonating all around.

Quiet settles over the cemetery once again, except for the sound of the wind. Something tells me it's not Bram. Then I hear it—a low laugh. A chilled feeling prickles my arm. I whirl around, expecting to see someone standing there. Instead, I see a flash of white, lying very still against a tombstone.

No.

I slowly walk up, eyes glued to the unmistakable curve of a fluffy white tail. "Oh, God, no." I throw myself on the ground at the cat's body, still and lifeless. Her tail, the only part of her that seems intact. "Coco." She's flattened and muddy in the middle. Her head is broken, fresh blood oozing from her ears and nose. Her tongue barely pokes out between sharp, small teeth. I fight to keep my stomach from rising into my throat.

She's been trampled but not by an animal. By tires. Someone driving, looking for a headstone, not being careful. I shut my eyes against the mangled mess. I remember Coconut as a tiny kitten with closed eyes and ears, nestled against Pumpkin's belly. I reach out and rest my hand on her head.

"Why didn't you stay home?" I whisper through tears. Who would do this to her? Why did she come all this way? Then I notice the stone on top of which the cat lies dead—

MARIA VASQUEZ BURGOS

Suddenly, I hear the laugh once again, calm and satisfied. A solid wave of rage starts between my forehead and the back of my head, overtaking my entire body. Teeth clenched so hard, I hear them grind. I scream, "What's so funny, you sick bastard!"

Then a new sound, so clear there's no mistaking it. A horse's neigh, followed by the woody, hollow sound of hooves galloping right toward me.

Thirsty leaves rustle on the ground like littered newspaper in the wind. I stand paralyzed over my mother's grave, eyes roving, searching for the source of the sound. A horse in the cemetery? Seriously? But there's no one here! Yet the galloping feels a blink away.

Run, Lela!

I break free of the invisible straitjacket immobilizing my upper body. I plunge through the woods, boots pounding the earth in time with my breath, eyes focused ahead, dodging grave markers, logs, rocks, and fallen limbs in my way. Who's charging me on a horse? The Headless Horseman is only a character in a story. A legend.

Isn't he?

I run straight for the bridge, my breath short and choppy. Isn't the horseman supposed to stop chasing his victims once they cross the bridge? How ridiculous that I'm considering the logistics behind a work of fiction. Maybe it's not a real spirit at all, but someone playing a trick on me.

It's unnervingly dark inside the covered bridge, but I have no other choice. The galloping is right behind me. I'll have to go through it if I don't want to sense a horse's hot breath prickling my neck. I avoid eye contact with whoever is chasing me, in case paralysis freezes my body again…then I'll get trampled like Coconut.

I charge through the bridge, my breath loud in my ears, panicked footsteps echoing against the siding, plowing along the musty planks until I blast out the other end, nearly tumbling onto the ground. I check over my shoulder. Nothing followed me through. But next to the bridge, a hazy mist hovers above the ground in the shape of what could be interpreted as a massive horse with a rider on top. It stands at the edge of the river, watching me escape.

That's no trick.

I tear my incredulous gaze away from the swirling shape and start dodging obstacles and jumping over grave markers. The marble angels watch me flee, their prayers falling on deaf ears. Suddenly, the horse neighs angrily. I peer over my shoulder in time to see it rear, its front hooves high in the air, land again, then take a few steps back for what quickly becomes a running start.

I don't wait to see the horse leap over the water or land on my half of the cemetery. I sprint again, pushing my body faster than I ever imagined possible, visualizing the west end of the property ahead to encourage me. Just then, another shape barrels into my view about fifty feet away, startling me even more. Someone on a bike. He seems to be fleeing the spectral horse and rider, same as me. Hooded black sweatshirt, black sweatpants, small and skillful on the low-riding mountain bike. The fat tires crunch over rough terrain, its driver expertly maneuvering over the challenging topography, using rocks and rotting bark as a springboard for leaping into the air.

Behind me, the horse and rider draw closer. From this distance, they appear more solid, real. Black shiny coat, brown leather saddle, black boots, gray pants, buttoned coat, and the rider's head—I want to laugh and scream at the same time—*missing?* As I gape at the phantom in utter fascination, I stumble over a gravestone and hit my knee against a massive rock, falling onto my side.

Damn it! I bite my lip to keep from crying out, but the pain is blinding. My jeans tear at the knee, and a deep scrape is already pooling with bright red blood.

The horseman will definitely get me now if he wants to. But he doesn't. He bounds on, through stones and bushes as if traveling on a completely separate astral plane as me. In fact, it's like I don't even exist. Up ahead, the Irving family plot marks the end of the property on the edge of a hill. If I jump off the hill to escape, I'll hurt myself even more. I have no choice but to lie perfectly still. I drag myself behind a tall gravestone and wait.

Watching the Hessian trooper carry on, I realize I'm caught in the middle of a different chase. It's the bicycle he's after. The biker pedals through the last section of the cemetery, heading straight for the edge of the short cliff. The horseman leaps over a low knoll, forcing the biker straight off the hill's edge. I watch in awe as the biker flies over the hill, laughing the same maniacal laugh I heard moments before I found Coco. He lands in a rough skid, swaying, nearly wiping out on the church property below. Seconds later, he regains balance and escapes through a grove of trees outside the cemetery.

As if pulled by invisible reins, the horse skids to a halt just short of the cliff, and a gruff voice echoes something like, *"Ved-peace dish!"*

The horse snorts, dancing in place while the rider reclaims control of its rearing head. I suck in deep gulps of air, trying not to faint. I peek and see the apparition still there, and, maybe I'm delirious at this point, but he's looking straight at me. How can he? He has no eyes, face, or head to speak of, but I just know that he's watching me. Is he coming for me next?

I really don't think he is. Especially when, after a minute of listening to the horse snorting air from its nostrils, the horseman calmly kicks his steed and trots back the way he came, satisfied, it seems, that his task of chasing out the unwelcomed has been successful. Was he protecting me when he saw I was in danger? Just in case, I continue to hide behind the tombstone. Until I'm sure, without a moment's hesitation, that my gallant guardian is completely gone.

...

At the apartment, sitting on the wobbly toilet seat lid, I press a wad of cotton balls soaked with hydrogen peroxide against my knee, staring at my dirty nails and hands, waiting for the solution to penetrate my wound.

"Ow!" The stinging pain sets off a wave of tears that have nothing to do with my cuts. I lost my cat in such a horrible way. Who would do such a thing?

My mind reels with a multitude of thoughts. How I should've kept Coco at the townhouse. Screw Nina's allergies. How I never should've come back to Sleepy Hollow, or *hey,* never should've left my mother in the first place. *Maybe*, if I hadn't been such a naive little princess under my father's influence, I might've helped my mother, and the poor woman might still be alive.

But that's not how my life is turning out, and now I'm smack in the middle of a colossal mess. I lift the cotton balls and blow on my knee, what my mother used to do. It feels worse than it looks. I can't remember the last time I ran that fast.

It had to be the biker who trampled Coco. She had tire tracks on her. Though I want to believe it was an accident, that no decent person would ever do that to an animal or to me, no matter how much they hated us. But it was so deliberate—the way she was left on Mami's grave and all—like a warning.

And I'm convinced the horseman was protecting me. I've heard older folks at parties before insist that the apparition exists. They talk about it with kids gathered at their feet, but I'd always assumed they were stories for a dark autumn night. He certainly looked real to me.

I don't know anything anymore. In fact, I'm starting to embrace uncertainty with the same sense of duty as a ship's captain sinking with his own vessel. One thing I know is that I can't stay at Bram's. Too risky. What if he's not really into me? What if it's all just an act to get to my mother's documents?

I open a packet of gauze and place it over the wound, ripping bandaging tape with my teeth and securing it in place. My tattered jeans go in the garbage. Carefully, I hobble to my bag and change into sweatpants, then I transfer my mother's envelope from my purse to my backpack, along with a few other things I've brought—a sweater, textbooks, an extra pair of shoes.

From the bed, my phone rings. I run over and grab it, noticing that Bram has texted me pics. I enlarge the first one, and—surprise, surprise—me and Dane at the lake! Of course! Because my day has not been shitty enough! The first one shows us walking through the courtyard. The other, us sitting together by the lake, my face twisted into a knot. And the last one, pure fodder for Bram, Dane holding my hand.

Bram's text—

You sure you want to do this?

The last pic is a screenshot of a text argument between him and Lacy. She tells him he's too stupid to realize that I have eyes for someone else, and it's clear that the photo came from her.

How did you get that?

What does it matter?

Because it matters.

> *Lacy is in color guard, Mica.*

What does color guard have to do with any— Ugh, stupid color guard. I knew we should've left the college. They were using the field to practice when Dane and I were there.

My fingers tap out a quick reply:

> *Do not pretend to know what this is all about.*

It doesn't sound very understanding. After all, it *does* appear as though Dane and I were having a quiet, romantic lunch together the very morning after Bram and I kissed for the first time, but after learning my mother was buried, might be a thief, plus finding my cat flattened beyond recognition, getting chased through the cemetery by a fictional ghost, and smashing my knee into a jagged rock, crap from Bram is the *last* thing I need right now.

A moment later, another text from him comes in.

> *I'm not the one pretending, Princess.*

Every time I think I can't handle another ounce of stress, more stress piles on. Screeching, I hurl my phone across the room, straight for the opening front door.

CHAPTER EIGHTEEN

"…a stouter man than he would have shrunk from the competition, and a wiser man would have despaired."

The phone clocks Bram right on the temple, bounces off the doorframe, and tumbles to the floor. "What the hell?" He drops an armful of things and rubs his head furiously.

"Well, I didn't know you were right outside the door!"

"I'm the one who should be throwing things, not you!"

"Really? And why is that?" I cross my arms. "Because your ex sends you a few pictures, and now you think you have it all figured out? Of course she sent those. She's mad at you! You broke up with her a month before I arrived!"

He closes the door and marches up to me. "Well, they do speak for themselves."

"No, they don't. That meeting wasn't a date or anything."

He throws his hands up, and I get a sinking feeling. "Look, Mica, you're free to be with whoever you want. I'm only worried about you, because you told me someone was after you. So don't come crying in the middle of the night anymore about how you need someone to protect you. I can't protect you if you're talking to strangers."

As much as I want to fall into his arms and forget this day ever happened, one glaring fact is, he *is* a Derant, and if all Dane said was true, the old Hollow families can't be trusted. My eyes land on the things he dropped when he came in—cans of spray paint, a gallon of fog machine fluid, and best of all, the brown leather saddle that was in the apartment before.

"What is this?" I point out the obvious.

"What does it look like? Stuff for the show." He picks up the items and dumps them in the corner with the rest of the HollowEve boxes. "It's all going to the manor house tonight."

"I only met with him because I wanted to talk about the items my mother left me. It's related to his theory."

He crosses his arms. "Like what? The picture of Mary Shelley? I can't believe you're sharing all that with him but not me, right after you told me someone's following you. What the heck's wrong with you, Mica? You don't know that guy from any other treasure hunter who comes through here."

Guilt gnaws at me. Is he right? Did I give away valuable info today to a thrill seeker? "I had to ask him questions."

"Ask me! I know more than that guy! Let me guess, you didn't, by any chance, talk about how he even *knows* all that stuff he talked about in class, did you? About the Engers' missing journal, did you?" He takes a step toward me.

"What does it matter who I talk to?" I say, sinking back onto the couch.

"What it matters is that my whole family and Jonathan's were responsible for that thing, and now it's gone, and the last one to see it was your mom!"

I've never seen Bram this upset before, and I'm just as unsettled knowing that I caused it.

But he quickly regains his composure, giving me a defeated smile. "I'm the *traitor* in my family for defending you and insisting that your mom had nothing to do with it. Same way Ellen took the heat for being her friend. Looks like we all get screwed in the end."

I don't know what to say.

"Why do you think I'm living in this paradise?" He spreads his arms out wide. "Huh?"

I shrug, tears threatening to spill over. "Because you wanted to live on your own? Independence and all that. I don't know, you never told me."

"While working my ass off still in school? Needing to shack up with Jonathan to pay for this piece-of-shit place? It'd be a hell of a lot easier living at home, don't you think? That's what you don't understand, Mica." He squats in front of me and takes my hands. "I'm here because of *you*. Because as long as I'm defending you, have always defended you, will *always* defend you, I can't live at home." His voice softens. "Got it?"

Flinging tears away, I feel like a total jerk.

"I love you," he says, and the words burn. "I always have. So I need to know right now…if you're just playing the flirt with that dude to get a rise out of me, because you wanted to see how much I'd care, that's fine, I can handle it. But tell me the truth…do you trust *me*, or do you trust an outsider? Because that's what he is."

Yes, Dane Boracich is a stranger, yet only hours ago, I saw him as the keeper of all knowledge, the one to trust if I wanted to stay safe. Was it all an act? Is Bram acting, too? I wish I knew the truth. "It's not that."

"What is it then?"

"I don't know." I fight back exhaustion. "I have to rest a while and think. I'm sorry." I drop his hands, get up, and brush past him into the bedroom. From the other room, I hear Bram's arms drop against his sides.

"That's great, Mica. Go and think," he mutters. "I'll still be here for you. Like always."

I pace the bedroom, taking in my surroundings one last time, the stain on the ceiling, the ratty desk, the bed where we kissed for the first time ever. But I can't stay. This was a mistake. I let myself get too involved when I said I wouldn't.

In the other room, Bram is still muttering. "I can't believe you talk to Boracich *one time*, and he turned you against me. I'm not to be trusted. I'm a Derant. Right? Isn't that what he said?"

I smash my lips together to keep from bawling.

"But what he doesn't know"—Bram appears in the doorway and calmly leans against the frame—"is that I know his little secret. I know why he's in town. And I can say the same about him."

He moves over to the coffee table and picks up his old, cracked iPad, pointing at the screen. An article headline reads: *Huge Cash for Irving Diary.* "Read it."

I grab the tablet out of his hands. A historical preservation society is offering five hundred thousand dollars for finding Washington Irving's private journal previously housed at the Historic Hudson Library in Tarrytown, New York, last seen in Andover, Massachusetts.

"He didn't tell you that part, did he?" Bram shakes his head at me. "Half a million? For a diary. All because it'll rewrite a famous biography and expose what should have been a high-profile relationship. I don't know about you, but I think a poor student teacher could use that kind of money. What do you think?"

Oh, God. A whole town, even treasure hunters from outside, vying for a chance to find a missing relic, not for preservation or to protect Irving's good name but for cold, hard cash. What else would awaken a sleepy, run-down village like this one? I should've known.

I have to get to my mother's storage unit.

Bram flings the iPad onto the couch with a huff. Then he runs his fingers along my cheek. "Don't believe everything you hear. It's fine if you don't want to trust me anymore, but don't think for a minute it'll change what I feel for you…because it won't."

With that, he grabs his keys and phone again and disappears from the apartment, leaving me alone with an article headline I can't bear to look at and the burning realization that now, I have no one left to turn to.

CHAPTER NINETEEN

*"He who wins a thousand common hearts is therefore
entitled to some renown; but he who keeps undisputed
sway over the heart of a coquette, is indeed a hero."*

I don't wait for Bram to come back. I leave for the
townhouse, hauling all my stuff across town like
a backpacker through Europe. When I finally arrive,
stepping up to the front door, I notice something stuck
there. A yellow piece of paper. Water's been cut. Next to
it is one from the power and light. Isn't this nice? I throw
open the door and toss my shit inside. "Nina?"

No answer. I head up the stairs, listening for the
sounds of bitching someone out on the phone, but all is
quiet. I turn the corner into her bedroom and stop cold.
The foreboding feeling I had when Nina first left to visit
her sister returns. The closet door is empty. All clothes and
shoes—gone. I open a drawer in the honey wood dresser.
Empty.

I can't say I blame her. I'm not happy with my dad,
either.

I feel terrible. Even though we weren't close, we kept each other company. Now, with Nina and all of her belongings gone, there's no reason to stay. At the bottom of the stairs, I find a note on the foyer table: *Micaela, I don't get paid enough for this. I'm sorry.* I stare at the note a minute then crumple it up, throwing it hard at the stairs. It bounces off the carpet and rolls back down to the floor again.

Furious, I call my dad for the fifty-millionth time. Of course, he doesn't answer. "Hey, Dad. Still waiting for that call back. I could be dying here, and you'd never know." I hang up.

Now what? Back to Miami? Maybe I could live with Emily, and even if I can't, I'd still be near her. *Tempting.*

No way I can. My mother would never forgive me if I left again.

When Dane's car pulls up outside, I take a last look at the townhouse. It's as empty as I feel. I close the door and lock it. Dane steps out of the car, grabs a bunch of bags from my hands, and sets them down on the porch. Without a word, he circles his arms around me. "I'm sorry," he says, holding me tight. The sincere action releases my torrent of tears.

"So much shit." I sob.

"I know. Shh. Give me all that. I'll carry it. You sit in the car."

Plopping into the passenger seat and closing the door, I sit in the dark, embarrassed. When I called Dane, asking him to please come get me, I rambled about losing Coco,

I complained about Nina abandoning me, and after a minute of hesitation, I even told him about my encounter with the horseman in the cemetery. He didn't judge, didn't ask if I thought it was an apparition or real—he just listened. Like a friend should.

Once we leave the development, back on Maple Street, I point to the only house I can think of where staying won't be a problem. "Halfway down on the left. Five doors from my old house. Where I met you."

As we slow past my mother's house, I gaze at the darkened windows with a clenched stomach, scanning for rogue wisps of light or shadows. Dane stops in front of Betty Anne's house. "Do you want me to come in with you?"

"No, that's okay. Thanks. I really appreciate your help moving my things."

"Not a problem. Call me if you need anything else. And listen, everything will sort itself out, okay?" He smiles sadly. Doesn't lean in for another hug. Doesn't push for a kiss on the cheek, nothing. It feels nice knowing I can trust him, that he doesn't want anything from me except for me to feel safe.

I close the door and face Betty Anne's house, aglow with light, a glaring contrast to my own abandoned home. Orange and black paper lanterns swing in the breeze off her porch eaves. Before ringing the doorbell, I listen to sounds through her open window. Running water, silverware thudding against plastic plates, the faucet stopping. A feminine shadow moves through the house, and the main light suddenly flicks on, drowning out the paper lanterns' feeble glow.

The door opens. "You gonna stand here all night?" I raise an eyebrow. How did she know I was out here? I drag all my bags inside, while she stands there, shaking her gray head.

Standing in her foyer, I ask, "How did you know I was out there?"

"Honey… Like I know. Come to Vanessa's room." She leads me down the short hallway into her daughter's old bedroom filled with photos, ballet trophies, elementary school behavior and academic certificates, and an old flat-screen TV.

"I'm sorry for this," I say. "I should've asked first before showing up."

"Sorry for what?" Betty Anne clears space on the dresser. "You're not pregnant, are you?"

I force a small laugh. "Not a chance."

"Then there's nothing to be sorry about. And even if you *were*, this is your second home."

"My only one now."

Her big round eyes pity me. She pats me on the back. "You stay as long as you like, Micaela Burgos. No worries. Got that?"

I nod, my cheeks tightening into a forced smile. I wish I would've stayed with Betty Anne from the beginning, but my father seemed to want me as isolated as possible.

She opens the closet and pulls out an extra blanket and pillow, placing it on the bed. "Rest for now, and we'll talk tomorrow. You need me to wake you in time for school?"

"No." I laugh to myself. The trivialities of school seem another world away. "I can't think about school right now."

"Whatever it is, hon, it'll pass. It always does." She backs out of the room. "Let me know if you need anything."

Seriously doubt this will pass, but… "Thank you, I will."

Once she leaves, I curl into a ball on the bed. If a year ago, someone had sat me down and told me that in the near future, I'd be lying in my mother's neighbor's daughter's bed like a sack of bones, thinking it strange to be spending the night just five doors from my mom's house with my old ability to hear and see ghosts on overdrive, I would've laughed my ass off.

But nobody did. And I fall asleep with the lamp still on before having the chance to lament it.

*F*or once, sleep comes peacefully. From the moment I lay down to half the next day, I more than make up for all the sleep I've lost. I sit up to find myself warmly covered with blankets, though still in my clothes. A glass of orange juice sits on the nightstand along with a note—*I'll call the school and tell them you need a few days. Going to run some errands. Eat something.*

A few days? Try a few weeks.

How nice would it be to wake up and find that the last week was only a dream—not a ghostly dream, just a regular, dissolved-in-the-morning dream. My sore knee reminds me that there's no such thing. Carefully, I stand and go about trying to act normal, doing normal bathroom, hair-brushing things.

I emerge and raid the fridge—yogurt, bread with butter, leftover rice with chicken, and garlic rolls that melt in my mouth after I warm them up in the microwave. I wash the whole thing down with the glass of OJ. Then I limp back to the bedroom and crawl into bed with my phone.

Right now, it's first hour, middle of Lit class. I wonder

if Dane has told the students about the historical society's reward money yet. I hope Bram has enough brain cells to stay away from Dane, not confront him or say anything stupid. I text Bram.

> *Sorry about the other night. Pls give me some time. Pls don't harass Mr. B. It's all my fault.*

I watch the local news at ten a.m. and see that there is, in fact, a lot of commotion regarding the reward money and journal. Now that my knee is slightly better, I'll visit the police department again, barge into an office if I have to, declare myself next of kin, ask for my mother's keys.

I will find the rest of the answers.

Unless, of course, the answers find me first.

I t's not the smell of cooking that wakes me in the evening, though after so few home-cooked meals this last month, it should rightfully stir my appetite. It's the text from Bram.

> *Went to school...doc T asked where u were...boracich was there at first then left... I don't know what to tell you mica except I freakin love u... tell me where u r...*

> *Can't do that right now. Sorry.*

The shutters over the window wheeze and slap against the panes. I peek through the slats. Something blustery is headed this way. The wind whistles against the glass, blowing leaves all over the front lawn. The paper lanterns bounce in protest. Are the last of the season's leaves, at this very moment, raining to the ground in the cemetery, covering Coco where she lies dead? It killed me to leave her there, but what else could I do? Soon the leaves and snow will completely cover her.

Ved-peace dish, the horseman had said. What does that even mean?

Footsteps sound down the hall, then a knock. "Coming," I call, hobbling to the door.

Betty Anne stands there, kitchen towel hanging from her belt loop and spatula in one hand.

"Hi." I give her a sheepish grin. "Sorry I ate all your food. I was starving. I haven't been sleeping lately, plus I had a really rough day yesterday. Not only that, but I—"

"It means 'piss off,'" Betty Anne cuts me off.

I narrow my eyes at her.

"*Verpiss dich.* It's German for 'piss off, get the hell out,' that sort of thing." Slowly, my mouth drops open. I rewind my memory twenty seconds and replay my every move. Did I speak aloud just a moment ago? "Where did you hear it?" Betty Anne asks.

I cross my arms. "Never mind where I heard it. How did you know what I—"

"You were at the cemetery?" she asks.

"Yes."

She turns and heads off. "Come eat something."

I follow Betty Anne to the kitchen and sit at the same flower-patterned, vinyl-covered dinette where I ate dinners as a kid. She stands by the stove, pressing a meat patty down so the juices jump and sizzle on the frying pan. Her face reflects internal torment.

"So you can hear thoughts," I say.

"Don't ask me how I do it, because I don't know."

"You can hear everything going on in my head?"

"Oh, goodness, no." Betty Anne recoils. "If I could, I'd be in a loony house somewhere, yelling at people to make the voices stop. No, I just pick up little pieces...bits...of conversations, thoughts, words, fragments. Like radio waves."

I clear my throat. "That's how I started, but since I arrived, it's been getting worse."

Betty Anne nods. "Your mother could, too. Since she was little, but she didn't develop better clairvoyance skills until she was older." She lifts the beef patty and places it on a plate alongside a scoop of mashed potatoes. "That was one reason we became friends."

"She never told *me* that. In fact, she never told me a lot of things, and I'm really resenting it, like really, really resenting it, Betty Anne."

"Can I just say something? In her defense, there are lots of things parents don't tell their kids. Deep down, we all want to be perfect in our children's eyes. Especially with something like this. It's not the sort of thing you go around telling people, not in a town where everybody's already judging you. Believe me, no parent wants their child thinking they're defective, but we are. We're all defective."

I think about that a while. I get it, but she still kept too much from me. "It's still frustrating. I don't always understand what I'm hearing or seeing."

"And you won't. The dead, they'll come around once they know. They'll want to tell you everything, but you can't let them. It's not fair to burden you like that. It's hard enough making sense of your own thoughts, much less someone else's."

"Why don't you tune mine out?"

"I can't tune you out when I'm worried about you."

She sprinkles something on the plate, then sets it in front of me with a fork and napkin. "Your favorite."

Bunless burger with mashed potatoes and peas arranged in a happy face. I want to cry.

"You know what I think?" Betty Anne sits across from me with a glass of water. "I think you and your mom probably communicated while you were apart without even realizing it."

I think she's right. I remember times my mother would suddenly pop into my head during a particularly hard day at school, or during times when my dad was away and I didn't see anyone all day but Nina. I thought I was just thinking of her in a normal way. But then…there was the note. I could see the words in my mind before I saw them on the paper. "I never wanted this ability. I didn't ask for it. And it scares the crap out of me."

"You get used to it," she says. "Once you realize most spirits are not out to hurt you. Most only want you to relay a message to a loved one, or they're trying to warn you. Those are the ones with experience in the astral ways."

"That happened yesterday." During my walk through the cemetery. "It was like my mom was trying to warn me that something bad was going to happen."

Betty Anne nods. "I always felt she was hiding something, but whatever it was, it's your burden now."

"She's not the only one who talks to me, though. I get other voices too."

"Forget the ghosts, Mica." She leans back in her seat and sighs. "It's real, *live* people you should fear."

I think of what happened to Coco. That was not the handiwork of a ghost. "Something else happened while I was out there…" Coco. I don't say it. But I don't have to. Betty Anne's eyes scan mine. She looks down at her water then away. "And you haven't been putting flowers on the wrong grave." I stick a fork into the mashed potatoes but can't eat. "I still don't know how it happened. Why she was there. Who would want to kill her…"

"And *verpiss dich*? You heard that in the cemetery too?"

I nod.

"Was he talking to you?"

I shrug. "I don't think so. There was someone else there. Someone on a bike."

She shrugs. "Ah. October in Sleepy Hollow. There's always someone in the cemetery this time of year. Let me guess…sound of horse's hooves and all?"

I set down my fork. "Go ahead. Say it. You think I'm crazy." I stare at her.

But Betty Anne is just an old wife of Sleepy Hollow, and all the proverbial old wives of Sleepy Hollow know the truth about the valley's unseen things—that they exist, that their energies are just as alive today as they were in the days of the Dutch settlers. I forgot, that's all, and I've been remembering it since I first arrived on that late-night train.

Her smile disappears into the smoothness of her cheeks. "Oh, you're not crazy, hon." She leans forward. "You're *home*."

CHAPTER TWENTY

"All the stories of ghosts and goblins that he had heard in the afternoon, now came crowding upon his recollection."

I lie in bed, listening to the wind coo over the house, shutters wheezing in and out, wondering if there will be any thunder to accompany this quiet lightning flashing behind my eyelids. Finally, the tranquil storm eventually lulls me to sleep.

The soft aroma of flowers filters into the room. I'm no longer in bed. I'm under a half moon in a beautiful silvery garden with patches of shrubs, curving stone walkways, fragrant herbs, and tall swaying grasses. Cold wind caresses my memory with scents of roses and English lavender, my mother's favorite. I feel like I know this place.

I scan the garden for her familiar presence, finding only a mouse scurrying ahead of me. My wrapped arms fight off cold air. Twigs snap behind me. I whirl around and spot a house—a tiny, charming house under the stars that I've seen many times—one room, gray walls, red roof, a sole window above the wooden door.

I might be able to place it in my memory if it weren't for the weeping I hear. A woman's sobbing, mumbling under her breath, sobbing again. I look around, fully expecting Mary's spirit to accost me out of nowhere, beg me to follow, push and pull me where she wants me to go, but I don't see her. The isolated weeping continues as another sound rises over the cries—a baby's piercing wail.

My bare feet crush a spot in the tall grass. The infant's cries ebb then start again, ebb and then again…the smell of lavender is stronger now, almost too pungent. I'm overwhelmed with a maternal instinct to find the baby and protect it. I crouch on the ground and run my hands along the hard earth, feeling for a warm body, a basket, blanket, anything.

"Shh, baby. It's all right."

Twigs snap again. I raise my eyes just above the level of the grass. Someone is there, rounding the corner of the house. I wait with suspended breath, forcing myself perfectly still in the squatted position. Then I see him. I'd know him anywhere. Only he looks older, a future version of himself, a hybrid of a man my father's age and the boy I grew up with, a powerful form hovering in the tall grass. *Bram? Dad?*

I've invested so much in you.

I know…

His words might comfort me if his voice didn't sound so twisted, manic, as if I wronged him. Like he's not Bram at all. I've had dreams like this before, where the person I'm seeing has an identity belonging to someone else.

It's a dream, I remind myself. *Anything can happen.*

My father–Bram hybrid steps out of the shadows on a mission. In his right hand, he holds something. A shovel?

Old, rusted, and black.

Bram…Dad…you're scaring me. Please stop.

He reaches me and grabs my wrists tightly with one strong hand. I feel his warm breath on my cheek. No one takes what's mine. He squeezes my wrists until I cry out, until my circulation is cut and I no longer feel my hands. Nobody.

I twist my wrists to set them free. *Let go of me!* I yell. Nobody can take me away from you.

He means me. Yes, of course he does. Why is he so angry? Because of Dane? Angry, like my father had been on the only night I've ever seen him enraged, the night I hid in the pantry, listening in on his jealous tirade.

Please let go of me. You're hurting me. This is crazy!

You're not crazy, Betty Anne's words echo, as Dad–Bram releases his hold on me and shoves me back onto the ground. *You're home.* For a flickering second, Shelley's ghost stands in the garden, longing to help but powerless.

Bram's look-alike lifts his other hand and brings it down with such force, I brace for the blow. But my eyes shoot open. I sit up screaming, realizing I'm still in Betty Anne's spare room, not a garden. Lightning flashes against the walls, the old TV, the pictures in frames everywhere bathed in electric white light.

"Jesus." I try regulating my breath back to even, but the lightning flashes again, and this time, in the second it takes for the room to light up, I see a woman in a white nightdress standing at the foot of my bed.

I take in the full horrific sight. Messy hair over her face and shoulders, chin hanging. She doesn't speak— or can't—though it seems like she wants to from the mournful look in her dark eyes. She should still be alive, should still be here to make amends with me.

"Mami," I say, a single sigh suspended between us.

I have a million questions for her, about the journal, about my father, about why she wanted me home, but the first thing that comes flying out of my mouth is, "Mami, I'm sorry. I was unfair to you. I should have stuck with you no matter what. But you didn't tell me what was going on. I didn't know." I cover my face with my hands and weep. She deserved the benefit of the doubt, and I never gave it to her.

...not your fault...

I uncover my face, realizing the mistake it is to look away, knowing she might not be there again when I look twice. But she's still here, gliding out the door, feet and legs bone white, nightdress trailing her knees. The outline of her body, the curve of her breasts, beautiful shape visible through the fabric.

I shoot out of bed. The wraith floats down the hall and out of the house through the door without even opening it. In awe, I watch her and unlock the door, stepping into a whirlwind of wind and leaves, electric light and cold air. "Where are we going?" I watch my mother's spirit float into the street and turn. "Your house?"

She looks over her shoulder disapprovingly, hair shifting down her back. I realize my mistake. "Home?" I notice the darkness behind her ear, the crusted patch of dark blood. *Blunt trauma to the head.*

"Was it an accident? Please tell me. I need to know."

She doesn't answer. Just leads me down Maple Street past our little gray house with the overgrown grass, the place I once loved, where dreams dried up and withered, past the barking dog on the corner, right and up North Broadway.

"Back to the cemetery?" I grow colder without my

sweater, or shoes for that matter. My knee hurts. Another walk to the cemetery in this condition just might set its healing back to square one.

No.

"So you can talk to me?"

Not both.

I understand. Until now, I've always heard my mother's voice without seeing her. But now she's visible with few words. She must have enough energy for one or the other—to be seen or heard—not both. She hasn't had enough time to learn *the astral ways*, as Betty Anne explained.

What if this is the last time I ever see her? I have to ask the right questions. "Everyone thinks you stole that journal. Did you? Is that the business you wanted me to finish, why you sent me that note? Just say yes or no."

She's preoccupied with her mission of leading me down the street.

"Mami, please, I'm not good at guessing games. You have to tell me what to do. Just tell me." I start crying again.

If she hears me, she gives no indication, just glides past the porches with turned-off jack-o-lanterns and white cheesecloth ghosts fluttering around in the wind. Her apparition is starting to lose strength. One moment, her legs are made of light, wispy, dissipating smoke. The next, her whole body turns to miniscule dots of swirling bluish light, and I'm walking alone down the sloping street.

"No! Don't leave me here like this. You have to answer at least one question, Mami, please!" I cover my face, shaking my head. "No, no, no." I wonder if I should sit and wait for her to materialize again.

But then, she reappears a moment later, like frames

on old black-and-white film, to reach out her hand toward
the west side of the street.

"What is it?" I follow her to a squat abandoned
building that looks a lot like the Hardee's that used to
be there when I was little. Now it's an empty shell with
nothing but an old parking lot and garbage dumpster next
to it. "What are you showing me?"

Is the journal there? Is that what this is all about?
Mami's spirit begins fading, her shape dissipating into
tiny dots of swirling light again. "Don't you leave! Tell me
what I'm supposed to do. Tell me!" But the blue dots swirl
faster until they blink out, and a tiny starburst of light
ends it all.

"Come back here!" I yell, flailing my arms. "I don't
believe this!" I close my eyes and try opening myself up
to the other side again, inviting the voices and visions
back in, but she's gone—faded, like the last warm day of a
bitter autumn.

"Where am I?" An insane asylum would be as good
a place as any. I cross the parking lot and walk up to the
building, placing my hands against the dark window to
look inside. Hardee's has been mostly gutted, only a few
planks of pressed wood lying on the dusty floor.

...dumpster...

"What?" But I heard her clearly.

Pulling away from the window, I peer at the metal
garbage container nestled in the shadowy corner of
the parking lot. Something in it calls to me. It's rusted
and partially covered with tree roots cracking apart the
asphalt it sits on. The more I look at it, the more I don't
want to approach it, but it dares me.

Slowly, I walk toward it. I wish I had a shovel or bat,
an implement to swat with in case something charges at

me. My breath is choppy and sounds annoyingly weak in my ears. *Stay calm.*

I stop a few feet away. This is not smart. I really should return some other time with Betty Anne and a flashlight. No, I'm not coming back here again, so I better get it over with now.

I force myself forward and notice it doesn't smell like other dumpsters. Good sign. In fact, it doesn't smell at all, and when I lift the lid and peek inside, emptiness stares back at me. I crane my neck over the edge for a better look. Except for a knotted-up grocery bag against the front wall, it's empty.

"What about this?" I ask. I pull my head back, and I pause—*the bag*—and lean in again. It's too far to reach, so I set down the heavy metal lid and circle the dumpster to rifle through the tree's droppings, finding a nice, long branch among the fallen foliage.

Lifting the lid again, I reach as far as I can with the branch on my tiptoes, sliding the end of it into one of the knotted loops and pulling the bag up. It feels light, another good sign that I'm not hoisting up a rotting animal or discarded head. The dumpster closes with a loud *clang.*

I throw the stick on the ground and begin unknotting the plastic, but when it doesn't loosen fast enough, I abandon all practicality and rip a hole in it. What I find crumpled inside is quite common—a well-worn, white cotton T-shirt, extra-large.

What I find spattered along the bottom edge of it— not quite as ordinary.

CHAPTER TWENTY-ONE

"The night grew darker and darker; the stars seemed to sink deeper in the sky, and driving clouds occasionally hid them from his sight."

"I spoke with the school counselor."

I peer at Betty Anne through crusty, slitted eye-lids.

"I told her you've been through a lot this last month, having lost your mother and all, and you needed to take care of her estate, so they're letting you complete your work at home."

I rub sleep out of my eyes. "When did you go?" *But Dane…I need to see him again.*

"This morning. They're only letting you home-school for a few months. Then you have to go back if you want to graduate on time."

"Man…thanks, Betty Anne." I really owe her.

She starts asking me a hundred questions—what flavor yogurt do I like best, which brand of coffee do I drink, which bread—white or whole wheat—would I like for my sandwiches. I can tell she's happy to take care of someone again. "Be back in a bit."

Once she leaves, I rip off the blanket and notice my feet. Filthy. *I didn't dream it.* I remove the tattered plastic bag from under the bed and stare inside.

A dull white T-shirt with spattered bloodstains along the hem. Spattered—sent flying through the air. Not spilled, not pooled. Last night, Mami showed me, confirmed what I've felt from the very beginning—her death was no accident. Now I feel terrible knowing I made her rise from the ground to come and spell things out for me, because I've been too naive to put it together myself.

But whose shirt is it? Looks like a man's. A washed-a-thousand-times undershirt can be anybody's. I get dressed, stuff the plastic-wrapped shirt inside my backpack, and head out.

Word Puzzle Girl is at her desk again, chewing on her pencil and looking mildly surprised to see me. In the back, outside an office door, a man in his thirties wearing a buttoned shirt talks loudly about a football game with an older man in a sweater vest who seems cornered and whose eyes flit between me and the guy talking about extra points and overtime.

"Can I help you?" Word Puzzle Girl's lazy eyes are bored with me already.

Demand answers. This is my mother—my dead mother—who no one seems to care about. "Did you ever give anyone my message that I was here two weeks ago?"

"I gave it to Officer Stanton. Didn't he call you?"

"No. Is he here?"

The older man enduring the younger man's verbal barrage looks at me again.

"I'll check." Word Puzzle Girl uncrosses her legs from her swivel chair and sashays between the cubicles in her plaid wool skirt. I watch as she quietly speaks to the two men, nods, and goes into the younger man's office to sit and talk. The older man comes out to the counter.

"Good morning, what can I do for you?" He grins politely but is clearly irked, as though he has better things to do.

"Officer Stanton?"

"Yes."

"I've been trying to reach you. I'd like to talk to you about my mother, Maria Burgos. 150 Maple Street. She was found in her bathtub back in Aug—"

"Yes, I know who Maria Burgos is. You're her daughter?" He looks at me from top to bottom. "This way." I follow him into his office. Officer Stanton sits behind his desk and closes a trivia quiz on his computer screen. Does anyone work around here? "Close the door," he says. I softly shut the door. He leans back in his chair to reach for a pile of folders on a table behind him, plucking a thin one out near the top of the stack. "Now, what is it you need from me?" he asks curtly, checking the name on the folder's tab.

I sit down and prop my backpack between my feet. *Don't let him dismiss you.* "A lot of things, actually. Which is why I left you a million messages to please call me."

"I only got three." He eyes me impatiently. So he did hear them? And just conveniently forgot to call me? "Sorry about that. Messages sometimes get lost in the shuffle here." He tries his brand of bullshit out on me, but I'm not having it.

"I've needed help," I say, betting he forgot that being a police officer means serving the people. "I have lots of questions."

"Right." He taps his pen on the table. "Why don't you start with one, and I'll see if there's anything I can do for you."

I clear my throat. "I came here before because my mother died this summer, and I wasn't here at the time. I'm her next of kin, yet no one has contacted me about her house, her belongings, or anything." I'm rambling, but hopefully the desperation in my voice will prompt him to do more than just sit there with that smug look on his face. "Where is everything? What do I have to do to get her things?"

Officer Stanton opens the file, quietly flips through some papers. "What things do you want?"

"What do you mean?" What business is it of his what things I want? They're my mother's belongings—now mine—that's all he needs to know. "Everything. Her furniture, her clothes…I mean, where is everything?"

"Storage." He puts down the file.

"Great. Then…where's the key for that? I need the key to her house, too. Doesn't it belong to me now?"

"Miss Burgos," he interrupts without answering. "Didn't your mother leave a will?"

"If she did, wouldn't I know by now?" I hear the frustration rising in my voice. "I mean, it's been almost two months."

"I don't know. Who's her lawyer?"

I feel my blood boiling. I scoot to the edge of my seat. "You're the police. Doesn't your file there tell you everything? If I knew about a will and her lawyer, would I be here asking you for help?" I smack the edge of his desk.

His eyelids fall to half mast. "Okay, relax." He opens the file again, checking something. He nods, closes it again, opens his hands in resignation. "I'm just a little surprised that you're here."

"Why? What is so surprising about her daughter being here?"

"Because according to this report, you're not next of kin." His countenance displays both his disdain and impatience. And truth to say, he's totally mocking me and reveling in my stunned silence.

"That's impossible," I say.

"I assure you it's not."

"But I'm her only child."

"But you're not her husband."

I almost laugh in his face. How lame a police department is this that their information is so outdated? "My parents divorced years ago." Did she remarry?

"Miss, the house is in Jay Burgos's name. He plans on selling it, even though, if you ask me, he's not going to get much for it right now, but hey, desperate times. He also rented the storage unit everything was moved to."

"But…that's a mistake. They're divorced."

He looks at his file again. "Estranged. Separated. Not divorced," he says, throwing the words into the vast expanse between us and watching them land like dice on one of those casino craps tables.

I can't reply. All I can do is think back, try to recall a time when my father might've said that he and Mami were officially divorced. I thought that he said so, but then again, maybe I just assumed they were? They were estranged?

"Miss Burgos?" Officer Stanton leans back in his chair and drums his fingers on the armrests. He's so done with me.

"I'm sorry. I didn't…"

He sighs and purses his lips. "Call your father," he says, tapping the edge of the file against his desk. "He would have the keys to the house and the storage facility. Then you can find whatever it is you're looking for. Is there something else?"

Something about his smirk and tone, or maybe because I'm so open and vulnerable right now, tells me he's talking about the journal. He knows about it. Of course he does. Everyone knows about it. According to some, I know where it is and I'm here to claim it, to cash in on it just as much as everybody else, even though clearly I don't need the money.

I think of my debit card declining at the store last week, how our water and power were cut, and how Nina said she didn't get paid enough. *Or do I?* "No, that's it. I'm sorry to have bothered you."

"Not a problem." Facetious smile from ear to ear.

I stand. I have to get out of this negative, accusing atmosphere, but then I remember the other reason I came. "There's something else…" I pull out the plastic bag containing the bloodstained T-shirt. "I found this. It belongs to whoever killed her."

Officer Stanton's eyebrows raise. He gives a short chuckle. "What makes you think your mother was murdered? She slipped and fell in her own bathroom."

"Because my mother didn't slip." I glare at him. No one will ever understand how I get my information. My mother told me herself. She came from the grave and showed me. "She just didn't."

He doesn't hold out his hand or offer to take a look at my evidence, just stares at my face, his brown eyes holding steady on mine. "Leave it there," he says, nodding to the edge of the desk. "I'll have someone properly collect it. Where did you get it?"

I went over this a thousand times on the walk over—where I found it, what I was doing rummaging through a garbage receptacle at an abandoned fast food restaurant—but I can't tell him all that without seeming suspicious. In the end, I decide on the truth. "I found it on North Broadway and Hemlock Drive, just north of the cemetery."

"The old Hardee's?" A slow smile spreads on his face, as well as an urge in me to lunge at him for his condescending manner, but instead, I un-crumple the shirt on his desk and point to the dried bloodstains. He smirks. "What makes you think a shirt you found so far removed from the scene belongs to a killer you don't even know actually exists?"

"Have it tested, and you'll see." I snap a few pictures of the shirt with my phone, just in case I never see it again. "Please call me if you learn anything else. You need my number?"

"No," he says, flipping up the note paper clipped to the file, the one I wrote on when I first visited this place. "Got it right here."

Outside the station, I let out a massive breath. Then I spot it—Dane's blue Eclipse pulling into the station, not from Main Street, but through the back parking lot. What is he doing here, of all places? It's the middle of school hours. Doesn't he have a class to teach?

Breaking into a jog, I hurry around the building, ignoring the gate bar that lifts whenever a police car enters the garage, ducking underneath it to get by. Is he following me? First the train station, then my mother's house, then hanging out at the coffee shop, school, here...

Anger blinds me, started by the news of my parents' non-divorce, now fueled by the truths that are starting to make themselves evident before my very eyes. I approach his car and see him halfway into the backseat. I'm about to call him, when he withdraws his long body from the backseat, toting his phone, a manila folder, and a leather case in the shape of a—

I stop cold.

What is he doing with—

He closes his car door and presses his key remote to lock it. He stops as well, surprised to see me. "Micaela," he says calmly, holding out a hand to placate the approaching guard.

I'm lost for words. Do teaching assistants usually go around with concealed weapons in holsters parking in authorized-only parking spaces? "Who are you?"

"Micaela, let me explain." He approaches me slowly.

I gaze into his face. *So stupid. I've been so stupid!* Mr. Boracich, student teacher teaching the unit on nineteenth century authors, touring New England to learn more about them. *Crud, crap, lies.* "Just—who are you? Obviously not who you say you are, or are you professor by day, police officer by night?"

"I'm not police." His words should calm me, but I've never felt this angry in my life.

"Then why are you here? This *is* a police station." I gesture to the building then let my arm slap against my side in frustration. "And *that* is a gun. How am I supposed to believe anything you say? You're not even who you say you are, so why shouldn't I trust someone I grew up with instead of you?"

Why does my heart feel like it's going to rip in half?

He blows out, cheeks puffing. "I didn't say everyone you grew up with, just those with a vested interest in the journal, people who never cared about your mother to begin with."

"How do you know if they care or not?"

"Aw, come on, Micaela, open your eyes! You know they don't care. I heard the way Bram's aunt spoke to you at Sunnyside. You're in direct danger, which is *my* main concern." His tilted head, his worried eyes, plead with me to understand. "I'm not police." He struggles, like he can't decide who to plead devotion to, me or whoever paid him to watch over me and stay hush about it. "I was hired."

I knew it.

"To watch over you and protect you."

So, when he warned me I was being watched, he really meant by him?

I clear my throat. "Hired by whom?" My father. This has to be my father's doing, adding to my status as princess, following me around with an extra pair of eyes. "Who, Dane?" I yell, wondering for the very first time if his name is even Dane Boracich at all. I wait for him to say what I already know.

"I can't tell you that." Carefully, he attaches his holster to a shoulder strap, so the weapon rests under his arm.

"Why not?"

"Because my task here is two-fold. Watching over you and looking into your mother's case." He flips up a palm. "That's already more information than you're supposed to know."

More than you're supposed to know. So he's a private investigator *and* bodyguard? Who can afford that but my father? "Well, if you can't tell me who it was, then at least tell me if you're aware that someone…" The words cling to my tongue, but I force them out. "Killed my mom."

He closes his eyes, almost like he's trying to control his emotions. When he reopens them, I see the answer written all over his face. *Yes, I know,* I can almost hear his thoughts. He nods an affirmation.

He's known all along. Not only do I detect guilt on his face, but something else. I can't quite figure it out. Is he mad that I'm mad, upset that I'm upset? Was he hoping I'd always be smiles and precariously close to flirting with him?

"I left something with Officer Stanton that might be of interest to you," I tell him.

He approaches me and brushes my cheek with his fingertips. I was right—he has feelings for me. No normal detective would do that. I should draw away, but I don't. I don't know what to feel anymore.

"I'll take a look at what you brought. Just…let me do my job, okay?" he asks. "Try not to interfere."

My legs are unsteady. I do my best to appear in control as he caresses me. If I can get past my anger, I think I might prefer this new role of his. It suits him better.

He withdraws his hand. "Now get out of here." I press my lips together and nod. "And Micaela?"

"Yes?" I watch him take a deep breath to regain his professional composure before walking off with a mission on his mind.

"Pretend you never saw me."

CHAPTER TWENTY-TWO

"Under cover of his character of singing-master, he made frequent visits at the farmhouse, not that he had any thing to apprehend from the meddlesome interference of parents…"

I should have come to Kingsland Point Park sooner, but I didn't want to stir up memories of those dark days when my parents would argue and I'd come here to meet Bram. Now I remember why the park had been my refuge—it was beautiful, right on the river, with a lighthouse to boot. A glowing emerald in the summer and a mantle of golden leaves on days like today. Quiet and calm, as if a storm hadn't just passed through here last night, or as if a tempest of my own wasn't now churning inside my head.

I pull out my phone and try my father, losing hope that he'll ever return my calls. It goes to voicemail just as I expect. "Hi, Dad! I miss you so much," I say, forcing a fake sweet tone, so he'll call. Sugar catches flies more than vinegar. "Nothing urgent, just call me." That should work.

Down the river walk, a tour group checks out the lighthouse. In a minute, my peace and quiet will be disrupted.

...damn tourists...

The dead. Their voices surround me day and night. Betty Anne is right. They won't leave me alone once they know. I wonder how Dane dealt with this ability when he was a young boy.

My phone rings, showing my dad's smiling face on the screen. No way. It worked. I take a deep breath and answer. "Dad."

"How's my beautiful girl?" his bubbly voice replies.

"Your beautiful girl is pissed off as hell." I've never spoken to him this way in my life, and it feels freakin' fantastic.

He clears his throat. "And why is that?" The effervescence in his voice fizzles out.

"You know why." There's never been any reason to be pissed at him before. He's been the perfect dad, the rock I've always depended on, not someone who would lie to me. But the last time I didn't give one of my parents the benefit of the doubt, she died. I have to at least listen.

"I'll be there soon. Tell Nina I wired her some money. It should cover a car for now, and—"

"Nina's gone, Dad."

"What do you mean?"

"Gone. Hasn't come back. Have you paid her? My card was declined, and the power and water are out, too. Want to tell me what's going on?"

Quiet, except for the sound of his fear. "Is this because it's taken me a while to call you back?"

"No. This is because you've been lying to me!" I yell.

"Lying to you," he repeats.

"Yes, lying to me." I get up and begin pacing out my frustration. "Why have you never told me that you and Mami were still married?"

Quiet, then a low sigh on the line. "You never asked. When you came to live with me, you never looked back, so why would there be any reason to talk about this?"

A pang of guilt comes close to hitting me, but I don't let it. "*I* never looked back?" I shout. "*You* never looked back, Dad! Even when my mom was trying to contact me. How is it that I got a note from her at Emily's house three days before she died—*Emily's house,* Dad—begging me to come home, yet she *supposedly* didn't want to talk to me over the years? Isn't that a little *off?*"

"Mica…" His tone warns me. "Lower your voice, or we won't be talking for much longer."

"You probably knew she wasn't cremated, right? Or are you going to deny that, too?"

"What are you insinuating? I didn't know that. And you know damn well that your mom was distracted. I'm not going to say that she didn't love you, because she did, but don't you think if she'd cared just a scrap about anything else besides her research—about you, about me—that she would've eventually come back to us?"

"Maybe she wanted *you* to believe in her and her work. To stick by her through thick and thin. Isn't that what married couples are supposed to do? You left. And I can't believe I went with you."

"That's why I never served her with papers, because I hoped that *one day* it'd hit her how much her family meant to her, and she'd join us. I loved her, I still do. Did I ever bring another woman into our life? No. Because I still had hope. I still believed in her. I waited until the very last day…" His voice trails off, and I hear muffled sounds of whimpering.

So odd to hear my dad so weak.

His words have always made perfect sense to me in the past. But that was before the dreams. Yes. Before the visions, the voices... Yes. Before Mami's visit last night. She was trying...always trying to reach me...even in death.

Yesss...

No parent ever wants their child to know how defective they really are.

I shake my head. "No, Dad. You're lying. My mother wanted me. Loved me. I know she did."

"She never called."

"She *called*, I'm telling you!" I shout again, pounding the side of the bench, expecting to hear him demand that I quiet down, but for once, he relents.

In the silence, I hear the tour guide explain to the group about the buzz around town, how it appears that Washington Irving had a secret journal, one that might be worth a lot of money, and how a lot of people are hoping to be the finders of the missing relic, and wouldn't it be cool if one of them found it? The group twitters with excitement.

"Mica?"

"What."

"Say something."

"You have it all in storage. It belongs to me. And I know you've sent someone to follow me. He's been doing a great job from the moment I arrived. You didn't have to go to such lengths. I *am* eighteen. I can take care of myself."

"I don't know what you're talking about."

I scoff. I don't have any proof that it's my dad, but who

else would it be? "I don't expect you to admit to it. Just know that it's lame, and your lying about it is really sad, too."

"Mica, if someone's following you, that makes me a little concerned. All the more reason you shouldn't be in Sleepy Hollow, but you went to that damn forsaken place anyway. You never listen to me."

"I *always* listen to you! That has been the root of my goddamned problem!" I smack the bench so many times, my hands sting. "It's a good thing I didn't this time, or I still might not know anything about myself!" I come close to shouting, wanting to tell him about the family tree, the rich history on my mother's side, that *these* were the reasons for Mami's obsessed behavior. From the sidewalk by the water, a few people glance over. The tour guide ushers his group away.

"Okay, you know what?" he says. "Your tone is upsetting me, so this conversation is over."

"And your denial is upsetting *me*, Dad! I know you were trying to paint this picture that everything was fine without Mami, that we were better off, but we weren't. I needed her." My eyes are glazed with tears. "I needed her."

My father's voice is low. "You needed a mother."

"I *had* a mother!" Whether or not Mami was perfect, there every night, or around when I needed her is irrelevant. I break into tears, sob, then quietly suck it back up. Enough crying. "Just send me the keys."

"What keys?"

"The house, the storage…the *keys*, Dad. You have them. Stop pretending like you don't know what I'm talking about. Everything's in your name, remember?" He's playing the fool, but I'm ahead of him now. "You're hiding things from me."

A burst of air escapes his lips.

All these years, he's vilified my mom. I can tell, from his huffing, that he's preparing to launch some more. "Your mother was the one hiding things all the time. Every chance she got. Have you found a will since you've been there? Did she leave you anything of interest?" He sounds like he's mocking me.

My mouth opens to say *yes*. "No," I whisper. There were papers, but no will.

"Exactly why I didn't want you going back. Because the truth hurts, because she probably left everything to that horse's ass, Tanner," he mumbles right at the end.

"What?"

His silence tells me he's said too much. Dr. Tanner? What does he have to do with anything? "What I meant was…ah, forget it."

If he hired Dane to follow me around, then he has to know that Dr. Tanner is my English teacher, yet not once has he asked me about my classes. "You know him? Why do you talk about him like that?"

The breeze shoots off the river, rustling the trees around me. With eyes closed, I can almost feel someone breathing near me. He lies.

As an historian, Mami collaborated with teachers and professors in order to put together the most comprehensive presentations on Washington Irving for field trips at Sunnyside. Did one collaboration go too far? Is *this* what Dad's jealous tirades were about? The reason he didn't serve her with divorce papers?

"I only know that I loved her, Mica," he says. "But she didn't love me back."

His voice, wronged and pained, centers me once again. So my parents weren't perfect. So they were always blaming each other for their woes. But they're my parents. And no matter what the truth is between them, I still love them.

My father fills the silence with a resigned sigh. "I'll overnight you the keys. So you'll see I'm not hiding anything."

I listen to his breathing as he shuffles around his hotel room, zipping up his suitcase, mumbling about another call he's getting. "Mica, you there? I have to go. I love you."

And then the line goes dead. I let the phone slide down until it lands in my lap. Then I stay at Kingsland Point Park, staring at the river until the chatter of tourists fades, the river walk is bathed in fiery orange light, and my heart sinks in time with the setting sun.

CHAPTER TWENTY-THREE

"What passed at this interview I will not pretend to say, for in fact I do not know."

What bothers me more than anything isn't even the lies. It's the fact that he won't admit to them. By the next morning, I'm completely convinced of what my father did and how he did it. After hiring Dane Boracich, he filled him in on all Irving-secret-journal folklore he learned from Mami, prepping him to understand the case from an insider's view, even training him for his role as Dr. Tanner's teaching assistant.

Amazing, the things people will do for truth.

But why couldn't Dane be an ugly old man who doesn't make my stomach flip every time I see him? No, my bodyguard has to be young enough for me to date with icy cobalt eyes that melt to liquid topaz every time his gaze falls on me. *Ugh.*

Being isolated at Betty Anne's house isn't helping the situation. She has no cable TV, and her army of knickknacks stares at me all day long. With as much as Betty Anne drives into town, I can't leave the house. I can't risk my dad's package being left on the front porch unattended.

I call the school, dialing Doc Tanner's extension. I'm ready to leave a voicemail, but lo and behold, he answers. "Tanner here."

"Dr. Tanner, it's Micaela Burgos. From your first hour literature class?"

"Micaela, is everything okay? We've been worried about you."

"I've been sick…"

He swallows softly. "I'm sorry to hear that."

"Thanks. I, uh…can I meet with you so you can give me any work I've missed?" I know that teachers—real ones—are not supposed to meet students outside of school, but I need to speak with him in person, and this is the only way I know how to get him to agree.

"How about I just email them to you? Let me have your email address."

"Actually, I need to ask you some questions, too, if you don't mind. Can we meet somewhere?"

He sounds hesitant but agrees to meet me at Ye Olde Coffee Shoppe tomorrow at four o'clock.

All day, I sit on the front porch swing, waiting for the package, assuming my father even sent it. I push with my foot, chains rhythmically creaking back and forth. I imagine Dane bustling around the police station, examining the T-shirt I found, working on my mother's case. Does he think of me in another way besides a young woman he's been hired to watch? Secretly, I hope he does. I think of Bram, too, getting last-minute preparations ready for this weekend's first day of HollowEve. I miss them both, but can't trust either. How lame is that?

My intuition must've been on track again, because

suddenly, my phone rings. It's Bram. I don't know if I should answer or not. I'll just hear him out. "Hello."

"Mica, where the hell are you? Please don't tell me Miami."

"I'm still here."

He sighs. "Thank God. Okay, look, I'm sorry about the way I reacted the other night. I just—*gah,* I can't explain it. Seeing you with Boracich in those pics after the way you gushed over him and how you asked me to watch over you...I know you said there's nothing between you two, but...I don't know...all I know is that I didn't like it."

I stop rocking the swing. "I don't belong to you, Bram."

"I know. I know that. But sometimes, it feels like you do. Don't take that the wrong way. We never got the chance to talk about this, but the night we lay in bed together was incredible. Kissing you was incredible. It felt meant to be. I've cared about you for so long, Mica."

I bite the inside of my lip. I agree it was wonderful, but maybe that was what I needed at the moment. "I know, and I don't regret that night. You calmed me, if only for a short while." Yes, we've known each other forever, but I don't feel possessive of him like he does of me. I remember Lacy at the coffee shop, how she told me she was free of his obsession.

"Are you there?" he asks.

"I'm listening."

"I guess I hoped that you'd feel the same way about me. Does that make any sense?"

"I understand, Bram. It's okay. You're a jealous baby, that's all." I grin.

There's a smile in his voice. "Fair enough. For whatever it's worth—I'm really sorry."

I appreciate his apology, his deep voice in my ear, and if I concentrate, I can imagine his breath on my cheek. But is this Real Bram or Actor Bram? Regardless, I'm glad he called. "It's good to hear your voice," I tell him.

"It's killing me to hear yours. Where are you? I have to see you."

Dane's warning creeps in again. Yes, yes, anyone belonging to an old Hollow family shouldn't be trusted, I know. The Derants and Engers guarded that journal for sixty years, I know. If anyone has the right to sell it to a historical preservation society for a good chunk of cash, it's them, not crazy Maria Burgos or her crazy daughter.

Wrong. It's yours.

I squeeze my eyelids tight, hoping it'll cast away Mami's voice. "Bram, don't take this personally, but I can't see you right now."

"You're at Betty Anne's, aren't you?"

My body stiffens. It's not as though I own a car that can be identified in the driveway. Has he followed me, or just a lucky guess? Is he nearby as we speak? I scan the street for his black Accord. "Where are you now?"

"At work, on a break. I know your mom was trying hard to prove some lineage that would make her and you the rightful owners of that journal. I know because she told Janice flat out when they were still on friendly terms. That's how she got in to see it at the library, how she met Tanner, whose former student works at the lab. But listen to me... *I. Don't. Care.* Where your family comes from doesn't mean shit to me. It didn't matter when we were kids, and it doesn't matter now. You have to believe me."

"Stop. You're making this harder." I press my fingertips against my eyelids. In my one dream, Bram was angry, forceful, jealous. I know it was just a dream, but Betty Anne says dreams are full of insight. What am I supposed to believe?

"Let's meet tomorrow before HollowEve. It's our last big rehearsal. I can pick you up wherever you are. Or I can meet you somewhere. Whatever you want."

I feel like a short rope in a tug-of-war. I shouldn't meet him. Dane is right. The man knows his job and the players in this case. Then again, I've known Bram my whole life, and he's never given me reason to doubt him. A quick hello and nothing more. "I have something to do at four, so afterwards would be fine."

"Six o'clock at the park?"

"Kingsland?"

The smile is back in his voice. "Is there any other?"

The next day, I'm up early waiting for the keys to arrive. I carefully unfold my mother's family tree, retrace all the names back through Cuba and Spain, and stare at photos of people I've never seen and yet known all my life, familiar strangers, a world just beyond this dimension. Whose spirit guide will I become when I die, I wonder? Whose job is it to decide that anyway?

Carefully piling the photos into a neat stack, I pray that my life ends on a happy note so that I'll never, ever have to go through the torment that Mary Shelley's and Mami's spirits are going through now.

At three thirty, I make sure everything is carefully put away, the most important documents tucked behind an old art portfolio in the closet for safekeeping, and I head out to meet Dr. Tanner.

I opt for the higher visibility of the main road in case the biker from the cemetery stalks me again. Even though the Headless Horseman forced him out a few days ago, I don't want to be caught alone with him in the forest shortcut.

Ye Olde Coffee Shoppe bustles as usual. The same familiar faces are there, along with tourists toting backpacks and poring over brochures of the area's attractions. Jonathan is there too, wiping down a counter. I try to avoid him, but he sees me.

He smiles awkwardly, probably knows all about my fight with Bram. Now, he's in the awkward position of displaying diplomacy. "Hey, you," he says as I approach him. "Haven't seen you all week."

"Been busy." I look around nervously. "Is Bram here?"

"He doesn't work today." Jonathan props his elbows up on the counter. "Hey, I was rude to you the other day. I said some stuff about your dad, and it was totally uncalled for. I was having a shitty day, so…sorry about that."

Well. I force a smile. "It's all right, John. I can empathize with shitty days."

"Truce?" He holds up his fisted knuckles.

I bump them with my own, just to get him off my back. Because really, the other night at the manor, he showed his true colors, and I will never be friends with him again.

The doorbells chime. I turn and see Dr. Tanner's head peeking in. When his scan of the coffee shop stops at my face, he waves me outside to a bistro table. "I'll see you later," I tell Jonathan, heading outside.

"Later."

"Hello, Micaela." Dr. Tanner holds the door open for me.

"Hi. It's a little cold out here," I say, hugging myself.

"Sorry," Dr. Tanner says, out of breath. "But it occurred to me that maybe we'd hear each other better outside." He slides out a chair for me then sits on his own with a big huff, propping his portfolio carefully against the table.

"Right," I say, noticing two missed calls from Bram on my phone before shoving it into my bag.

Dr. Tanner pulls out papers from his portfolio and lays them on the table. "I brought you the work you missed. I hope everything is okay." He raises an eyebrow.

"Not exactly." I notice that half the locals in the coffee shop turn their heads now and then to peek at us through the window. Did not miss the nosiness of a small town *at all*. "I didn't really come here to get make-up work. I have a few questions, and considering the buzz around town these days, I didn't want to risk you turning me down."

His big chipmunk cheeks suck in a rush of air, which he then releases slowly. "I gathered as much. Miss Burgos, if I may say so…about that, I want you to know that you have my help in any respect. The families of this town are very protective of their history, but if you have anything that could help your case, or if this becomes a legal matter, I am here to assist you." He bows his head gallantly.

"I appreciate that," I say. As much as I want to believe him, I have to wonder if his presence at the bank that day had anything to do with *my case*. I almost expect him to ask for half the reward money in exchange for helping me locate the missing journal. "But I didn't come to speak to you about that, either."

"Oh?"

I hold out my hand to a sparrow hopping near my feet

on the brick-paved patio. Anything to avoid his straight-on gaze. The way he's looking at me makes me a bit nervous when I'm already stressed over what I'm about to ask. Dr. Tanner moves his thick leg, and the bird flies off. "How do you know Dane?"

He shrinks back, like it was the last thing he'd ever expect me to ask. "I taught a literature class on weekends at University of New Haven years ago. Mr. Boracich was in my class. This was before he went to graduate school at Harvard."

Before he became an investigator, I see…

Fair enough. Now the toughest question of them all. "And what about my mother? You knew her well, didn't you?"

Silence for a moment. He clears his throat. "Yes, I've been meaning to catch you after class, but there never seems to be a good time. I'm so terribly sorry for your loss."

"No, I don't mean know her the way everybody knows her name when they hear it. I mean, you knew her, as in—you *knew* her."

"I'm not sure what you mean."

You have the right to know, my brain pesters me. "What I mean, at the risk of sounding way over-personal, is…" I pull my hair forward so it shields the side of my mouth from any lip-reading regulars of the coffee shop. "Were you and my mother having a…you know…"

He waits for me to finish, but when I let him figure out the rest on his own, he sits back and sighs. "No, Miss Burgos, your mother and I were not having an affair. She was a great woman, very intelligent, persistent, honorable, but we were not involved in any romantic way."

For some reason, his words sit right with me. I want

to sigh in relief. "I'm only asking because I have reason to believe otherwise."

"Don't listen to everything you hear. This town likes to talk."

"I didn't hear it from this town."

He holds up his hand. "Would you like some coffee?"

"No," I reply. "Not to be rude, but I only want answers."

"Understood." He stares at the table for the right words. "Your mother and I, after meeting at Historic Hudson Library and years of collaborating on projects and sharing a passion for the same subject matter, became friends. Close friends," he stresses. "But nothing else."

"You swear by it?"

"I..." He chuckles. Something about my question resonates with him. "I swear by it."

"Then why would my father insinuate it?"

"Because people believe whatever they want. Whatever makes sense to them. Whatever makes them feel *happier* about their own lives. But you should know better than anyone, Micaela, that things are not always what they seem." His expression challenges me.

"I understand that, but like the locals here, I'm also very loyal. To beliefs I've had for so long. Everything I've ever thought to be true has been challenged since I arrived here two weeks ago, Dr. Tanner. So I'm sorry if I seem a little untrusting."

Dr. Tanner purses his lips, does a little flourish with his hand. "Completely forgivable."

"Then would you mind explaining why you were at South River Bank in White Plains last week? It's not exactly a local bank, mostly housing safe deposit boxes."

He peers at me through a surprised expression that

softens the more he thinks about his answer. He scoots his seat closer to me and grabs his cane. "You have to understand something. Your mother and I were good friends, so yes, I was privy to the details of her life. But, make no mistake, Micaela, she was fearful."

Fearful? I absorb his words reluctantly.

"I know you think the world of your father, and I would never do anything to change that, but as your mother's friend, and because she is no longer here to present her side of things, I feel it's my duty to let you know that your mother tried repeatedly to stay in contact with you."

"How so?"

"Let's just say she didn't take kindly to threats."

Who does he mean? But my father's not an aggressive man. He might have been a little overimaginative, maybe even oversensitive, but he wouldn't have threatened her. I don't think.

"Your father assumed the worst, that we were more than friends, because we spent time together working on projects, Sunnyside events, etcetera. She insisted there was nothing going on, *I* told him there was nothing going on, but once a jealous man has it in his head that his wife has been cheating on him, there's little anyone can do to convince him otherwise."

That I'll buy. But how does this answer my question? "What about the bank?"

"I was at the bank because Maria wasn't hopeful she would ever see you again."

Stab my heart, why don't you. I stare at him through watery swirls. The sunset's sheen is breaking through the trees behind me, creating interesting shapes and patterns on Dr. Tanner's face and jacket.

"So she took things that mattered most to her," he goes on, "things she didn't want Jay ever touching, and locked them up in the box. She left Betty Anne with one key, in case you never made it back to Sleepy Hollow." He sighs and folds his hands on his belly. "And she gave me the other key."

Dr. Tanner and Betty Anne have been guarding Mami's prized belongings. In case something ever happened to me. Because Mami felt things could, or would, go wrong. She took care of me more than I thought.

"Micaela..." Dr. Tanner reaches across the black bistro table, his hairy, burly arm a strange complement to the lacy ironwork, his hand patting mine. "After hearing the news about the reward money, I was there making sure the journal was still safe. For you. For whenever you went to find it."

I stare at him and try to process his words.

But there was no journal at South River Bank the day I went with Bram.

There was a medium-sized box, a big open space where more could have fit, but no journal. *Unless...*

"Would you excuse me?" I rip my hand out from under his and sprint across the street with my backpack. I dodge cars blaring their horns, cut through the college campus, pass the lake and joggers, and burst out the west end, taking the shortest route back to my mother's things and the woman Mami was fool enough to call a friend.

Chapter Twenty-Four

"It stirred not, but seemed gathered up in the gloom, like some gigantic monster ready to spring upon the traveler."

I pound the shortcut through the yellow birch trees, dark shadows mottling along the ground. It's sunset, a breath away from darkness. I focus on reaching Maple Street as quickly as possible, but it's not long before I hear voices fighting for attention inside my head, one of them familiar above my own choppy breath.

Hurry...

So stupid to leave everything! God, what was I thinking? No wonder she's been so nice to me. The journal *was* in the safe deposit box. It had been right on top of my other things! But it wasn't there when I took the rest. Now it's gone.

Bram calls me again, but I have no time to answer. I leap over branches, wincing in pain every time my knee absorbs the shock as my feet crunch over the blanket of leaves. The old wives know these woods are haunted, all the woods in Sleepy Hollow are haunted, but I get it now.

Ghosts can't hurt me. *It's real live people you should fear.*

The sickening *click-click* of a loose bike chain is all the motivation I need to hurry the hell up. He's back. And somewhere behind me. If he maneuvers expertly in the cemetery, he's going to maneuver all the more expertly in the flatter terrains of these woods.

I cast a glance over my shoulder. Obscured by shadows in the fading light, my follower is back, a good forty feet behind me, wearing the hooded jacket again cinched tightly around his nose and upper cheeks, legs pumping pedals up and down. In his hand, a tight fist holds a wooden baseball bat.

Horseman! Where the hell are you? Dane!

Damn it! How great are these protectors that they're not around when I need them most? *I don't need them,* I remind myself, crouching as I run to pick up a branch, thick and heavy. I hurl it hard behind me. It lands far to the right. A young man's voice cackles. It sounds like nobody I know, yet every guy in high school and college combined. I try again, this time running alongside the brook, picking up a heavy rock that can damage a skull if chucked just right.

I fling it hard with all my strength. "Get away from me!" I yell, hoping at the very least that someone might hear me in these houses I'm running past. Glancing back, as my feet pound on, I see the rock as it hits my follower's tire and bounces aside. The mountain bike wobbles but regains its course.

Faster...

I pump my legs. *No pain, no pain.* I'm racing fast now, but my knee can't be an issue right now. My irregular breaths beat in time with my pounding heart. Bike Guy gains speed. He's about twenty feet away, but the exit of the woods is now within my sights.

I pummel toward it, the opening in the wire fence like a magical portal to transport me to safety. But the closer I get to it, I notice the fence opening has been sewn shut with wire. Cold hard truth descends on me like a python on a cornered mouse.

"No!" I slam into it, pounding with fuming fists. "NO!"

I glance over my shoulder, gauging the number of seconds I have before my enemy reaches me, when I catch a glimpse of his wooden bat barrcling straight toward my head.

I duck, the whir of the spinning bat hissing as it flies over my head and then hits the metal grid behind me. It tumbles from the fence to my shoulder to the ground. I leap up, grab ahold of the thin metal wiring, and hoist myself over the top edge of the fence.

Landing in a squat, I watch the biker skid to a stop, roll back, and lift his middle finger at me. *Whatever, shit for brains.* I want to spit obscenities, hurl my fury at him, then realize he's just as capable of jumping fences as I am. My gaze locks on the only part of his face exposed by his cinched hood—his eyes—clear and jeering.

A familiar neigh comes from behind me. I whip around to see a gray mist swirling out of nothingness and quickly become a massive, black horse and headless rider leaping over me. Cold wind whooshes over, blowing back my hair, as the apparition leaps over the chain link fence straight at my attacker. The biker fumbles with the handlebars but regains control of his bike just in time to ride off ahead of the horseman by a good ten feet.

I would love to stand here and see how this chase ends, but the horseman didn't show up just in time only for me to stand here. I run off for Betty Anne's, reaching it a minute later, stumbling up the steps and slamming into the front door.

"Open the door. It's me. Open up!" I pound hard with my fists.

Footsteps shuffle across the wooden floor. "For heaven's sake, I'm coming!" Her voice filters through the screen. The irony of seeking shelter from one enemy on the front steps of another slaps me hard.

The door unlatches and opens. "Move!" I shove Betty Anne aside, lock the front door, and all the windows at the front of the house.

"What on Earth?" Betty Anne backs against the wall. "What happened?"

"Did you take it?" I demand, spitting hair out of my mouth.

"Take what?"

"The journal. The journal that was in *my mother's* safe deposit box. The box with *my* name on it, *not yours*!"

"My name is on the account, Mica, but I don't know what journal you're talking about." Betty Anne is on the verge of tears.

I stomp into my room. The bed has been made. *She's been in here.* Throwing open my closet and pulling back the art portfolio, I expect for my envelope to be gone or in a new position as if searched through, but it's not. It's in the same position I left it in. Betty Anne hovers in the doorway, fingertips nervously touching her lips. I open the envelope and shake everything onto my bed.

A quick inventory confirms the family tree, the photos, even the little sticky notes that keep popping off from me unsticking and sticking them so many times. I whirl around. "Something should've been in the safe deposit box that wasn't. Did you take it? A book, something with pages in it?"

At first she's shocked. Does she really have no idea what I'm talking about? Then, slowly, her eyes gloss over. She nods, leaves the room. I follow her down the hall to the master bedroom alight with two bright lamps, needlepoint frames on the walls, and lots of lace curtains. She walks to a shelf by her dresser, pulls something off the wall, and brings it over.

A moment later, she plops it into my hands. An old doll, a ratty thing with blond hair and hazel eyes. Uglier than sin. More beautiful than life. "Sofia?" I'm hit with a hundred memories at once. I caress her white dress and then look up at Betty Anne. "What were you doing with this?"

She flings away tears. Her face has turned a deep pink, and I think she might choke from not breathing. Finally, she draws in a deep breath and mumbles something incoherent. After another breath, she tries again. "Your mother told me that if you didn't come back, I could have her. She knew you never liked her dolls, and I guess I was the only one who did."

"*This* is what you took?" I want to cry, too. The journal is still lost. Or did Dr. Tanner just prank me and is now on his merry way to the historical preservation society to claim his half-a-million-dollar check? I scream, "Where is it, Mami? You can speak to me, can't you? You can even show yourself, so tell me where it is!"

Betty Anne covers her ears. "Oh, honey, don't do that. It's negative energy. It'll invite unwanted spirits. Let's take this to the kitchen." She tugs at my arm, but I yank it away.

"Are you *sure* this was all you took? I need to know, Betty Anne. I need…to know. There was something else. Something *important*."

"That was it, Mica. I swear I was going to give it to you now that you were back. Oh, what have I done?" She shakes her head.

Silhouetted by the lamplight and in tears, Betty Anne looks old and frail. I feel terrible for yelling at her. Yes, she took Sofia without telling me, even as I slept in her *very* house. But that was it. That was her crime — appreciating my mother's disturbing handiwork.

I look at Sofia again, stroke her hair. *Uglier than sin.* But Mami made it for me with love because it had my color eyes and my color hair. Slumping under the weight of my immense failure, I amble to Vanessa's room and sit on the bed with Sofia in the crook of my arm.

Soft shuffling of slippers on the floor follow me. "I'm sorry, Mica," Betty Anne whispers from the doorway. "I thought you didn't want her anymore. I shouldn't have assumed I could keep her when she's not mine to keep."

"It's all right."

"I feel awful."

"Don't." I hear my phone ding a text message. I reach my backpack on the floor and check it — from Bram.

> *Can u meet me earlier? They're shorthanded at holloweve.*

> *On my way*

I reply with a sigh. I stand, handing Sofia to Betty Anne. "Here. Have her. I wasn't talking about her anyway."

"No, I couldn't, not after — "

"Take it." I stare at Betty Anne's swollen, pink-rimmed eyes. "You'll take better care of her than I would." And just as she's about to squeeze past me in the doorway, I throw my arm around her. "I'm sorry I yelled at you. I'm just losing it."

"You've lost your mother is what you've lost." Betty Anne sniffles. "Yell at me all you want."

Walking to Kingsland Point Park, I remove Dane's business card from my wallet and punch his number into my phone. "To what do I owe this honor?" he answers right away.

"I was almost killed a while ago, and considering you're supposed to be my bodyguard, I'd like to know why I was left to fend for myself. Or did my dad forget to pay you, too?"

His voice sounds less stern than concerned. "Do you mind telling me where you went? One moment you were at the coffee shop talking to Tanner, and the next thing I know, I lost sight of you."

Oh. He really does track me. "I took a shortcut. I had to get back to Betty Anne's house as quickly as I could."

"Well, rule number one from now on is no more shortcuts. If you *must* walk, walk where the rest of the world can see you. And for clarification, I'm not a bodyguard. Yes, I've been asked to keep an eye on you, but my main responsibilities involve your mother's case."

"Are you keeping an eye on me now?" I scan the street. "Because I'm crossing North Broadway into Kingsland Point Park to meet someone, but it'd be good if you had my back."

"Who are you meeting?"

"Bram."

A moment's pause softens his tone. "You are a

stubborn one. You feel that's wise?"

"I feel it's safe enough. But if you are so inclined to spy on me, please do so from where he can't see you."

"I'll do my best."

"Thank you. And…I'm sorry." I enter the park through the east entrance. "I'm very angry and confused at the moment, so please forgive me for going against your judgment and indulging just this once. He's my friend—I need him."

"Suit yourself," he mutters. "Call me if you need me."

"Sorry, Dane. I hope you'll understand." I know he's doing his job, but I have to do what feels right, and ignoring my closest friend in town doesn't. I hang up, hurrying into the heart of the park. The light from a yellowing lamppost casts a shadow on the figure ahead, reminding me of Bram-Dad in my garden dream. Dark and intimidating.

Until I hear him. "You're a vision. Even when you're not trying." A minute later, his arms are around me, warm and enveloping. "What happened? Are you okay?" he asks.

"No." I grip his jacket by the sleeves. "Someone is after me. I don't want to stay in town anymore. I feel like I should leave soon."

His body blocks the cold breeze drifting off the river. I want so much to stay shielded by him. "Who's after you?"

"Someone on a bike."

He huffs. "You've just named half the people in Tarrytown. If someone's following you, you need to report it to the police."

Somehow I get the feeling that Sleepy Hollow police couldn't care less about my safety. "They know," I say. If Dane is informed, then Officer Stanton knows by now as well.

"You reported it?"

I pull away. "Yes."

He smirks and caresses my face. "You're not the same. You've changed."

I push his fingers aside. "I'm just being cautious, Bram. You have to understand that."

"And you have to understand that I won't let anything happen to you. Don't you see that?"

I nod and close my eyes. I do see it, but I also thought my mother didn't love me, and I was wrong. I thought my father would never lie to me, and I was wrong. Clearly, I've been wrong about a great number of things and need to wake up.

He squeezes my shoulder, inching closer, as though hoping I'll take him in for a full hug. "Things will get better soon. You'll see."

I shake my head. "They have to. 'Cause they sure as hell can't get any worse."

Apparently, they can. Suddenly, Bram's body goes rigid, and he spots something behind me. "What the fuck?" His voice booms through his chest against my ear, making me gasp aloud. He shoves me aside and charges toward a side street.

"Bram?" There, in the dark behind a slew of maple trees lining the sidewalk, sits the old blue Eclipse.

CHAPTER TWENTY-FIVE

"He would double the schoolmaster up, and lay him on a shelf of his own school-house."

"**B**ram! Where are you going?" I watch, lump in my throat, as he strides across the lawn, climbs over the low wooden fence, and charges over to the Eclipse, pounding on the hood.

"Come out!" He rounds the car to the driver side door. "Where you hiding, teach?"

I run after him, hoping to serve as damage control, and see that Dane isn't inside his car. "It's not even his. Let's just go," I call out.

"Of course it's his. How many blue Eclipses have you seen around town?" As he scans the park, the familiar hint of rage from my dreams makes my stomach sink. "Boracich! Stop playing games." His voice echoes throughout the park. A teen couple on a nearby bench gets up and walks off. "You wanna spy? Get a life, dude!"

"Just leave him alone."

"Leave him?" He turns to me, and I see a wave of

forced self-control settle over him. He smiles. But it's not a genuine smile, and I suddenly feel like running. "You've told me that he follows you. I've seen him staring at you like a lost puppy." He's ranting, eyes wide and raving.

"He's not the one I should worry about," I say, hoping it'll calm him.

He points to the parked car. "Don't let him fool you with his I-have-everything-figured-out attitude. That's exactly what he wants you to think. I've watched him. I've given him serious looks, and being a guy, he knows what looks I'm talking about, and still, he has the balls to come around here?" he yells.

"Calm down. It's not like that." I want so much to tell him what's going on. I'm so scared he's going to hurt Dane.

He charges up to me, his stare weighing on me. "Calm down? I've invested a lot in you."

My body tightens. What did he just say? Is he kidding me right now with this act? "What are you saying, that I owe you?"

"You don't know all I've been through," he mumbles through gritted teeth.

"I appreciate your going against the grain for me, but it doesn't give you the right to act like an asshole. I didn't ask for you to defend me. It was all you. As for Dane, he's only keeping an eye on me. That's all. Leave him alone."

"Keeping an eye on you," he repeats. "Are you crazy? Make up your mind. Do you need my help or not?"

"Yes, but he's not the one to watch out for."

"How do you know?"

"I just—I just know, Bram."

He blinks softly. He's listening. Still, he scans around the park. Where did Dane go? Then I see a tall, skinny shape moving under an oak tree across the street. He's been leaning against the trunk in the shadows the whole time, hands in his pockets. Cool and collected.

"Let's just go." I grab ahold of Bram's arm and yank him the opposite way.

God forbid someone should touch him when he's upset, though, because he suddenly pushes me back, and I stumble a few steps. "Don't...grab me like that," he says.

Dane jumps out of the shadows when he sees me rubbing my arm, but then he realizes he's out in the open now. "Don't touch her like that again."

Bram whirls around. "Oh, yeah?" He launches at him like a cannonball, and Dane steps out into the street to meet him, holding up his hand to stop Bram from coming any closer. Bram grabs and twists his arm, using his free hand to plow a fist into Dane's face.

Dane's head flies back then returns as if he's used to this sort of thing, a thick spot of blood dripping from his nose. He swipes at it, like it's nothing. Calmly, he grabs Bram by the shoulders and plows a knee into his stomach.

"Stop it!" I run to the middle of the road, torn between separating the two, scuffling on the street, or staying out of the way to avoid getting hurt. "I said stop! You're acting like little kids!"

The punches continue to fly, the pounding and body-slamming against the car. As good as Dane was at the start, Bram is all lean, heavy muscle, and something inside him snaps. He pounds and punches and pummels Dane in the face, pulling his head forward then banging it against the car window. Something in his eyes...he could kill him. "Stop! Bram! Please! He's...*damn it*...he's *not* stalking me..." Bram stops hitting him, and he looks up. "He's a detective."

I watch my betrayal fall across Dane's face like an eclipse over a full moon. *I'm so sorry...*

Bram gasps for breath, his gaze shifting from Dane to me and back to Dane. He shakes his head, releases his death hold on Dane, and doubles over to catch his breath. Dane watches me, completely shocked and hurt. He throws his hands in the air, resigned, and flips over to hug the car. After a minute, he circles it and pauses to look at me again before getting in, as if saying, *You're on your own now.*

I can't believe what I just did. But Bram was hurting him.

What just happened? Dane might've known who's been chasing me, he might've been close to figuring it all out. But I blew his cover. Now, Bram will tell everyone who he really is, ruining my protector's chance of getting to the bottom of it all.

The guilt kills me. But I was just tired of everyone's pushing, pulling, and shoving instructions. What if *everyone* is wrong but me? What if, deep down, only *my* intuition is the right one, and I don't follow it? Can I live with that?

For once, I can't listen to anyone. Not to Dane, not to Bram, not to my parents, not even to Mary Shelley's poor tormented soul. What I need now is to listen to my own instincts—given to me at birth for a reason. And if that alienates everyone I love and causes me to make huge mistakes, so be it. But at least the mistakes will be my own.

...

It's raining when the small brown bubble envelope finally arrives. I sign for it, watch the delivery man run back to his truck under the deluge, and then stare at it.

Wiping beads of water off the package, I take it to my room and close the door. On the bed, I pull the tab to slice open the envelope and two key chains slide out. One holds a green key, the one Mami always used for the front door as well as the back one leading into the kitchen. The other ring has two smaller, identical silver keys with a plastic key chain marked *Hudson Storage #301*.

Hudson Storage is on Route 9 a half mile south of Sunnyside. I remember driving past it on the way to the bank. I throw on dirty jeans and tie my hair into a tight ponytail. Then I grab my keys and head into the living room where Betty Anne is finishing her latest needlepoint—a carved pumpkin with a black kitten poking its head out of it.

"I like it." I peer over her shoulder. Sofia now sits perched next to Diana the Dutch doll on the shelf. I smile sadly. At least my evil stepsisters can now commiserate together.

Betty Anne smiles at her handiwork. "I thought it was cute, too. Are you heading somewhere? It's raining awfully bad."

"I know. I was thinking, if you weren't using your car, maybe I could borrow it today? Would you mind?"

"Not at all. First hook on the right in the kitchen. It just needs gas."

"Thanks." And though I haven't done it in quite some time, I lean over and kiss Betty Anne's cheek. I still feel awful about having yelled at her when she did nothing wrong.

She touches her face. "Careful in the rain, okay?"

"'Kay." I grab an umbrella from the kitchen and sprint under the rain to Betty Anne's dark blue dinosaur parked out front.

Down Route 9, I'm so lost in thought, I plow through a yellow light turning red. Thoughts of Dane plague me. What is he doing now? Will he ever forgive me? Will I see him again? He was right about here last night when I lost sight of his car.

Driving through town, I know exactly which cars will be parked outside Mario's Tex-Mex Restaurant, which stores are open now, and which patrons I'll see sitting at which windows. Whether or not I meant to become a Tarrytown girl again, it somehow happened over these two weeks.

In ten minutes, I arrive at Hudson Storage and use my key to get through the front gate where a security guard barely looks out from under his visor to nod at me. I search for Building 3, since the unit key is marked #301. I find it in the back, facing another woodsy area that makes me cringe. Hopefully, Dane is still following me around, checking on me, even though I completely blew his cover.

Pulling into a parking space, I wait for the rain to let up and stare at the unit's roll-up door. I'm about to find out what's inside. If the journal everyone is looking for is in there, what will I do with it? Keep the money for myself? Share it with my dad, as angry as I am with him? Find Nina and pay her for her lost time?

Would $500,000 make me happy when money was never what I truly wanted in the first place? It can't bring my mother back. The Derants and Engers could use it, judging from Jonathan's apartment and Bram's shitty car. But do I deserve the journal? I've done nothing to keep it safe all these years the way Bram and Jonathan's families have.

But Mami gave me the family tree for one reason and one reason only—*to prove it belonged to me*. She would've cared for the document had she known for sure it was our family's. I do know one thing—if and when I find it, assuming it's not in someone else's hands right now, I'll share its contents with the world. For Mami. For Mary. So their souls can rest. That's all that matters to me.

When the rain stops swishing against the windshield, I turn off the ignition and get out of the car. Taking a deep breath, I insert the key and twist it. The deadbolt clanks open. I roll up the big orange door.

My life, the one I left behind, flashes before my eyes. My childhood. My memories—the dark wood furniture my grandfather gave my mom when she got married— Mami's bed and dresser. In the back is my white wicker bedroom set, the one that used to sit in my yellow room with the holographic stickers. The dining room set with scratch marks all over one side from where I used to bang it with a fork when I was a toddler. Boxes of toys, yearbooks, and games.

It'll take me days to go through it all.

For hours, I rifle through kitchen items, bakeware, sewing equipment, scissors, fabrics, buttons, thread, newspapers, microfiche slides, books on various historical events, even the colonial dresses I used to wear at Sunnyside. At one point I stop and gasp—a hatbox filled with old snapshots, some stuck together from humidity, of Bram and me as kids, eating ice cream in his kitchen; of Bram riding Apple, his grandfather's horse when he was about ten; in Halloween costumes through the years; in my room doing homework.

Wow, he's really changed. Not the same skinny little runt as before. And my hair! So long and braided. *Ha!*

Reminders sprout everywhere, like flowers from the cold, hard ground after a harsh winter. Yet, at my dad's house in Miami, I have not *one* reminder of my childhood.

Then I find the dolls.

Big and clumsy, too big for any little girl's arms to really wrap around. Blond dolls, brunette dolls, red-haired dolls, white skin, dark skin, caramel skin. Amber dresses, purple dresses, gold dresses, zigzag trim, beaded trim, lace, lace, and more lace.

Too many things to go through in one day. I'll have to come back.

I pull out the boxes with the most research papers, books, and work-related items and carry them out to the car, taking as much as I can. I pack the dolls into the trunk. Betty Anne will have a field day with them.

But four hours and twenty-two minutes later, I've still found no journal. Nothing to show for my search efforts but a nice stash of junk to dump at Betty Anne's house, a pounding headache from not eating, and the dawning awareness that it's probably lost forever.

I'm in the apartment again, the old one in some dark city, probably London, but I don't see Mary's spirit anywhere. It's night, and rain sprinkles against the window. Under it is a small desk with a lit candle that flickers erratically, creating shadows that dance and leap against the glass panes. On the desk are many books, a dried-out ink well, and some blank pages, as if someone has just been writing here.

The rocking chair is back again. A baby cries.

Mary? I call out. *Are you here? I haven't found it yet, but I'm trying.* The crying continues. I remember how Mary led me out of this apartment in the last dream, how we soared over the countryside in search of something— her baby, I think. Was that train headed for Spain? With Cristóbal? My great-great-great-grandfather?

People will know, Mary. You can rest now if you want, I tell her, but I have a feeling that Mary doesn't live here anymore. As if everything that was once good for her— hopes, dreams for the future, a chance for a better life— was ripped out from under her, sending her tumbling underground where nobody would ever know the truth about how much she loved Irving, wanted to share a life with him, but was left behind.

If Mary's baby is gone, then who is crying?

I look around.

Double creation, someone whispers—a deep, solid voice. Suddenly, I feel as though someone is in the room with me. Not the spirit I'm used to. Someone else. I know him. I turn around, expecting to see a man standing behind me. An important man. A man who spent long nights with Mary here and complicated his life.

But of course, there's no one there. Only a cradle softly rocking and creaking in the corner of the room. Cristóbal isn't the only one they created together. There's another. The dark voice says, I was in way over my head, lured by her weakness, her need for me, entirely past what was acceptable, sensible. It never should have happened.

I can't see whoever is speaking, but I know him, and I've loved him for a long time. So did my mother. And even though I've never met him, I can sense that the rest of the family wouldn't have approved of the match, so he dealt with it the best way he knew how.

Inside the cradle.

Slowly, I float up to it. The cries grow louder. *Shh, baby. Shh, it's all right.*

The window shutters open, and the wind blows the remaining papers off the desk, sending them fluttering all around the room. My heartbeat sounds loudly in my head. I close my eyes. When I'm inches away from the cradle, I hold my breath and open them again. At once, the crying and rocking motions stop.

I peer over the edge. My heart pounds inside my rib cage. Inside the crib is a shovel. Rusted. Old. And black.

Chapter Twenty-Six

"Just sufficient time had elapsed to enable each storyteller to dress up his tale with a little becoming fiction…"

I wake up drenched in cold sweat. The man in my dream was Washington Irving. I know it was. He showed me a shovel. But he doesn't want me to dig up a baby's remains straight out of the ground, does he? Sounds like something Mary Shelley would ask me to do.

And there is absolutely no way. I'm not Victor Frankenstein, and I will not be exhuming any dead bodies anytime soon, thank you very much. Not in this lifetime. The glare from my phone's light burns my vision when I check the time: 4:45 a.m.

He's coming, Lela.

I sit up straight in bed, blinking in the darkness. "Who is?" I strain my brain to listen, shutting off as much external stimuli as I can to focus, but Mami doesn't respond.

Listening to the creaks of Betty Anne's walls and floors contracting and expanding in the cool night, I finally settle back down under the covers. I wait, no longer afraid of falling asleep to face my ghost. Let her come.

As the sunlight edges its way into my room, I fall into a conscious slumber, not waking for any good reason, not for Betty Anne stirring in the kitchen or for her gasps of delight upon seeing the mountain of dolls I left her on the sofa, not for Bram's ringtone going off under the blankets, not even for my mother's voice somewhere in the recesses of my mind…

…*hide it, hide everything.*

*D*ays later, I finish sifting through the piles of my mother's research. I'm a lot closer now to understanding adoption procedures in Spain during the nineteenth century, Mary Shelley's loss of three children with husband Percy Bysshe Shelley, and the fact that Mary had an older half sister, Fanny Imlay, who was her mother's illegitimate child, a woman unable to cope with her biological misfortune and thus committed suicide.

It makes sense now, how Mary could give up her last child to Irving. She didn't want her baby, or babies, to suffer the same fate as her. Society was ruthless then. No one would've accepted the child unless their parents legitimized the union through marriage. And even then, Mary had little to gain, already hated as she was. Irving, big celebrity and hero *he* was, had everything to lose. Tragedy any way you looked at it. The right thing to do was to give Cristóbal to a good family.

Dane was right. Washington Irving was a hero. In ways no one could ever imagine.

If Dr. Tanner is the new proud owner of our journal, he had plenty of time to turn it in, and word of its return should've been on the news by now. Bram would've called me. So would've Dane. I hope. But I'm starting to believe Dr. Tanner didn't take it. Maybe it was the tone of his voice at our meeting, the way he spoke affectionately of Mami, the genuine referral to her as a good friend, but my instincts believe it wasn't him.

On the floor, surrounded by papers, I realize tomorrow is opening night of HollowEve. Bram is probably neck-high in last-minute responsibilities. Since the incident at Kingsland Point Park, we haven't spoken. Only his single voicemail. "*Some bomb you dropped on me the other day, Mica. If you were told to stay away from me, that's fine, but know that my intentions for you were never anything but pure.*"

I reach for the hatbox and open it. Eight-year-old, eleven-year-old, and nine-year-old Brams and Micas stare back at me, innocent, unburdened. I reach deep into the pile of photos and pull one out. There it is—eating apple crisp at Bram's house, tongues out to touch the ice cream on our spoons. I never noticed Bram's mom in the photo before, leaning against the kitchen counter far behind us and to the left, eyeing the camera in the most annoyed way. Pesky Micaela was sitting at her kitchen table.

I've invested so much in you, he said the other night.

I don't know that I owe him my life, but maybe an explanation, at the very least. I grab my phone and text him.

> *I understand you're angry with me. I'm sorry for not explaining more.*

Not thirty seconds later, he replies:

> *Make it up to me by joining me at holloweve tom nite. Ily.*

Sadly, I don't think I can do that.

I stand, collect the papers, photos, books, and copies and stack it all in my closet. I remember my mother in one of her most bizarre moments right before a weekend trip to Lake George. She spent the better part of the day hiding things—money, jewelry, passports, valuables under mattresses, behind the linings of her jewelry boxes, even inside some fake cleaning products. *So burglars can't find anything,* she'd said.

I remember thinking *holy crap, my mom is crazy,* but now that I think about it, it was brilliant. Damn good way of hiding things. I take out her safe deposit box envelope, the keys to the box, and the storage unit key. *Trust no one.* I slide manila folders under the mattress, behind the framed certificates on the wall, and the keys into the hollow base of Betty Anne's daughter's ballet trophies. My mother seemed so insane that day, hiding things, but I get it now.

Hide it, hide everything...

In the mirror's reflection, I see myself. The younger, prettier version of Maria Burgos. I stare at the person I've desperately tried *not* to become the last six years. Not to be like Mami. More rational. More sensible. Yet here I am, hiding things from burglars just like her.

Obsessively.

The only way she knew how.

I stare so hard, my eyes dry out. *No...way...*

Frantically, I pop off the felt base of the trophy, grab the storage unit keys and my backpack, and dart to the kitchen. I swipe Betty Anne's car keys, bolting to the front door.

"Going out?"

I rip my sweater off the coat rack. "Be back in a sec." I

won't be back in a second, of course. I'll stay at the storage unit all night if I have to, tearing into mattresses and sofa cushions, twisting open cans of bug spray, starch, and bathroom cleaner. I yank the front door closed, catching it right at the end.

In a matter of minutes, I'm back at Hudson Storage, making a sharp left past the empty guard house and careening into the parking lot. I had only looked for the journal, not *searched*. I bound out of the car over to the unit roll-up door, unlocking and throwing it up with superhuman force.

Everything is where I left it. I enter the center row and plow into my mother's mattresses, pulling off fitted sheets, smoothing fingers along the edges for any open slits, sewn slits, or holes in the borders. It must be here somewhere. A soft and bulky black garbage bag sits atop a nightstand. I rip it open, squeezing pillows, feeling for a notebook, hard or soft—I don't know what I'm looking for exactly, anything out of the ordinary. I let those fall and try another set of pillows from the linen closet boxes. Nothing.

Next, I try the dresser drawers, both my mother's set and my own wicker one. Maybe it's not hidden, maybe it's in plain sight or simply stuck behind drawers or underneath them. One by one, I pull them out, flipping them over, checking the undersides. I do the same with the china cabinet drawers, nightstand drawers, every drawer in sight.

Where else?

Bookcases. I looked through the books the other day, but not *inside* them. Maybe the journal is tucked inside a larger volume so its spine doesn't show. One by one, I pull out every book and shake it, catching little slips of paper as they fall out. I flip through the scraps. They're jotted dreams in shaky handwriting, written in the dark. All of them about me. She wondered what I was doing, how my school work was going, whether or not I heard her messages when she tried sending them with her heart, and the worst scribbling of all, about a dream—that she'd come home, wrapped her arms around me, but only awakened to an empty house and the reality that she'd lost her daughter for good.

"Mami." I fight the tears, but they come. With them comes something else. A painful kind of peace. No, my mother is no longer here in the flesh, but I'm more connected with her now than ever before. It took separation, it took death…it took empathy.

I look around the storage unit, opening myself up to messages from beyond, anything Mami might suddenly point out to me. After a minute of silence, I start rubbing my eyes. Where is it? Where is that goddamned journal! Only Sofia was in the safe deposit box with the other items, not a jour—

Crack.

A match illuminates the darkened tomb that is my brain. It was always clear. But I was crippling myself. "Oh my God." No one would ever think to look inside her. Not in a million years.

Because she's horrible. Uglier than sin. More beautiful than truth. I slam down the storage unit door, lock it, and rush back to Betty Anne's as quickly as humanly possible.

• • •

My feet pound up the steps, key barely able to slide through the keyhole from how much my hands are shaking. *I'm right. I'm so right. I know I am.* It's just past eleven. I shouldn't make any noise, but I don't need to worry. She's awake. The familiar sound of slippers shuffles toward the door, which pops open just as I manage to get the key in.

I stumble into the house.

"Are you all right?" Betty Anne's face takes in what must be flashes of madness in my eyes, because she holds me by the arm and delicately leads me through the foyer.

Yes, better than ever, I want to say, but the words are stuck in my throat. All I can do is stride right up to Sofia on the shelf, flanked by Diana the Dutch doll and now the array of others having multiplied overnight. I pull her right off the shelf. And there, before Betty Anne's horrified eyes, I grab her crafting scissors from her needlepoint basket and proceed to slide the shears underneath the back of Sofia's dress.

"Oh, honey, no!" Betty Anne cries.

Laying her flat on the counter, I cut straight up the doll's white dress. Her body feels crunchy underneath the soft sculpture exterior. Once I cut straight through the dress, I notice the closure in the back. A thick scar, carefully sewn shut, runs from the base of the neck to where the legs begin. I snip away at the stitches.

All at once, Sofia's spine opens. Fiberglass filling blooms out. I yank it out and see, not a book or booklet like I imagined would be inside, but a rolled-up sheet protector containing old, yellowish paper. I gasp, blood pounding against my eardrums.

I think of Mami in the basement at night, cranking these ugly dolls out as if anyone cared for them. As if anyone wanted those horrible little sisters, anyone besides Betty Anne, that is. Mami spent late hours underneath the lightbulb's glare in the basement, arguing with herself for hours. She wasn't maniacal after all.

She was *methodical*.

"Ha!" I jump into the air. I pluck the plastic sheath out and unroll it. Another one of Mami's notes, bigger with more writing, stuck to the plastic:

> Lela,
>
> The flesh and blood he spoke of is you. Use the family tree to prove it. More pages inside the girls. Did you dream of what lies beneath the lavender? I think the rest is there. Stay protected. I love you.
>
>
> —Mami

I close my eyes. "I love you, Mami. I'm sorry I left without telling you that." Then carefully, I slide out the slightly thinner, aged papers and read the familiar typeset:

26 March, 1826—These pages must never see the light of day, as long as we traverse this earth, until the flesh and blood which follow us should one day learn of them—she has endured enough torment for one lifetime; I cannot contribute to her misery—whereupon, our decision is the correct one; I am mostly certain, however—as I take pause to reflect on her whereabouts with Percy at her heels, I am disheartened by the prospect that I may have failed her and will live to regret it.

You did what you could, Great-Great-Great-Grand-father. They were different times.

"What is it, Mica?" Betty Anne jolts me back to the present.

"My great-great-great-grandfather's diary. One page of it." I lay the sheet down on the counter and lift my mother's note back up again. *More pages inside the girls.*

"Why was it inside Sofia?"

She dissected it. She dissected it and separated the pieces to make it harder to find. I stare at Betty Anne, as if I've never seen her before in my life. "Huh?"

"Never mind. I heard you."

In tune again, together in one room, both worried about the fate of my mother's creations. Of course she could hear me. "Because it's rare. Because he's famous."

"Irving."

I take her hands and give them a gentle squeeze. "Yes."

Sprinting over to the shelf, scissors in hand, I quickly grab Diana the Dutch doll, turn her around, and slice into her as well, blue and white dress slitting down the middle. More fiberglass fluff aside, and I find more protected sheets of the journal, also dated 1826. I lay them carefully on the sofa and proceed to pluck the rest of the dolls, one by one, off the shelf and line them up for mass surgery.

"Can you please bring the rest of them?" I ask Betty Anne, who's gone white and horrified. "I think I gave you more than what's here."

"I just picked my favorites to display." She shuffles down the hall, voice disappearing into the distance. "But I guess it doesn't matter now."

I stare at the line-up, as Betty Anne returns time after time with roughly forty more dolls. My plan is to open up all my evil stepsisters, retrieve the pages, and read through them. So I do, way into the night, occasionally crying over more of Mami's words. Each doll contains four to five typed pages, enough to cover the undocumented year of Washington Irving's life.

Betty Anne reads one of the pages, palm to her chest. "Oh, my."

Around the thirty-fifth doll—a ghastly life-size thing with a crooked grin that would frighten any little girl—I find the journal's original leather covers, back and front, and the strips of rawhide to bind it all together. I go on this way for a few hours, meticulously decimating each and every doll, laying out her contents, then piling the empty corpses on the couch, until finally, around three in the morning, with eyes burned from exhaustion and fiberglass entrails everywhere, it's done.

And there, on the floor of Betty Anne's little house on Maple Street, in glory so haunted and justified, it deserves to be seen by all the literary world, lies the whispered, the forgotten, the *real* legend of Sleepy Hollow.

CHAPTER TWENTY-SEVEN

"…his heart yearned after the damsel who was to inherit these domains."

In the late morning, sunlight slivers through the shutters, forcing my eyes open. Not only to the sound of the front door opening and shutting, but to the realization that I'm wide awake. That my life suddenly *means* something. What will I do with the journal, I don't know yet, but I succeeded in helping my mother with the last request of her life, and that's all I care about.

But there's more. Mami said there was. Rolling toward the nightstand, I pick up the note that was inside Sofia:

> Did you dream of what lies beneath the lavender? I think the rest is there.
> Stay protected. I love you.

"Yes, Mami. I did dream of lavender. Was it a garden near a little house?" I whisper. "Is it far away or nearby?"

Her reply doesn't come. But something else does. A knock at the door.

"Come in."

In walks Betty Anne, still dressed in pajamas, brandishing...*a gift*? "What is that?" I sit up in bed.

She places a medium-sized box in my arms, cold and slightly humid. "This was on the porch for you. Doesn't look like it was mailed or anything."

My name is written in orange and black alternating markers flanked by bad drawings of a jack-o-lantern on one side and a bat that looks more like a chicken on the other. "Must be from Bram. Thanks."

"Hmm." Betty Anne turns to leave. "If you want breakfast, I'll have it ready in five minutes, or lunch instead, considering the time."

"What does that *hmm* mean, huh?" I smile at her. It's been a while since I even mustered up a smile, and it feels foreign on my face.

"Oh, I don't know. *Hmm* just means *hmm*." She leans against the wall and rests her head. Then she leaves me alone with my curiosity and some serious clear tape to start peeling.

I finally get it open, tugging the tape off, and find a little white envelope sitting on top of brown shredded paper. I open it and slide out a printed HollowEve entrance ticket and a note card with Jack Skellington on it, arms raised against a full moon. It reads:

The Pumpkin King reigns tonight.
Be my Sally?

I'm not sure if I can ever be Bram's Sally, but once this is all over, maybe we could start again. I toss out the paper. Lifting it up and over the edge of the bed where I can release it is the most beautifully rich, gothic-inspired, floor-length gown I've ever seen. Dark amethyst and black with beadwork, scrolls, and a fitted bodice that would put even the wench version of Katrina Van Tassel costumes to shame. I can almost hear Bram's wicked laugh.

I've always told myself that no man could buy me with bribes and gifts, but this, this is an excellent attempt. Though I'm not in the mood for HollowEve, this dress is too beautiful not to show off. And I could use a night away from the stress. But I won't tell Bram I'm coming. I'll just show up and surprise him.

*G*athering the folds of my dress, I stride up to the entrance of HollowEve at Philipsburg Manor, a long and stunning walkway perfectly lined on both sides with massive oak trees and lit jack-o-lanterns hanging from their branches.

I acknowledge the looks of admiration I get from men as I walk in and smile at the women, too, some in fanciful dresses, some without costume, to let them all know they look their best as well. It's Sleepy Hollow's shining moment. Having curled my hair to form wavy golden tresses and swept the sides up into elegant swags, I feel like the princess Bram always calls me. Somewhere in this living nightmare of ghoulish faces and literary characters come to life, Bram thinks I've ignored him.

Heart beating with anticipation, I show my complimentary ticket at the door. Things have changed quite a bit since I was a kid. In six years, the event has gone from a plantation museum decorated with typical Halloween decorations to a morose wonderland of the macabre. A thick layer of dreamlike fog covers the ground, breaking into slow-moving curls as visitors walk through. Ghastly masks, fangs, blood the color of rubies, and capes abound, but the most amazing spectacle of all is the hillside. Sloping toward the river, facing the armada of boats that have come to see it, is the Blaze with *thousands* of glowing jack-o-lanterns the likes of which nobody has ever seen.

Carved by hundreds of artisans, they dot the landscape for a mile, pumpkins of all different contours and silhouettes shimmering in ethereal resplendence.

"Micaela?"

I turn around. Natalee Torino touches my arm with long black nails, deep red lips, and eyes wide with an expression torn between admiration and envy. She wears a black fitted dress with open slits at the thighs, fluted sleeves, and a thick choker studded with black beads. Easily the prettiest I have ever seen her. "Hey, you look beautiful!" I say.

"Me? Look at *you*, oh my gosh! Where did you get that dress, it's incredible!"

"A friend got it for me."

"Nice friend!" She pulls in close to me as a couple of friends wait nearby. "Hey, is it true that things went down between you, Bram, and Mr. Boracich? I mean, none of you have been in school for a while. Bram, I figured because of HollowEve prep, but why did you leave?"

He hasn't been in school? "I've been dealing with my mom's stuff. You know…"

"Oh, right," Natalee whispers. "So it didn't have to do with Mr. Boracich? 'Cause like, we all miss him."

"I'm not sure what you mean. I haven't seen him, either," I say. Why add fuel to the fire? "Everything's cool."

"Oh." Natalee deflates, like she was hoping there was more drama to it. "Well, you know about that diary, right? The one Mr. Boracich mentioned in class? Well, supposedly, it's *real*! Everyone's talking about how he was only in town to find it and keep half a mil all for himself. Do you believe that? I think he already found it, which is why he hasn't been back."

No one's seen him around? I really drove him away.

I cross my arms, satisfied I know the journal's whereabouts. It's safely put away in a deposit box at Betty Anne's bank. We went together this afternoon and used an alphanumeric password no one will ever guess. I'm still not sure what I'll do with it. "Seems likely. I mean, it makes a great story. But don't believe everything you hear." I pat Natalee's arm. "I have to find Bram. I'll see you later."

"I saw him a while ago."

"Where?"

"Somewhere in there." She points to the hillside. "Beware of Lacy, though." She makes a creepy face with claws.

I laugh. "Thanks for the warning." I keep my eyes peeled, hoping I don't run into her, and head for the staging area. Regardless of what role Bram was given, he'll be there getting things ready for the night's main event—the Headless Horseman's annual appearance.

When I whirl around, I'm momentarily taken aback to see a man behind the crowd of people, shrouded in darkness under the trees, wearing a long black coat and demon mask. His eyes glow with actual red lights, and under normal circumstances, it might seem like a cool costume, but considering he's intently focused on me only, it makes me shudder.

Is he my follower from the cemetery and the birch tree shortcut, waiting for the perfect moment to snatch me? More than ever, I need Dane and his protection. For a moment, I think I catch a glimpse of him, or someone who looks like him, sitting on the manor house steps underneath the very chandelier I painted last week. But when I look again, he's gone.

So is the demon-faced man.

I hurry through the fiery jack-o-lantern field, swishing and shifting my dress around to keep it from brushing against the pumpkins, and head straight toward the north side of the manor. Gentlemen hosts in knickers and waistcoats stop to offer themselves as escorts, seeing that I'm a lovely maiden alone on a diabolical night such as this, but I refuse them each with a coy smile. As much as I know Bram will love it when he sees me in my dolled-up glory, I find myself wishing Dane could see me in it, too.

Far off to the right, on one end of the back porch, I see the demon-masked man again. Yes, it's an ordinary mask, and there could be more like them, but he stands behind everyone watching me with glowing red eyes. He averts my stare after I've noticed him twice already. I break into a hurried walk, bumping shoulders with someone.

"Again? I guess you're here to stay."

I'm face-to-face with Lacy wearing a Katrina Van Tassel outfit, the slut corset, boobs-popping-out kind. Ugh. Figures. "I'm sorry. Excuse me."

She gives a short scoff. "You think you can just come back to town and take whatever you want like you own the place, you know that? Even though other people have put in the time and effort."

"Listen, I didn't mean to hurt you. I didn't come back for…" My voice trails off. She's not talking about Bram, is she? Behind her, I see the demon man is getting closer. "I'm sorry, Lacy. We'll talk about it later." I rush away through the crowd. Where did he go?

"Not if I can help it," she calls out, her voice swallowed by the din of the guests.

He's watching me. It's him. Some of the voices pop out from the background, behind the sound loop of ghostly moans and rattling chains. "That's Micaela. Right there. See her?" People from school, familiar faces. A man dressed as Ichabod Crane in knickers and a long braid makes me look twice. I think it's Dane, but I know that's just wishful thinking.

Run, Lela.

"Mami..." Biting my lip, I push straight through the end of the Blaze, casting a glance to my right again to notice the demon man keeping up with me. Not running but advancing as I do.

Dig it up, Micaela. Dig up the rest.

Mary?

The image of an old shovel barrels into my consciousness. My dead mother, buried two months ago, and my spirit guide, departed a hundred and fifty years now, are taking turns speaking to me about digging. They want me to run, to dig someone up from right out of the hallowed ground, but who? "*It*, Mary? What is *the rest*?"

The double creation.

I scan the landscape for the demon again. Is it worse to keep glimpsing him, or to not know where he is at all? The staging area is behind a wooden fence flanking a row of trees, and there's a NO ADMITTANCE sign on the open gate. Familiar volunteers slip in and out. I reach the gate, out of breath, where a small woman with a walkie-talkie, who should look less menacing than she does, blocks my way.

For a moment I think I see Bram somewhere behind her. "Bram!"

"Sorry, no one's allowed."

"I'm looking for Bram Derant. I'm his best friend."

The woman shakes her sour head at me. "I said no."

Her blunt bangs and glasses pushed hard down against her nose remind me of Edna Mode from *The Incredibles*, except with zero charm whatsoever. Who is she to tell me no? "Excuse me." I push past the woman, who begins to offer a few choice expletives.

Sorry, but I need to see Bram. Need to know where I stand with him. Need his help digging up whatever is under the lavender bush. Assuming that's the right location. But it's his big night, so I doubt he'll be able to help, even though there's no better time to exhume a dead baby's bones than when the entire town is captive at the spookiest event of the year, if you ask me.

Without warning, a hunchbacked lab assistant blocks my path, taking in every inch of my being with his oversize, weird eyeballs. "Hey, Mica. Looking for something?" Fake-stained, crooked smile. *Ugh.*

"Jonathan?" I shrink back. "Nice costume. Hey, uh… where's Bram?"

"Bram…not available," he says in a hunchback voice. "Maybe I can *hel-lp* you instead?"

"No, I need him. Just tell me where he is." I try moving past him, but he hops in my way again. "Don't make me shove you like I did the lady back there. Move, it's urgent."

"How urgent is it?" His voice deepens, his face conveying something I can't quite grasp. Is he serious, or just playing a part? "Urgent enough that you'll risk your life? Is it really that important to you?"

"I don't know what you're talking about."

"You know *exactly* what it is…" His hand shoots out to grab my wrist tightly. "…I am talking about."

"Don't touch me, you freak." I twist my hand out of his clutch.

"You already found it, haven't you? You're holding out. You little bitch. Same way you always have." He reaches out and slides his nasty hand along my arm, pursing his putrid lips.

I shove him hard, and he takes a few steps to regain his balance. "Don't…touch me. Screw you. You have no right to judge me. None of you do. I haven't found anything, but even if I have, I have plenty of ways to prove it belongs to me. Look at me like that one more time, and you're going to have more than just your back hunched."

As I huff off, Jonathan calls out, "You're nothing, and you'll always be nothing! Especially now that Daddy's world has fallen down!"

He may as well have punched me in the gut. I wish I could whip around and tell him to go to hell, but I don't feel like giving him the satisfaction. Even though I wonder… Between Nina leaving, Jonathan saying my dad owed people in town a visit, and the only trips he makes are business ones, my mom's house being up for sale, his dozens of trips to Bogotá, and my debit card declining, I have to wonder…is my father still okay financially?

Can't stop to think about it now. I have an atrocity to commit.

Nearby, a horse neighs, which can only mean one thing. I follow the sound around a path leading to a stable and find two people gearing up a massive black horse with a saddle.

"Is Bram here?" I ask, and one of them, a woman

helping to fit the saddle, points toward the stalls. I can't tell which stall she means, so I go one by one, checking each.

At one stall I pause to stare at something bathed in the darkness, a hulking massive shadow. As my eyes adjust to the dim lighting, I see a man standing feet apart in a wide stance, boots planted firmly on the ground. In one hand, he holds a long blade. In the other, a small dagger he's using to sharpen his sword. His head is missing.

My skin prickles with fiery heat. "Bram?"

He gives no reply.

Drawing back, I tear my stare away from the towering shape and move to the next stall. Empty. Another stall. Empty. "Hello, Bram?"

"In here, Mica," he finally replies from another stall.

So, if that horseman wasn't Bram, was that…?

I find Bram and a man with long gray hair helping him into a costume. Bram wears black pants, a black-and-silver vest, and they're fitting him into a riding jacket with a wire frame that rises over the top of his head.

Wait, so…he *did* get the horseman part?

Bram spots me and his eyes widen. "Wow, you are without a doubt the finest thing I have ever seen, Micaela Burgos. That dress is sweet perfection on you. Isn't it, Russ?"

Russ glances at me with a knowing grin. Bram extends a hand to me. I take it and rise on my toes to kiss his cheek. "What's wrong?" He zeroes in on my face. "You look like you've seen a ghost."

"Who's the horseman?" I ask, glancing back at the other stall. No one comes out of it. No one goes in.

He laughs. "Isn't it obvious? You're looking at him."

"No, I mean, who's the *other* horseman?"

"There is no other horseman. I'm your one and only, baby." Bram does a rascally chuckle, then goes back to Russ and the fitting of the structured jacket.

Under normal circumstances, say, a year ago, I might've thought that four stalls away was another man in a horseman costume, waiting for the show to start, no big deal. But I know better now. Life has completely changed.

I have protector spirits here in the Hollow.

They're everywhere.

And this one, I never got to thank when he ran the biker out of the cemetery. I hold up a finger. "Be right back." Lifting the hem of my dress off the dusty ground, I inch my way back to the first stall, pulse beating in my throat, every cell of my body terrified of what I'll see again, but I do it anyway. I can't be afraid of ghosts anymore. They're just ghosts.

When I reach the edge of the stall, I slowly crane my neck and peer into the shadows again.

Gone.

Nobody.

Empty.

Like he was never there in the first place.

"What's wrong?" Bram steps out of the stall in full headless costume, tattered cape fluttering in the breeze, talking to me through the small rectangular screen in the neck. His voice echoes inside the suit.

"I—nothing."

Just then, another vision wracks my brain so hard, I grip my temples and bite my lip to keep from crying out. Mary Shelley, eyes intense, wringing her hands, stands in a field of flowers pointing to the garden, an English garden with lavender bushes, near a little gray house. *Sunnyside.*

"Bram, I need your help."

"Okay. But can it wait? I'll be done in an hour." He slides a boot into one of the horse's stirrups, grabs the horn to hoist himself up, and takes his shiny metal sword and glowing fake jack-o-lantern from Russ.

"No, you don't understand. I need you to come with me somewhere. I need you right now."

"I like the way that sounds, Mica, but I can't. Less than an hour. Watch the show, and then we'll go?"

I'm not sure why I feel so panicky, except for the fact that Mary keeps asking me to hurry, and I can't dig by myself. I'm a weakling, and as much as I hate to admit it, I need Bram's brute strength to help me.

"Horseman, you're on." The woman from the staging area gate appears from around the corner, giving me a dirty look. "You, I said you can't be here. Bram, get her out of here."

"Princess, I'll see you out there, okay? Tell me later how I did?"

Tears linger at the corners of my eyes, but I nod. Of course. It's ridiculous, not to mention selfish, to lure him away from his most important night of the year. I watch as Headless Bram takes the horse's reins and saddle horn in one hand then places the sword in its scabbard at his waist with the other. He holds up a hand. "Actually, wait there," he says, handing the pumpkin back to Russ.

The gate lady heads back to her post with her walkie-talkie as Bram practices a few laps around the yard. I can't stand here and watch him practice. I have to go, even if I need to find the lavender bush alone.

Sunnyside.

Yes, the lavender bush is at Sunnyside. That's where Mary was standing the day we visited. Whatever is buried there, Irving must have done it after coming home to

America and settling at the house.

Bram's horse gallops all around the yard then suddenly comes up behind me, and my brain, remembering the same trotting echo in the cemetery the day Coco was killed, flies into a pounding fit. Is he coming up on me? I turn, horrified.

"What are you doing?" I yell. All I can do is stand and gape at him charging toward me as he leans to one side with his arm outstretched. A second later, he hooks it around my waist and sweeps me off my feet, pulling me onto the space in front of him.

His practiced, maniacal laugh echoes inside his costume. He pulls back on the reins and turns the horse around. "That *so* could *not* have worked out the way it did."

It's a little hard to answer him with my stomach lodged in my windpipe. A miracle I'm conscious at all. His horse trots over to Russ who offers up the flaming pumpkin to me with a smile. "This'll be a nice twist from every year."

"Thank you, sir." Bram trots off to the staging area where volunteers are already gathering in droves to take photos of us as we approach. "Don't worry, I got you, Mica. Just hold the pumpkin and look like you're my Katrina Van Tassel."

"I *will* be throwing this thing at someone, right? Please tell me I am."

He laughs so hard, I think he's going to lose his grip on me. "Man…"

"What?"

"You really can't take Sleepy Hollow out of the girl."

CHAPTER TWENTY-EIGHT

*"The lady of his heart was his partner in the dance, and
smiling graciously in reply to all his
amorous oglings."*

The show begins as a slow waltz, our horse prancing in circles, us posing for photos and waiting for our time to come. The speakers throughout the manor grounds pump standard spooky sounds, but once Bram and I hear the fanfare that cues the start of the show, he kicks his heels, and the volunteers break apart to let us through.

When we begin charging, Bram is no longer Bram. He morphs into his part—my captor and protector, my reason to fear and to love, all at once. I play the damsel in distress, his arms pinning me tightly, and I hold on for dear life. I cradle the pumpkin, scared to drop it, as the steed bursts through the gate to the roar of cheers. Bolting toward our track, we stay along the perimeter of the manor grounds, and every twenty feet, security guards stand ready to intercept anyone who tries to get in the horse's way.

Immediately, the event attendees clap and take pics, flashes going off like twinkling stars. It's a beautiful dream, the kind I wish I had more often, an exhilarating trance that suddenly makes me forget my problems. I feel alive. I've been dormant for way too long, believing lies, living a half existence.

Sleepy Hollow has awakened my core, and I will *never* be the same again.

I should be uncomfortable sitting side-saddle with little room for my body, rising and bouncing hard onto a leather seat, but I'm not. Bram keeps me in place snugly. He unsheathes his sword from its scabbard with his other hand, and it sings a high-pitched note that highlights the dark musical score blaring in the background. Crazy horseman laughter echoes on the speakers, and the flashes dazzle the landscape.

Bram wields his sword in circles high above his head, and if I didn't know better, I might have felt genuinely afraid of this madman rocketing through the woods. I externalize this fear by acting the part of a pained and suffering damsel. We ride several laps, disappearing into a thicket of trees to turn around and then bolt out again. Each time, more and more people gather to watch, and for one brief moment, I see the demon-masked man.

"Hold on tight!" Bram says inside his costume. A moment later, the giant black horse rears up on its hind legs. *Holy crap...* I curl up against Bram's chest to keep from sliding off. "Oh my God...don't drop me, please!" I shut my eyes and try not to look at the HollowEve landscape standing up on its side. How ridiculous would it be for me to tumble off this horse and be the laughingstock of the town *again*? But I'm lying if I don't admit this is, all things considered, the most fun I've had in my life.

The horse snorts through its nostrils and lips. It lands back on its feet, and Bram says, "Okay, now you see that guy coming this way? The one on the horse?"

Cutting through the crowd from the opposite direction is the Ichabod Crane look-alike who made me do a double-take earlier. He's wearing knickers, a shirt, coattails, and a tri-cornered hat with a long braid, and he's atop a gray horse, looking at us very worried. "I see him."

"Okay, we're gonna chase him one time around. When he comes back to the middle here, he's gonna pause and wait while we rear up again. Then you throw the pumpkin at him. Got it?"

"Got it." I love this interpretation, how the Headless Horseman has stolen Ichabod Crane's crush straight from under his nose. Or as in the original story, is the horseman really Brom Bones in disguise, leading the fair Katrina to the altar? Either way, I'm a part of it. I didn't expect to be, but here I am.

"Here we go!" Bram kicks the horse, and we're off, hooves pummeling the ground at a medium clip, Bram baring his sword again, slicing and swinging at the air. We follow poor Ichabod Crane all around the grounds, and I have to say that whoever is playing the part of the lanky schoolmaster is pretty spot on and super funny. Finally, after a few minutes, we make our way around the last bend, cut straight into the middle of the field, and wait as several staff members keep the crowd at a safe distance.

The horse rears, and that's my cue. I lift the pumpkin, heavy in my hands. Can I even throw straight? *Please let me do this right...* For a moment, I wish Bram wouldn't have pulled me into this without as much as one rehearsal, but it's too late now. I raise the pumpkin higher into the air. Cameras flash all around us. *I can do this.*

"Do it!" he says. I do as he says. Then, with all the strength I can muster, I pull back my arm as far as it'll go, as even Ichabod Crane nods at me in encouragement, and using my body for support, I heave it at him as hard as I can.

The pumpkin head goes whizzing through the air to more camera flashes, applause, and cries from the crowd. Then Ichabod, raising his arms up to avoid getting hit, cleverly positions himself to look like the flaming missile is really striking his head. He pretends to fall off his horse and tumbles to the ground. The crowd cheers.

The Headless Horseman's laughter echoes again from the speakers, and that's Bram's cue to turn the horse back to the staging area off-grounds. Only he doesn't head back to the staging area. He pivots and disappears into the south woods, the cheers and noise level from the festival melting away behind us. Once we're a safe distance from the festivities, between two streets outside of Patriots Park, Bram slows down long enough to unbutton the top part of his costume.

"Mica, that was wicked." He smiles. "Incredible."

I turn my face up to him. "Why did you do that? Take me with you?"

"What kind of headless gentleman would I be had I just left you there?"

"The kind that had a job to do? I would've understood."

"That's not how it works. You showed up for me tonight. Now I'm all yours." He bends to kiss the top of my head. "Besides, it was dramatic as hell, wasn't it? Now tell me where we're going."

Remembering my purpose, I point toward Sunnyside. "That way."

"Sunnyside?" Bram sounds disappointed.

"Yes, to dig."

"To dig," he repeats. "And what, pray tell, are we digging for? Treasure? Dead bodies?"

I shrug, readjusting myself so that I'm straddling the horse same as Bram, my dress cascading on either side of me. "Maybe both." He pauses to think. I can feel his mind going a mile a minute. "Just take us to Sunnyside, will you please? I have to get this over with, or I might never sleep again."

Soon, silence, except for the sound of the horse's clop, envelops us.

Bram's arm wraps around my waist. He holds me closely, and not because he's keeping me from falling off his horse. I feel his warm breath on my neck in the cold night, and it makes my skin prickle. "Well, we can't have you losing any more sleep, can we? So if my Mica wishes to dig at Sunnyside, then digging at Sunnyside we shall do."

I begin thinking about the logistics of the plan we're about to execute. Where do we even begin digging exactly? Where do we find a shovel? Do I really want to see a tiny set of bones? Or maybe, Irving and Shelley's second child had been older when Irving brought him home. Maybe he didn't die as a child at all, but as a fully grown man (or woman!).

I ask Bram to move the horse a little faster and punch it down the road. Once we turn into the familiar driveway, more darkness settles on us as we traverse underneath the canopy of trees that seems so peaceful during the day. At night, however, the whole path takes on an ominous tone that makes me want to turn back around.

Crickets and frog noises surround us, fighting for

attention with the horse's footsteps and the sound of our
own breathing. Once, Bram stops to fix his costume.

"What are you doing?"

"The guard is less likely to ask questions if he sees I'm
decapitated, don't you think?"

I lean my head back against his chest. "True."

But there are no guards tonight. Maybe they're all at
HollowEve in case things get out of hand. Bram leaps his
horse over a low gate then leads him down the curving
path around the gift shop. Owls welcome us with soft
hooting, and the grounds take on a holy splendor I've
never before experienced.

Listening to the hooves crunch over gravel, I close my
eyes and try to visualize the exact spot we need to start
digging. Lavender bush. Start of the foot trail. As soon as
we're near the little cottage in the English garden north of
the main house, my heart skips a beat. I stare at the house.
That's it—the little house from my dream. How come I
saw this house every day for the better part of my life, yet
I wasn't able to recognize it?

I swing my leg over the horse and slide onto the
ground while Bram tethers him to a wooden fence. I help
him remove the wire-framed jacket off his costume.

"Mica, maybe this sounds like a crazy question, and
I'm all for going along with your loco scheme, but, uh…
what the hell are we doing here?"

"I told you, we're going to dig."

"For?"

"Bram"—I sigh—"something's buried here. I dreamed
it. My mother dreamed it. Whatever it is, it's the other
thing that Irving took from London with him. He spoke of
two things he called a double creation. I think it's code for
two people. One is his son, Cristóbal—"

"You know about Cristóbal?" he interrupts, and I'm totally not shocked that he knows, too. I was probably the last one here to find out.

"Yes, so you can stop pretending you don't know. Seems like everybody did but me. My mom wanted me to know about my heritage before I left, but I think she wanted to be sure of it first. And in finding all the proof she needed, things went wrong. Bram, my mom didn't fall in the tub. She was murdered."

Bram gapes at me, a glint of mistrust in his eyes. "What makes you say that?"

"I had a feeling from the day Nina told me she died. Something wasn't right. Plus, she showed me in a dream. I don't know who it was, but if you know, please come clean."

"I swear, I don't. I mean, a lot of people didn't like her, but enough to kill her? You're talking someone with a serious axe to grind."

"Or someone who'd do anything for the journal."

"Or someone who needs the money, or just plain crazy. You think she stole it?"

"I know she did," I say, as painful as that is to admit. "Bram..." I have to tell him. He's my best friend. I have to trust, give the benefit of the doubt. "I know, because I found it. Not only did I find it, I have more—papers that'll set me free from all this, documents to stop people from questioning once and for all."

"You what?"

"I found it."

"You found the journal?"

I nod.

Bram takes off his riding gloves and sets them on top of his jacket on the wooden fence, breathing out a huge sigh. "Wow."

"Are you upset? I know everyone thinks it belongs to Historic Hudson, but—"

"If that thing belongs to you like your mom said it did, hey—more power to you. I don't give a shit. I know where I stand." He looks around. "Which currently is in this stupid garden while HollowEve is going on, but whatever, no beef. I'm here for you. Let's get this done."

I take his hand and lead him to the garden house. "I dreamed of an old black shovel. If we find one that looks like it, then I'm officially psychic." I turn the doorknob to the cottage. *Locked.* "We're going to have to break the door in."

Bram stands on his toes and reaches up, plucking a little gold key resting on the doorframe. "Or not." He unlocks the house.

There's not much to steal—two old lawn mowers, gardening tools, watering cans, rope coiled on the wall, and a multitude of other things I can't see well in the dark. Bram moves past me into the center of the room. He reaches up again, and in seconds, light from a single bulb burns my night vision.

"Light," he sings.

I shield my eyes.

"And you're psychic, because here's a black shovel. You do lottery numbers, too?"

I take one look at the garden tool hanging off the wall. Old, black? Gray maybe. Rusted, definitely. I stare at it a long time. Not sure I can go through with this. It's one thing to dream about it. It's another to do it for real. "Whatever happens here tonight, promise me one thing."

"I'll still respect you."

"Stop, I'm serious."

He laughs quietly. "Tell me."

"Promise me you'll never talk about this to anyone, ever. Not your mom, not Janice, not Jonathan, not anybody. I don't care about me, I really don't. But my mom's memory doesn't need any more bad press than it already has. I happen to think she was pretty freakin' brilliant, and that should be enough, you know? No need to try and convince others."

Bram comes up to me then, holds my face in his hands, and lowers his for a soft, sweet kiss. It feels nice to reconnect with him. I know the last two weeks have been stressful for us both, but now that the dust is clearing, I see who's still here for me. "You have my word," he whispers, taking the shovel from me, walking out of the shed.

I realize how much I love him. How much I always have. And how if anyone can make me consider staying in Sleepy Hollow after this is all over, it's him. And I would be just fine with that.

Following Bram out of the shed, I close my eyes to drown out external stimuli. *Concentrate, Mica,* I tell myself. Roses, jasmine, and something else I can't quite place, fill my senses. Visualizing the exact lavender bush in my dreams, I move to the spot where my heart tells me it should be and open my eyes. Under a starry night, just like I imagined it, a jasmine tree sways in the breeze. "Here."

"Here?"

"Yes."

"All right." Bram rolls up his sleeves and slams a boot firmly on the ground. With a heavy breath, he swings the shovel high over his head. He could be a gravedigger from an old monster movie, the way his shape falls dark against the dim light from the cottage, arms and shovel against the sky. He brings the shovel down with force, just barely cutting into the hard earth. He takes one irritated look at me.

I smile sheepishly, shrugging. "You want me to go see if there's another shovel in the shed? I can help."

Shaking his head, he starts again. "I got this."

And again.

And again.

And again.

Until the earth slowly begins to come loose, the lavender bush wilts beside a growing pile of dirt, and I have plenty of moments over the next few hours to wonder if ever, in the history of best friends, has there ever lived one so dedicated, crazy, and sweat-drenched exhausted as Bram Derant.

CHAPTER TWENTY-NINE

"If I can but reach that bridge…I am safe."

Sitting on the grass, ripping purple lavender petals apart, keeping a wary eye on the horizon for any interlopers—besides us, that is—and listening to Bram's labored breath, I finally hear the sound I was starting to think I'd never hear. Except it's not wooden or hollow, like I thought an old coffin might sound. It's more like—*clink*.

"What was that?" I sit up and peek into the seven-foot hole Bram has dug.

"That," he says between gulps of air, "is the sound of the shit I'd do for you."

"You found something?" I gather up my dress and jump into the hole, using my hands and nails to remove dirt away from the spot where the shovel made contact. Bram scrapes away more earth and pulls out his phone to shed a tiny bit of light on it. Something silver—a box protrudes from one side of the hole. If Bram would've dug slightly to the left, we never would've seen it. "You found it."

He leans back against the wall of the trench and wipes soil and sweat from his brow. "Thank God. I was about to tell you that I don't care how much I love you, I'm not digging anymore."

"Glad you believed in me." I stand and face him, taking in the sight of his soaked, filthy form in the shadow. I take his face into my dirty hands and kiss him, not caring about his sweaty face or the stubble that seems to have grown since the night began. I never would've been able to do this without him.

He sweeps a limp ringlet of hair from my eyes. "Open that thing already," he says, pointing at the box. Together, we work to dig it free, scraping and scraping, until I finally yank it loose. It's a flat metal container no bigger than a shirt box with a small lock caked in dirt. I pry the soil loose with my nails until the lock hangs freely. *Are there cremated remains inside?*

The double creation, I hear Mary's voice.

"Yes. Now promise me you'll move on," I mumble. *Go toward the light and free yourself.*

"Who are you talking to?" Bram eyes me sideways.

I set the box down on the most level part of the ground and move aside. "Break it, please." He grabs the shovel again, lunges at the lock, and bangs on it several times until it cracks and falls away. With the sharp edge of the shovel, he flips up the rusted latch.

I fall to my knees. "Please…" *Whatever is in here, let it be worth it. To my mother…my family…*

"Shh, what was that?"

"What was what?" I gaze up at Bram. Billions of stars hover over him.

"Somebody's out there. Hurry."

"On the grounds?"

"Somewhere. Just open it. I'm dying to know what's in there."

"Me, too." I loosen the corners with my nails and lift the lid to find a dark brown leather satchel cinched on one end with rawhide. Carefully, I insert my index fingers and wiggle the rawhide apart, lifting the satchel out of the box. Whatever it is, it's nothing like the bag of bones or dried flesh I imagined. I reach in and try sliding out the contents, but there's another leather satchel, and together, the two pieces create a sturdy bind that's difficult to separate.

"What is it?" Bram asks.

"I don't know." I grab the inner bag, which feels about two inches thick, and tug, wiggling side to side, until it finally slides out of the outer satchel. This one, lighter in color than the outer one, also has rawhide strips cinching one end, and as soon as I peek into it, I pause, remembering my dream. The last one, where papers fluttered around the room, sucked out of the open window by a rogue gust of wind.

Important papers. Written by important people. Two important people. I widen the opening. "It's a book." I pull out a thick stack of decaying paper, its outer edges rank with dead, black mold.

"You dreamed about this book," Bram says.

I run my forefinger along the edges. "How did you know?"

"The first night you woke up screaming at my apartment, remember? You said there was a book. Turn it over."

"That's right, I did." I flip over the stack of pages as Bram illuminates it with his phone screen again.

It's a manuscript. Typeset in the middle of the page reads:

"The Double Creation"
by
Washington Irving and Mary Shelley

1825 - 1826

No...freakin'...way. Two of the world's most famous weavers of words, lovers whose paths got tangled in a nasty web of rules and expectations. They worked together to create something unique, beautiful, untouched by daylight—a legacy unseen by even the most devoted readers of romantic literature.

This thing has traveled from its London birthplace to Spain, across the ocean to a new home underground in the Hudson Valley, buried by one of its very creators and unearthed by me, his awestruck descendant.

And sure to be worth millions. If only Dane could be here to see this.

"You gotta be shittin' me." Bram runs his fingers along the top page. "How did you know this was here? How did you figure this out?"

I take it back and feel its weight in my hands. "I don't know, but Dane would flip if he could see this!" I clap my hands in delight and lift the valuable collaboration to my chest, hugging it carefully. *I got it, Mary. I'll keep it safe, I promise.*

When I look over at Bram, he's staring at me, jaw clenched. "Why do you say things like that?" He shrugs and shakes his head. "Why do you care what Boracich thinks? The dude is gone, Mica."

"I was just thinking aloud. I mean, it's what he talked about in class that day. I didn't mean anything by it."

I can feel his resentment through the silence like

poison spreading through blood. It doesn't matter anyway. Dane Boracich *is* gone. I shouldn't have said anything. Bram reaches up and hoists himself out of the hole. He grabs the shovel, readying himself to clear the area of evidence, reaching a hand down to me. "Here, give it to me, then give me your hands."

As I reach up and begin handing Bram the papers and satchel all askew, a fleeting, morose thought occurs to me—a shovel slamming down, knocking me unconscious, the way he—or my father—or whoever was in my dream did.

No. He wouldn't.

"Hurry, Mica."

He's the only one I can trust. He and Betty Anne.

With trembling hands, I lift the bundle up to him. It only takes a moment. One hesitant breath to let it out of my hands. My prize, my reason for coming back to this forsaken valley. My mother's reason for losing everything she had—even her life.

Carefully, Bram wraps a hand around it, eyes gleaming even in darkness, and places it on the ground next to him. I reach up for his hands, and then...

A flash of disappointment flickers across his face. "You were always gullible, Princess." For a moment, his gaze holds mine. Familiar but dark, different. *This isn't happening.* A fraction of a second later, the time it takes for a house of cards to come crashing down, for one heart to shatter into billions of splintering shards, his shovel comes flying at me so hard, I feel the rush of air preceding it.

"No!" Without a moment to think, I lift an arm to block the blow, and the dull metal bites into my flesh. There's an awful cracking of bone, and I stumble to the bottom of the earthy pit, crying in pain. Pain and confusion. Dull lights inside my eyelids, a tornado of thoughts attacking me.

What is happening?

Bram's voice is somewhere above me. "Sorry, Mica, but you made this more difficult than it needed to be. Believe me, I'm not enjoying this." Shovelfuls of dirt rain onto my head, shoulders, all around me. I can't move. Can't speak. "Then that *Boracich* dickhead didn't know when to stop meddling."

Bastard.

Bastard.

Derant bastard.

"It's our families—*our* families..." Blinding, searing pain radiates from my arm. My chest heaves underneath me. "...who've guarded that journal for sixty years. If the money it fetches belongs to anyone, it's us. Us. Got that?"

He dumps more dirt into the hole that's going to become my grave if I don't scream soon, don't try to move. Yet all I can do is crouch, clutching my arm, listening to sounds of dirt and shoveling, footsteps, and something else.

Bastards.

Derants. Engers.

How did I let this happen?

Another voice. A voice accompanied by a familiar sound, but I can't place it, can't... *Say something, Mica!*

"Did you deal with her?" A voice, not Bram's.

Jonathan's. *Deal with her?*

A bike chain. The other sound was a bike chain.

My stomach rises into my throat, and I empty its contents right into the dirt. I lean over and lie next to the mess. Double the dirt now hails onto my head and all around me. *Move, Lela, move.* I force my face to turn upward and look at the inevitable. At Bram Derant and Jonathan Enger peering over the edge, working together to fill the hole a hundred times faster than it took to dig it. "Nice capture, buddy."

Nice capture.

"Shut up," Bram bites back.

"Who are you texting?" Jonathan asks.

"Shh…" Bram says then mumbles something I can't hear.

I can't believe it. I can't believe the secrecy and betrayal, but there's no time to dwell. If I don't at least *try* to do something, they're going to bury me now that there's two of them. And even if they don't bury me, if they just leave me here, who will care? Not one person in this town gives a shit about me, except for a lady— *one* lady—too far to help me, and a man—a friend, I now realize—who I stupidly drove away.

"Please don't," I manage to say.

"What?" Jonathan sounds surprised.

"Don't do this." I glance up at him. Clearly, I see what's in his hands. Long, wooden, and twirling. Baseball bat. The same one that came spinning at me in the woods, the same one that crushed Coco's skull. I grit my teeth, rage building inside of me.

I can imagine him smiling at Bram during all this. I can't be sure, since they fall out of my range of vision every time he scoops a shovelful of dirt. "Dude, wasn't that the *exact* same thing her mom said?" Jonathan asks.

I feel sick to my stomach. My mom?

"Yes," Bram says coldly. Calmly. "But don't talk about that."

"Why not?"

"I said shut up."

I can't believe what I'm hearing. What I'm seeing. Everything I thought I knew. The words coming out of their mouths. This has to be one long, insane nightmare.

Only it's real and much worse than I could ever imagine. Against my will, the pressure inside my head forces tears into my eyes. Stupid, weak tears. All I can do is lie here and cry, tears and dirt-filled air choking me. Meanwhile, a storm brews inside of me, but I can't let it out.

My mother's last breath, stolen by the boy I loved. The boy I believed loved me.

"Bastard."

"What? What's that, Micaela?" Jonathan chides.

It hurts to talk, hurts to think. Maybe I should just let them finish me. Finish me like they finished Mami. But I can't. I let go of every ounce of hatred bubbling through me right now. I tilt my chin back and scream, "You *bastards*!" That hurt my side like a bitch.

"What?" Jonathan laughs. I hate him. God, I hate him.

"You bastards," I hiss. I can't look at them.

Jonathan clucks his tongue. "I think she's upset, Bram."

"Leave her alone." Bram, even as he works diligently to bury me alive, keeps defending me. "I hit her pretty hard. I was pissed. She's not going anywhere."

"What? You feel bad about this?" Jonathan quips. "Then forget it. Let's just go. What'd you find down there anyway?"

There's a moment of no talking as I imagine Bram gesturing to the leather pouch containing the manuscript on the ground and Jonathan picking it up and examining it. Together, they'll take it back to their elders, claim they found it, and get a ton of money for it, while I only got to hold it for a second. They'll probably tell everyone I left town again when they ask where I am. Meanwhile, I'm slowly asphyxiating six feet under the ground. Make that seven.

A dark haze sweeps over me then, my pulse ringing in my ears. Can I scream? Or did I use all my energy just now? Will anyone find me here?

"What was that noise?" Bram asks.

"It came from over there."

If my orientation is right, Jonathan is pointing to the thicket of trees joining Sunnyside with Lindhurst, the neighboring property.

"No, man, it's coming from that way." Bram glances up at the bluff, atop which sits the Sunnyside parking lot.

"We gotta go," Jonathan says, peering back at me. My heart sinks. They're going to leave me here half buried in this ditch. I force my eyes open and examine the side of the hole. There are crevices I could place my hands and feet in to climb if I weren't in so much pain.

"No, dude," Bram whispers. "It's probably him."

Jonathan fusses and fumes. "Here? You couldn't have told him to meet us somewhere else? Come on, dude." He scoffs.

"What's wrong with here? Where the fuck did you want me to tell him?" Bram argues in a hushed tone.

"I don't know, someplace without a guard who might come back?" Jonathan replies.

"I didn't know she was going to lead me here, you idiot!" Bram snaps, and I hear the sound of gravel crunching under their feet as they leave me behind and head up the path. Nearby, Bram's horse protests their departure with a snort.

Someone is up on the bluff. Who? Then comes another

voice, low but clear from the parking lot. "Okay, you guys called me here. Now where is she?"

"Dad?" I cry, my voice cracked and weak. I have to get out of this hole to warn him. I stand, a little bit at a time, wincing in pain, ignoring the blinding ache in my arm and shoulder. I burrow a bare foot into the tightly packed soil. I feel bone rubbing against bone. "Rrrgghh." I keep my teeth clenched.

Vaguely, the voices mix and argue above me. "Money first, then your daughter."

"Daddy," I call again. My voice is lost in the breeze. Bram's horse neighs quietly.

"I'm not playing games with you two."

"...not playing either..." Bram trails off. I know he's speaking through a tight jaw. I saw him do it in my dream, the dream where I believed my father was the one holding the shovel. "She's hurt, but Jonathan will hurt her more if you want. So, money first, old man. Everything you owe. All of it."

"Hurting her was never part of the deal."

I grip chunks of soil with my free hand and try pulling myself up, getting so far as a few inches from the level ground. "Daddy." *Not good enough. Ugh!*

"The whole thing..." Jonathan is saying. "Everything you owe. No more bullshit."

I stop, two feet in the soil, one hand above me, and my arm tight against my chest. The pain is too much. *But I have to. Push through it.* "Daddy!" I yell louder. He has to hear me. "Dad!" I yell again. "Owwww!"

No answer. From any of them. The arguing continues. The chunk of earth I'm holding comes apart in my hand, and I fall back against the other side of the hole. "Shit," I mutter.

One more time. I reach up and grab a new spot, bring my foot up, and manage to reach the ground. Carefully, I reposition my other foot against a rocky spot in the hole's wall and, fighting back excruciating pain, use one arm and shoulder to hoist myself slowly until my chest barely balances on the dirt patch next to the hole.

"Fine…" I hear my father saying, trailing off. Where is he going?

"Daddy…" I drag myself one last time, pulling the length of my dress along the ground, beads scraping dirt, until I'm finally out. Bram's horse eyes me from his post and whinnies. I stand and limp over to the bluff's access ladder instead of the footpath, dirt and rocks and grass falling off me as I lumber along.

The voices are right above me. "Dude, why'd you let him go back to his car? What if he's packing?" Jonathan whines. Slowly, I climb the ladder, but it really hurts.

Bram spins the shovel in his hands. "Then we're packing, too."

"Dude…" Jonathan says. Something about a shovel and a bat being no match for my father's bullets.

I'm almost to the top, five more rungs, but I save my energy to cry out. *Or should I?* What if my father really is going back to his car to get his gun? Should I foil his plan right as he's about to execute it like I foiled Dane's back at Kingsland Point Park?

Four more… I press my body against the ladder to keep balance every time I reach my good arm up again. One rung at a time. I know I'm making the damage in my shoulder worse, but I have to do it. When I finally reach the top, I peer over the edge and see my dad leaning into a car about ten feet in front of Bram and Jonathan, who are a few feet in front of me. By Bram's shoes, the packaged manuscript lies on the asphalt.

"No tricks, old man." Bram replaced his sword back into its scabbard at some point while I was in the hole. His hand covers the hilt protectively.

Jonathan stands feet apart, bat ready. Their focus is all on my dad. Maybe I can run when they're not looking. My father is taking a long time. *What are you doing back there, Daddy? Please don't do anything stupid.*

Bram nudges his chin at Jonathan, as if asking the same. *What is he doing?*

Jonathan shapes his hand like a gun and shrugs nervously. He mouths something I can't hear, and together they make signals to move toward the car.

"I told you he's packing. Let's go," Jonathan whispers, and he and Bram approach my father's car with slow, deliberate steps.

Daddy, Daddy!

If only I could lift myself off the access ladder without crying out, I could scurry over to the thicket of trees on the edge of the property and hide.

"Did you hear me?" Bram warns, stepping closer. "I said no tricks."

Dad mumbles something like, "No, no tricks, I'm getting it together." And before I can completely pull myself to my feet, my father turns around. In his hands is proof that Bram and Jonathan were right. "Move, and I win," my father says calmly. A small pistol gleams in his hands, its aim somewhere between Bram and Jonathan.

"Dad!" I yell without thinking. In the moment my father looks past the boys at me, Bram and Jonathan move into action. Bram pulls out his sword and charges straight for my father. At his side, Jonathan brings his bat.

"Don't." My dad tightens his grip on the gun.

At that moment, a blood-curdling cackle penetrates the atmosphere, and every hair on my arms stands straight up. Everyone pauses to look toward the dividing forest on the edge of the property. A familiar sound heads straight toward us, the galloping hooves of a familiar black steed, only there's nothing there. Suddenly, he materializes out of thin air. On top of the horse is the headless ghost of a Hessian trooper who protected me several times before. I watch as his ethereal shape comes charging at us, an amoeba of swirling black smoke. A dark sleeve reaches out to one side, brandishing a gleaming silver sword. His laughter echoes from somewhere unknown.

I'm not afraid. I've never been more thankful to see him.

"Mica, get down!" my father yells.

I don't need to. *He's not here to hurt me, Daddy. This one is on my side.*

Bram and Jonathan watch, dumbfounded, eyes wide with revulsion, as the realization settles in that the rider has come for them. Their heads, their souls. The trooper laughs an all-encompassing, maniacal cackle that reverberates throughout the property. His sword whirls in the air with lightning-quick looping motions.

Bram stands his ground, sword in hand, ready to fight, while Jonathan takes advantage of my mesmerized stupor to come charging at me. "Stay where you are," he says.

"Mica, run!" my father screams again. Where is he?

The giant black steed is almost upon Bram, its crimson eyes glowing in the dark night. Jonathan laughs even louder than the ghost, rushing at me. Someone fires. I scream, covering my ears.

Jonathan's bat misses me by inches. The horse is a few feet away, charging a straight line toward Bram, Jonathan, and me. Another shot fires. My dad is trying to help. But I'm tired of his help. I don't need it. I don't want it. As soon as Jonathan swings his bat at me again, I think of Coco, his everyday taunting of me, and what he did to my mother.

I duck, the bat whooshing over my head, and then I push, shoving my body into his torso with all my strength. He loses footing and stumbles backward.

The horseman brings his sword full circle at Bram.

Bram swings his to block the horseman.

Jonathan falls between the two razor-sharp edges like a sheet of paper between the blades of a pair of scissors. His hateful blue gaze falls wide upon his fate, and his scream is cut off sharply by a thwack.

Slice.

I cover my face. I can't look, but I hear it. The sickening thud of his head toppling to the ground like a coconut gone rolling off a ledge. His screams echo in my mind. The horseman's laughter heightens then fades, as do the galloping sounds, and when I dare to look through my fingers again, the ghost has vanished.

My head feels like it's going to explode. My stomach lurches.

Bram, having fallen to the ground, struggles to his feet and surveys what happened. He shakes his head, covering his mouth. Was it the horseman who killed Jonathan, or did Bram? Or both? Doesn't matter. He's dead. Bram stares at Jonathan's headless body, lying so close to my peripheral vision, and gags.

"Mica…" I hear my father's urging tone, and I know he means it's time to run or hide. Bram doesn't care anymore. He doesn't care, and he's going to come for me next.

I fall to my stomach, so that my feet find the ladder behind me, vaguely aware of headlights coming down the path on the road behind them. *Who's here at this time? The guard?*

I lower myself back onto the ladder. I'm scared I'm going to fall with how weak my limbs are. When I look up, my dad has one foot in the car, and Bram has decided to go get him first. Dad is in the driver's seat, turning the ignition, but Bram grabs the car door and slams it against my father's leg. He cries out in pain, and a metal sound chimes off the floor. His gun has fallen.

My dad reaches down for it, but Bram kicks it away. It slides across the ground and stops right at the Irving–Shelly manuscript bundle.

"Get it, Mica!" my dad cries out.

I want to curse at him for calling my name, for alerting Bram to the fact that I'm so close to both the gun and the manuscript. Bram sees me and rushes straight over. Somewhere nearby, tires screech. To my right lies the gun and manuscript. Bram locks his sights on them, too. He shifts his track slightly and heads for them.

Oh, no. I don't think so. I am *very* sorry. But my mother did *not* die a violent death making sure her documents were in safe hands, and Mary Shelley did *not* haunt my family for a hundred and fifty years, only for me to let him take that.

I pull up to my knees, pushing the pain behind me, and pounce.

A second later, I hear a whir, and the silver of Bram's sword flashes at me. I hit the ground. The blade just misses my head. My fingers wrap around the warm metal of my father's weapon, and I aim straight at him.

So it's come to this…him or me…

One last blast tears through the night.

I think of home—the little house on Maple Street, my beautiful mother, the father I love, Coconut's soft belly, holographic stickers, and an idyllic life by the river, a woeful life I left behind for an even lonelier mirage by the sea.

The boy I once loved falls to the ground, his face mere inches from mine, brown eyes leaking life, looking right at me, or past me. His gaze goes vacant, and then...he's gone. I stare at the gun in my hands.

But I never pulled the...

Someone moves just behind my father's car, elbows poised on the hood of a blue Eclipse, driver door flung open. Gun barrel smoking in his hands. Black pants, black jacket, demon mask gone. Even in the dim light, I recognize the familiar icy blue gaze, conflicted with love and duty. Dane stands to his full towering height. "Sorry, Micaela. I had to."

CHAPTER THIRTY

"And it is a favorite story often told about the neighborhood round the winter evening fire."

Kingsland Point Park two weeks later, I'm on a bench listening to Dane's soothing tone with a heavy soul. I'd forgotten how cold Novembers are here. "Your dad needed that journal money to pay off his debts. And he had a *lot* of them. He owed the whole town. A Ponzi scheme."

I hear him, but his voice is miles away. The seagulls over the river screech and swoop into the water. "I had a dream that made me think he'd killed my mom."

"Your father?" He pauses, but I don't answer. "Well, we're looking to see how much involvement he had. He might have paid Bram, sent him to hurt your mom, promising half the journal's value. Don't really know yet. But he was definitely in financial trouble. He filed for bankruptcy a couple of months ago after getting hit with a lawsuit from the Engers hoping to reclaim the funds they lent him."

"How did you know it was Bram who killed my mother?"

"I didn't at first. We only suspected. We didn't know for sure until the shirt you found. His DNA matched. The results came the morning of HollowEve. One reason why I followed you all night."

The words chill me more than the freezing air around us. "You tried to warn me," I tell him, staring out at the river. "But I didn't listen."

He doesn't say anything for a while. Then, "You were giving him the benefit of the doubt. Hey, he was your friend. I know, it's hard. But your father was on his way. His phone bill showed calls to his assistant, and then he bought a plane ticket. Something bad was going to happen. I couldn't leave you alone."

My eyes are cold, wet. I blot them with my sleeve. *I guess this leaves me with nobody.* My shoulder still hurts. I'll be wearing the cast another few weeks. I know I shouldn't say or think this, but I miss Bram. I know it was all an illusion, but still—it's hard telling that to my heart.

"Mica, I'm going to be leaving town soon," Dane whispers. His hand covers mine lightly on the bench. Long, slender fingers lightly caressing mine. His skin slightly paler than mine. His eyes reflect little bursts sparkling from the water. I turn my hand in his and hold onto it.

Will I ever see you again? I want to ask, but I shouldn't. I know what he does for a living now—a real living. Besides, what if he doesn't feel for me the way I'm starting to feel for him? What if this is just protective affection? I focus back on the water, the boats, anything but him.

"When do you take the cast off?" He touches the wound on my shoulder.

"Two weeks." My voice doesn't sound like mine. I wonder how long before I sound like myself again.

"Who's going to take care of you, now that your dad's in custody?"

"I can take care of myself."

He laughs softly. "You can, huh? I don't know about that."

I shrug and try not to care anymore. Seems all I've done the past two weeks is cry in isolation at Betty Anne's. "I'll go back to Miami, maybe move in with Em, graduate, go to Yale, be a lawyer, live out the rest of my days in disbelief. Whatever. Don't worry, I'll be fine."

"I believe you. You're stronger than you think you are." He squeezes my hand hard then lets go. It slips away, and I suddenly feel forsaken in a frozen wasteland. He stands up slowly. "Well, I guess I should be going."

"Wait." I stand to face him. Do I really want to move in with Em? I feel like she belongs in a different time and place. Can I really live with someone so far removed from everything I experienced here? I wish I could keep Dane around, always protecting me. "If it wasn't my dad who hired you, then who was it?"

He blinks slowly. "You know I can't tell you that."

"It was my mother, wasn't it? She wanted to make sure I was taken care of when I came home. You were there from the moment I stepped off the train."

He doesn't say yes. He doesn't say no, either. A flock of fifty, sixty birds in the tree nearest us begins screeching. "The authentication came back, you know."

I nod. Yes, I know. They called me yesterday. The genealogical document is solid. Real. As real as they come.

"What are you going to do with all your treasures?" He smiles.

"I don't know." In the morning, I'll be gathering my belongings to meet the appraiser from Sotheby's at Dr. Tanner's office. Then I'll decide what I want to do with it all. It's a lot of stuff. At the very least, I want to share the profit with whoever helped me, the ones I know love me and have always had my best interest at heart. There aren't many.

Dane purses his bottom lip and stares out at the river. "All right, well…" He hesitates. "I'll be at the station another few days if you need me."

I stare at him a long moment. Then I throw my arms around him, reaching high for his shoulders, feeling his arms enclose me tightly. His body is different from Bram's. Strong in a gentle way. His heartbeat slower, more even. Even his breathing and scent are different. Holding him, waiting for something to happen, I realize I could get used to him.

This is killing me.

As if Dane understands, the way he seems to always know everything, he lets me go with nothing more than a smile, a tap to my nose, then walks away. I watch him go, powerless to stop him.

The people at Sotheby's drool when they lay eyes on *The Double Creation*. Irving and Shelley's collaborative novel turns out to be about an estranged husband and wife who raise twin boys on two different continents, unaware of each other's presence until they fight against each other in the Revolutionary War. I don't finish reading the manuscript penned by my two famous ancestors before accepting the five-million-dollar check, but I also know it won't be the last time I see it, either.

Days later, I show up at Historic Hudson Library, and despite my father's insistence that I keep all artifacts to myself, I donate ten of the rare photographs and the family tree to the Washington Irving Collection. It already served its purpose, and the old Hollow families do deserve *something* for keeping the journal safe over the years. It's not their fault their sons were psychopaths willing to hurt people for that fortune.

Betty Anne won't go without, either, and I leave her a decent-sized check on the countertop when she's grocery shopping. Then I slip out with my bags. I suck at good-byes. The last of my reward-giving endeavors comes the day I visit the police station five days after holding a certain someone's hand at Kingsland Point Park, a seven-figured check sealed in an envelope made to the order of Dane Boracich.

Officer Stanton comes out to receive me. "Can I help you, Burgos?" he asks, rolling his eyes at Word Puzzle Girl.

"Is Dane here? Officer Boracich? I wanted to give him something before he leaves."

Officer Stanton shakes his head. "Sorry, he's gone."

"Gone?" Does he mean for the day, or...

"Yes, gone, as in, you know...gone?" His crooked eyebrows mock me. God, I dislike this man very much.

I blink at him, watching him smirk as I conjure up a response. "But—but I have something for him." I'm on the verge of tears. Would he really leave without saying good-bye? "Where did he go?"

The police chief chuckles to himself. "You're kidding me, right? First of all," he scoffs, "as if that's even his real name. Funny. And second, as if I'm going to tell you where a private detective is headed next. Come on, Burgos. Anything else I can help you with?"

I can barely believe it. Apparently, Dane sucks at good-byes too. Doesn't he even want a slice of this pie? I look down at the envelope containing his check in my hand. Or of me? Is it because I was standoffish toward him when I really knew in my heart that I cared for him? How couldn't I, after the way he watched over me from the moment I arrived?

"No. That's it." I turn, nearly losing my balance.

Before I reach the front door, Word Puzzle Girl *psst*s at me to come back. I give her a questioning look and return to the counter. The secretary waits until Officer Stanton closes his office door. "*Dane Boracich*," she tells me, chewing on her lumpy, bitten pencil, "is an anagram."

"An anagram," I repeat. Yes. When letters are switched around to spell something different.

"For Ichabod Crane." She waits for me to absorb this little fact and make it mean something. The darkest of clouds slides off my mind. "And you know where Ichabod Crane is from, don't you?"

Of course. Where Doc Tanner said he met him. Plus, I'll always be a local, like it or not, and *all* locals know their Irving trivia. "Connecticut."

Word Puzzle Girl points her pencil at me and winks. "Exactly."

The next day, inspection of my mother's house passes, and I watch a real-live realtor hang a FOR SALE sign with an actual photo and verified contact number on it. Before leaving, I stand in the middle of the house and open my mind one last time to messages, memories, visions, or lingering thoughts from another place—Mary or Mami.

Is there anything else you want to tell me? I'm leaving now.

I wait for the voices, but there are none. 150 Maple Street is quiet, for once. Quieter than the sleepy Hudson breeze blowing through it.

"Thanks for everything," I tell the house, taking in its empty walls one last time, and step into the waiting cab. On the way to the train station, my heart feels heavy and regretful. I soak in my surroundings one last time. The swaying treetops, the gently sloping streets, same power lines, Route 9, the station itself—same log cabin from when I was twelve.

I pay the driver and pull my bags into the station. Same old wood paneling, same dusty chandelier. I move up to the window, dragging my bags alongside me. The ticket seller mumbles, "Where to, miss?"

Back to the city? To catch a plane for Miami?

No, that doesn't feel right. Nothing does. Home could be anywhere now. Except...someone out there knows me. Could love me, I think. I could love him, too, in time. I don't know his real name, but no matter—I'll find him. And when I do, I'll tell him.

"Miss?" The ticket seller's eyebrows slope as he waits.

Excitement flurries in my belly. "New Haven, Connecticut."

Acknowledgments

In the fall of 2008, I began writing this story and "finished" it a few months later. Little did I know I'd be shaping it for another eight years. Since then, it's been through countless revisions, but the core of it has remained the same.

Along the way were some important people who read it in its various stages, people I owe a huge thank you to, particularly Linda Rodriguez Bernfeld, Danielle Joseph, Marcea Ustler, Adrienne Sylver, Alex Flinn, Christina Diaz Gonzalez, Alexandra Alessandri, Marjetta Geerling, Jodi Turchin, Joyce Sweeney, and Curtis Sponsler who both critiqued an early version and made my kick-ass book trailers. Thank you all for your wise words and direction, for opening my eyes to what needed changing while confirming what I always felt was strong and needed to stay. Thank you also to Chris Nuñez for working two, sometimes three jobs, so I could continue toiling on this book and for believing in me. To my agent, Deborah Warren, for putting up with my emails and not giving up on me nor this story, and to my editors, Stacy Abrams and Lydia Sharp, for picking my diamond in the rough out of the miry clay and polishing it 'til it sparkled.

These acknowledgments would not be complete without a nod to my kids—Michael, Noah, and Murphy—for staying busy, being understanding, and not killing each other downstairs while I slaved away at my laptop. I adore you crazy boys. To my family and friends for asking how the writing is going and attending book signings. And lastly to my mother, Yolanda, who accompanied me to Sleepy Hollow for research and is always the first to critique my books. When finished with the first draft of *Wake the Hollow*, she said, "*Muy bueno*. From the moment Mica stepped off the train, I felt like I was watching a movie." Those words have fueled years of hard work, Mom. I thank you and love you.

WAKE THE HOLLOW READERS' GROUP GUIDE
Prepared by Nancy Cantor, media specialist, NSU
University School

1.   Micaela had visions of spirits that haunted her, day and night. Did the supernatural elements of the story feel realistic? How did the residents of Sleepy Hollow react to her visions? Have you experienced any supernatural phenomena?

2.   In the novel, the humans were strikingly more frightening than the ghosts. Give examples. Why would the author present the story in this way?

3.   Rumors and gossip played an essential role in the novel. The residents explained them away by stating that that was life in a small town. Do you believe rumors and gossip are more prevalent in small towns? Could your high school be compared to a small town?

4.   How did the rumors and gossip affect Micaela and the other characters?

5.   The title indicates an awakening. Discuss how Micaela's return to Sleepy Hollow awakened both the town and herself.

6.   Both the original Legend of Sleepy Hollow and Wake the Hollow involve a love triangle. Before Bram's betrayal became obvious, which suitor did you think Micaela would choose, and why?

7.   When Bram first reveals his jealousy toward Dane, Micaela asks herself, "Does first love ever die?" What are your thoughts and experiences with first love?

8.   Micaela had trust issues with almost everyone she encountered in Sleepy Hollow. Why do you think this was the case? How did her discoveries contribute to the atmosphere of horror that permeated the novel?

9. Betty Anne tells Micaela, "...no parent wants their child thinking they're defective, but we are. We're all defective." How do parents shield their children from their flaws? Should they?

10. Micaela discovers that her parents never legally divorced. Discuss their marriage and how it affected Micaela's choices.

11. In her meeting with Dr. Tanner, she questions him about why her father believed his wife was having an affair. Dr. Tanner states that "People believe whatever they want. Whatever makes them happier about their own lives." Do you agree? Give examples from your experiences.

12. Micaela states that, "...my mother is no longer here in the flesh, but I'm more connected with her now than ever before. It took separation, it took death...it took empathy." Do you believe this can be true? Have you experienced the loss of a loved one?

13. Quotes from the original short story began each chapter. Discuss how they added to your overall understanding of the novel. Which was your favorite?

14. The affair between Mary Shelley and Washington Irving was never proven. In fact, they were acquaintances and nothing more. What were your thoughts on the "Double Creation" before you learned the truth? Did the author create a believable story line using this rumor? How?

15. Both the original short story and Wake the Hollow end ambiguously. Do you think Micaela will find Dane? What does her future look like to you?

Sunrise Valley, Vermont, late 1800s

Briar Rose's life has never been a fairy tale. She's raising her siblings on her own, her wages at the spinning mill have been cut, and the boy she's desperately trying to get to notice her has started dating someone else. Most days it feels like her best friend Henry is the only one who supports her, though his jokes about secretly being in love with her are starting to sound less and less like jokes…

When Briar meets a local peddler offering her a "magic" spindle, things finally start looking up. The new spindle works so well, sneaking it into the mill seems worth the risk. But then one by one, her fellow spinner girls come down with Polio, commonly known as the sleeping sickness. When Briar becomes ill, too, the only way to stop an epidemic might be to start believing in fairy tales…and in the power of her best friend's kiss.

Don't miss these other fantastic titles from Entangled Teen!

Cinderella's Shoes
by Shonna Slayton

The war may be over, but Kate Allen's life is still in upheaval. Not only has she discovered thatCinderella was real, but now she's been made Keeper of the Wardrobe, her sole responsibility to protect Cinderella's mystical dresses from the greed of the evil stepsisters' modern descendants.

But Cinderella's dresses are just the beginning. It turns out that the priceless glass slippers might actually exist, too, and they could hold the power to reunite lost loved ones like her father—missing in action since World War II ended. As Kate and her boyfriend, Johnny, embark on an adventure from New York to Italy and Poland in search of the mysterious slippers, they will be tested in ways they never imagined.

Because when you harness Cinderella's magic, danger and evil are sure to follow...

TARNISHED
BY KATE JARVIK BIRCH

Genetically engineered "pet" Ella escaped to Canada, but while she can think and act as she pleases, back home, pets are turning up dead. With help from a *very* unexpected source, Ella slips deep into the dangerous black market, posing as a tarnished pet available to buy or sell. If she's lucky, she'll be able to rescue Penn and expose the truth about the breeding program. If she fails, Ella will pay not only with her life, but the lives of everyone she's tried to save...

OLIVIA TWISTED
BY VIVI BARNES

Tossed from foster home to foster home, Olivia's seen a lot in her sixteen years. She's hardened, sure, though mostly just wants to fly under the radar until graduation. But her natural ability with computers catches the eye of Z, a mysterious guy at her new school. Soon, Z has brought Liv into his team of hacker elite—break into a few bank accounts, and voila, he drives a motorcycle. Follow his lead, and Liv might even be able to escape from her oppressive foster parents. As Liv and Z grow closer, though, so does the watchful eye of Bill Sykes, Z's boss. And he's got bigger plans for Liv...

Thief of Lies
by Brenda Drake

When a super-cute guy disappears into thin air at the library, he leaves only a book behind—a book of world libraries. With that, Gia Kearns stumbles upon the world of the Mystik, where there is magic, the ability to travel through" gateway" books to other libraries...and Arik, a Sentinel charged with protecting humans from malovolent creatures. There are also those who long to destroy both worlds, and Gia will have to find a way to save Arik's world—and her own—even if it means losing herself in the process.

True Born
by L.E. Sterling

After the great Plague descended, the population was decimated...and humans' genetics damaged beyond repair. But there's something about Lucy Fox and her identical twin sister, Margot, that isn't quite right. No one wants to reveal what they are. When Margot disappears suddenly, Lucy is forced to turn to the True Borns to find her. But instead of answers, there is only the discovery of a deeply buried conspiracy. And somehow, the Fox sisters could unravel it all...